by Maureen Howard

Not a Word about Nightingales
Bridgeport Bus

Before My Time

Before My Time

Maureen Howard

Little, Brown and Company
Boston   Toronto

THIRD PRINTING

T 01/75

Portions of this book were first published in slightly altered form in
Partisan Review, Winter, 1971-2, and *Ms.* magazine.

The author gratefully acknowledges the following for permission to quote
from previously copyrighted material:

Alfred A. Knopf, Inc., for permission to quote from "Debris of Life and
Mind" from *The Collected Poems of Wallace Stevens*. Copyright 1947 by
Wallace Stevens.

Macmillan Publishing Co., Inc., M.B. Yeats, and Macmillan Co. of
Canada for permission to quote from "The Coming of Wisdom with Time"
from *The Collected Poems* by William Butler Yeats. Copyright 1912 by
Macmillan Publishing Co., Inc., renewed 1940 by Bertha Georgie Yeats.

Library of Congress Cataloging in Publication Data

Howard, Maureen, 1930–
  Before my time.

  I. Title.
PZ4.H8524Be [PS3558.O8823]   813'.5'4   74-6212
ISBN 0-316-37468-7

Designed by D. Christine Benders

*Published simultaneously in Canada
by Little, Brown & Company (Canada) Limited*

PRINTED IN THE UNITED STATES OF AMERICA

I would like to express my sincere gratitude to the John Simon Guggenheim Memorial Foundation and the Radcliffe Institute for Independent Studies for their generous support.

To David

There is so little that is close and warm.
It is as if we were never children.

Sit in the room. It is true in the moonlight
That it is as if we had never been young.

— *Wallace Stevens*

I

HISTORIES: *The Cross to Bear*

THE FEARS HAVE MOVED IN for the first time. Laura Quinn puts out her cigarette in the dirt of a potted plant. Nasty, but she has felt all day that she is not to blame if she's not altogether there. Her fears absorb her — fears that she would be willing to think about if they could only be defined, like hair gone gray at the roots or dwindling expectations. But nothing surfaces.

"It won't happen," she says aloud and looks out to the yard. Rain was predicted. The sun is there in the sky but filtered through a haze so oppressive it seems to smolder out of the lawn and hang in the low branches of the trees. Looking out from the sun parlor, as though from an observation booth, Laura watches her children quarrel. She has failed at something: the children most likely. Their lives seem complete on the lawn without her. They enjoy picking on each other — the boy, who is seven, kicks his sister out of the hammock over and over again. The girl is older, but no

3

match for him, a docile child. She has been his victim, Laura thinks, since the day he was born and she will be someone's victim always. There is no reprieve.

The sky darkens. She can see a faint reflection of herself in the plate glass window. "Christ," she says and comes round enough to laugh. She sees herself as wilted suburban, one of those silly faces that never made it beyond girlhood. Clean fingernails, decorous clothes, a trim framework of sexual insignificance. Usually she has a brightness in her eyes and a vitality that substitutes for beauty in a woman near forty. Lady of high degree, a type of patrician energy that is not valued in youth. Today she is as ordinary as any housewife. Getting old, she thinks, oh, nothing more than *that*. She tidies the cigarette out of her Boston fern. In the yard her little girl's plain round face is distorted with anger, but Laura is quite safe from her cries behind the thermopane windows. The air-conditioner hums in the sun parlor.

If, in fact, it's only age she's afraid of, she sees that she can turn all the fears of the day to her advantage. Why not do it up as an article on the monkey gland doctors or the old double standard? Certainly that applies here. How many gallons of hair dye per head, per year? How many tons of hormonal night cream seep over the continent like the great ice floe, reversing time? But her writing is no refuge today, a secret she keeps from herself. For years her "work" has been a kind of thin flowing-out from herself, a false abundance. She has dealt with the specifics of her time — race riots, the androgynous spirit, set theory, abortion, transformational grammar. She can turn her pen to anything. The great problems of the day unfelt, half-understood and rendered harmless. Perhaps she has expected more from one of these pieces of journalism — an elevation of the spirit? A repellent moment she has not thought about in years: a long time ago, before Mary was born, she had turned the radio on one

4

day for the weather report and the voice of a sophomoric disc jockey said: "Come closer. A little closer —" The voice whispered: "That's it . . . are you listening now?" The voice said: "YOU ARE NOT GOING TO MAKE IT."

Laura looks at her watch and moves around in a daze, gathering up the car keys, a white pocketbook. The mood begins to slip away and now she savors it — what does it mean? But it's time: she goes out into the yard and calls the children, orders them into the back of the station wagon and they drive to Logan Airport.

Laura Quinn's gloom is not a total mystery. On this torpid afternoon she is to go to the airport and pick up Jim Cogan, her cousin's boy, a teenage kid they hardly know. The Quinns have taken him on for the next few weeks. They got what's coming to them, Laura thinks, for she and Harry both like to bill themselves as warm, wonderful people. Warm in print, wonderful in public, but recently so careful in their private life. They are not given to taking in waifs.

She waits with the children near the runway where the shuttle from New York will come in, squinting into the sun.

"Are you mad?" the little girl asks.

"No. What makes you think I'm mad. Look, there's the plane."

A tremendously hearty scene follows. First, a smiling boy, Jim Cogan, runs down the ramp. Unnaturally loud greetings. The children squeal. Then the whole thing fizzles and they walk to the car in dead silence.

"I've never been on a plane before," Jim Cogan says.

"I wouldn't have known you," Laura looks up at his square face. The family resemblance is very strong — the Murrays' broad nose, green eyes, high coloring. She means that he has grown to six feet, a shaggy young man, straightforward in manner. His blue jeans are torn at the knee and

5

he carries a duffel bag stamped with faded peace symbols. Laura thinks that his mother might have put him together better than this to come up to Boston, but then of course the Cogans never have an extra cent.

The trip back home is awkward for them all. . . . He has fogotten the children's names. The boy is called Sam and the girl Mary. "We really stuck them with sensible names." An empty defensive thing for Laura to say to the boy. She babbles on — a whole theory — about the chastening effect of the early sixties. It was over: she and Harry had wanted to be plain people when the children were born. They didn't want to be caught like fools thumbing through their scrapbook of the New Frontier. Jim Cogan keeps his own counsel like one of those gorgeous laconic studs in a Western. She goes on about her aversion to names like Heather and Christopher, Melissa and Melinda and all that pretentious topping, so much ersatz whipped cream out of an aerosol can. At the end of her spiel she remembers that Jim Cogan's brother and sister are twins with ridiculous Gaelic names.

Laura points out the beautiful spires of Boston on the murky landscape. Then in Cambridge, Dunster House and Eliot and a lone boy punting on the Charles. They turn off to the green lawns of the suburbs and finally in a thick silence come to the Quinns' house. It's a dream cottage: a half-timbered, mullioned, hollyhocked, adorable cottage blown up out of all proportion. Laura loves the house, though it reeks of the past. Gumdrop trees, bushes clipped and trimmed to a soft rounded perfection like the arty shrubs in her fairy-tale books of the thirties. A playhouse big enough for real people. A terribly dishonest house, she's the first to see that. Still, she finds it moving to think that there was a time in America, not long ago, when the man who built it believed the story had a happy ending. The house is set on a lawn tended like a putting green. Laura

6

takes a visceral pleasure in this perfect sweep of green, skill-fully broken up with "natural" plantings. It is the kind of place that families like the Cogans ogle on a Sunday drive. "Gosh, will you look at that one!"

Jim, who's been to visit a few times with his family, says nothing. As he gets out of the car he looks back down the length of drive and up at the slate stone roof, blank and cool. The rain finally starts, the first heavy drops like beads on their faces. The children begin to whine and run for the back porch when Jim Cogan catches them up, one on each arm and runs them off to the bottom of the yard, around the swings and out to the field with the three apple trees. He looks such a healthy boy to Laura Quinn, but he's been in with a bad crowd, picked up by the police in New York, and until his hearing comes up she's responsible for him. The children clown with him, free of the constraints of the day, soaked with warm rain. It's all so easy for them. Their fascination with the boy seems to her sudden and cheap. He is "beautiful" — she sees that. From the back steps she waves out to them and smiles: she isn't sure she's done the right thing at all, to have the boy here. She remembers, fondly, the hours before he came and wishes she were back inside the sun parlor again with her fears, back before he came, unavailable, enclosed and dry, looking out helplessly at her children. If she can't run around the field like a laughing fool, she has only herself to blame.

Laura

I WOULD LIKE TO THINK that I am sensible about the whole thing, but I find myself suffering as I have not suf-fered since my brother's death. Then there was good cause. When Robert was killed the world fell away, but now the world is quite substantial — suppertime, the roof leaks over the porch when it rains.

It's a week ago today since Jim Cogan came to stay with us, Millie's son. He's a surly, appealing boy. There should be nothing more to say, except that at times I am reminded of Robert, just a slight independence of mind Jim Cogan displays — nothing like my brother's genius. It rained the day he came and has been raining ever since (the announcers, spreading their false cheer, call it intermittent showers) — long depressing storms, the flowers all battered down. The lawn has turned the rich deep green of a billiard table, but I don't give a damn. How it all comes back — that I was left to fight it out alone after Robert's death. In this mood the Cogan boy seems like a dark angel of the Lord sent to ask what I've been about all these years and have I kept my contract? I don't know.

Jimmy Cogan is a boy of seventeen who lives at home in the Bronx. His story is the usual one of adolescence: endless tortures and temptations, insatiable desires, a satisfying rebellion and at rare moments an exhilarating freedom. These things don't change. I don't believe they change. They had better stay as they have always been or we will be lost.

Jim Cogan knows how to make a bomb in a cigarette pack. I don't believe that he has done it, but he has seen bombs being made and whatever is needed he could easily buy and put together. Surely there must be something which I knew at seventeen, some dark wisdom that he can't know, nothing to do with my time — the Second World War wrapped up and the United Nations Plaza laid out with frail trees. Oh, and the World Federalists — what a sunny group we were! (The other night I dreamed that Harry Truman, a diminutive wax figure of himself, but alive, was carried on a sedan chair into a famous restaurant in Los

Angeles where Presidents dine, but they would no longer serve him.) It's unfair to throw history in the face of a boy. My wizened dreams are nothing to him — still, there must be something I knew at seventeen, some fact about my world, like Jim Cogan's bomb in the cigarette pack, which I knew but my parents did not, though nothing comes to mind.

At forty, there is a good deal that I do know that a kid will never believe: that life is hard — so hard that young Cogan's anger at his mother and father, loathing of the American way, heartache for a lovely receptive girl (seen on the subway and lost forever), will pass and be replaced all too easily by other, more worthy sorrows. I know that children are hard on their parents, that my freedom is hedged neatly and necessarily by responsibilities. I know that you can escape from this hellish and beautiful country but I would never want to, never: and I am contemptuous of those who do. I know many other stuffy, and to the young, impossible truths: I would match my desire with theirs. Yes, put it to the test — for quality, intensity. Ha! I have not made my peace with the world after all, and never will. And I will be considered a bitch to insist that I do know, at forty, Jimmy Cogan's story — so special, wild, wonderful to him — to be absolutely ordinary.

I've come on too strong. Not to be sentimental, that's all I intend, neither about my own compelling history nor about this boy who is prepossessing, vulnerable. But weren't we all? Singling ourselves out in high school photographs, doesn't it seem that we were all *amazingly* young, and we laugh at the arrangement of our hair or at a strange jacket because we cannot believe, without terror, in our own faces so open to the world. Jim Cogan is like this, soft and good-looking. The softness is not his fault, not a moral flaw, but the simple blankness of his years which are only seventeen.

9

Not shy or apologetic — he looks too directly at me. There is less behind Jim's look than I imagine. It's clear that I've forgotten what a trial I was at that age with my frankness, my great honesty that reflected little beyond a rampant ego.

Look at *me*, Jim Cogan's eyes seem to speak to my years, as I look at you: don't give me all the guarded smiles, the dissembling glances that you have learned. Really, it is all in myself for he can't possibly know why I have learned my tricks. His eyes are green and set so wide under dark brows that they appear like separate untroubled seas. His hair is black and thick, shaggy rather than long because he played high school basketball until recently and knew that since his height was against him, six feet, he had best appeal to the coach with something like a regular haircut. A practical boy in many ways: he has to be. His father is a loser (quite literally), a small-time gambler, horses and cards — and Jimmy's unwonted control reflects the integrity that is missing in the man. The boy's features are snubbed, handsome and unmistakably Irish. At first sight the girls are wild for him but he does little to encourage them. Not that he doesn't look up every skirt and wallow in dreams of breasts big as balloons, but he is a private, quiet sort of boy.

For the past two nights Harry has come home from the office, fixed himself a drink, and talked heartily at Jim. "We've all made mistakes," and so forth. Swiped a car when he was young, with some Harvard friends, Harry did. Luckier that's all. It looks bad for the boy now, but believe me, Harry says, we've been there, jiggling the ice in his glass like a lawyer on television. Jimmy nods and looks grateful when Harry tells him exactly what he's arranged with the defense in New York and says gravely that it's a tough case, but the charges against him will be dropped. Rational and to the point. That whole world we must support, give our continuing support as the good liberal causes cry to us every day in the mail. I want to throw something across the room while our honeyed voices are closing us in with sticky maturity, but then I realize that the boy is nodding mechanically and our words never reach him.

All these discriminations. Christ — my attitude towards the color of the lawn, the soulful matter of the rain, that rhetorical lie about my youthful honesty. I want to be direct. To say a thing simply: I am my history, but the story of my life is always guarded, self-conscious. It is finally the only story we give to someone we love. I relate here the agony of getting to that story and how a stranger assaulted me with his impudence, his youth, until I opened to him as I have not opened to anyone since Harry Quinn discovered me shut off from air and light in a library, imprisoned in the great romance of my family. We *are* a trading of stories, like travelers on the road or the figures in the Book of Hours, rich with our details and our particular. . . . Mannered. Awful. To say it simply, I am afraid of growing old. There's no more than this — we have taken my cousin's boy to stay with us, to get him away from his family for a while. I am not the boy's mother so what's it to me, the life he sullenly proposes to waste, except I must have been ready for a stranger to ask me questions and he, with all his promise and the years ahead, would just as soon ask and not listen, make light of the past. This is how he took the advice of his parents and the parish priest — without a fuss.

He's got himself into a lot of trouble for a quiet boy — running with some mad religious sect who induce a state of malevolent innocence in themselves; babes, pure babes, we are to believe, trapped in the mire of our civilization. Spiritual onanism that leads these fools, these mindless children, to glorify themselves, or the self and its own ignorance. Romantics without ecstasy or joy, just sour, tag-end romantics who look at the world without imagination and see

11

crap. No torture, only dissatisfaction, their own scab to pick at, and themselves writ large. No synthesis: only themselves, tiresome and unredeeming. No one has ever grown a bean or baked a loaf or sung a song before they came along. Poor Jim, he does not seem cut out for that, a bright, clearheaded boy who got mixed up with an awful girl. She challenged him to be Jesus. I leave it to Jim's mother to call her a tramp. The grumbly lusterless girl who betrayed him. In this way too, the boy is like my brother — done in by a woman in the first round. Robert has been dead for years, but the girl he cared for was only a cut above Shelley Waltz — she did not begin to know how to love him. But Jim Cogan's story has nothing, of course, like the scale of my brother's life, the grand design.

Until this spring he always managed to have one nice girl at a time to take to rock concerts and dances, much to the pleasure of his mother who sees this as healthy, that is, the way things were done when she was young. In the daily tribulations of her adult life she forgets the past humiliations, the erratic behavior of youth — wanting for her son the bittersweet strains of "Dancing in the Dark," crushed camellias, a forbidden rye and ginger ale. Please! What is the use of this glittering trip down Memory Lane? It brings *her* back, Millicent Cogan, to a time that never was, not really, but she wants the best for her son and her best is a crazy quilt of nostalgic snippets. I remember, I hope with honesty, for that's what Jim Cogan asks of me, the passion, the uncontrollable flights of my imagination that were thrown away on a neighborhood boy. I should thank Mill's son then, to the depths of his wide accusing green eyes for this — the confession of my first loss. Where has it gone? — the art to construct a whole world, detailed, alive, moving, out of a tawdry teenage crush. I am sure that my first girlish obsession (and others that quickly followed) created a heightened universe, vivid and more complete than any of my adult imaginings. Now I see that poor old Proust must have been relieved to send Marcel off alone on the last train ride into a depleted future.

At fifteen I haunted the parking lot behind the First National Market for what seemed an endless spring, but was in fact one week, ten days at the most. Carefully combed and dressed — should I touch you, have you see as I have tried to make Jim Cogan see — a pale top-heavy chubette, her pompadour, though anchored with an arsenal of bobby-pins, wobbling in the April breeze, immensely unbecoming. Her sloppy-joe sweater in a shade called hunter green is worn with a sweet string of graduated pearls. On the gray cement steps that lead to the loading platform of the First National Market, she is reading a French grammar, a book which makes itself attractive to young people by interrupting the subjunctive verbs with dim frontal photographs of Versailles, Les Halles, a Paris café, etc. That alone is astounding, that they, the perpetrators of *Leçon de Grammaire II* did not reach out for their dwindling audience. But she reads on, a good girl doing her homework through a surge of violent emotion.

The gray cement was cold and punishing to my bottom. A strange place to study, but by a fortunate twist in the road the boy for whom I yearned lived in a house which sat on a wry lot facing the rear of the market. A small, one story house, barely respectable, with a rickety trellis on the porch and warped front steps. So I waited for him, hoped that he would come or go out on some errand. The sight of him would sustain me. Growing bold I took casual walks through the parking lot, a natural cut through to Main Street, and planned to say "Hi" which seemed cute and seductive at once. We met half a dozen times, smiled and, as I rehearsed it, I did say "Hi" and went around the market and down Whitney Avenue to my home parading an orgasmic flush for three blocks. Combed and dressed for the encounter, I waited for him — this you *can* see, even sense the familiar heart throb as the door of his house opened or he came down through the parking lot with a mysterious canvas bag that held some athletic equipment — and with a stab I realized I did not know what sport he played.

Of course it was creepy to be loitering at the back of the First National Market and I had in mind to say that I was waiting for my mother who was shopping but that I loathed all the meat and parsley and had fled with my French grammar to this cement haven midst the tranquility of packing crates. I waited for this boy daily, combed and carefully dressed, a whited sepulchre in saddle oxfords. My underwear was sour and gray. There were a couple of years when I gave up bathing and let my undergarments grow in filth with the passing days. Some fear possessed me of washing my frail identity away in the tub or perhaps I was frightened of my physical change and wanted the second skin of silk to stay forever the same, to comfort me. In any case I was dirty. Under the thick white bobby socks my ankles were ringed black. When I washed my hands the water dribbled white streams up the grimy skin of my forearms. My scalp was encrusted — but enough. No one bothered me. I don't think anyone cared to look closely at me. The trouble of my adolescent years coincided with my mother's anxious menopause. She was forever napping or off at the Women's Art League trying to bring meaning to her life, to compensate for an enormous loss by hooking rugs or glazing an amateurish pot.

To avoid sex, my fantasies about this boy (I cannot, by the way, remember his name) took a public turn. How could a scene unfold in which I excitedly whipped off my sweater to reveal my dingy underwear, safety pins gleaming at every juncture through the gnarled gray lace. I imagined (with hot yearning thighs to be sure) that my father and his, both Democrats in the same ward, would strike up a friendship to unite us. His father I remember well, florid, unsuccessful (insurance, real estate?) — a marginal man in his worn suit, soiled tie. A man of no importance to my father who was then a judge in the criminal court. My pale mother, dependent on her weekly liver injection, even she did not escape the elaboration of my dreams: she would be drawn out of her lethargy by some traffic with that boy's mother and though he is now faceless as well as nameless, the woman is clear to me, a bright little soul, quite dressy, chirping through the crowd after Mass. Crocheted gloves, a broad hat with cherries knocking about and her two men, the red-faced husband and that boy dragging after her. My God, how I wanted to make up to those people! A few months ago I sat next to a lively couple from Des Moines on a flight to the coast and, breaking all rules about getting caught with insufferable strangers, opened to what I thought was their glamour: the man's alcoholic ruddiness, a whiff of the heartland betrayed in her flirtatious low-cut blouse. After hours of boredom (they owned a Chevelle, ranch house with washer-dryer-freezer-stereo, three boys, problematic power mower, African violets under fluorescent light, two Sting Ray bikes, *World Book Encyclopedia*, and a black dog named Nindo) it dawned on me why I had let this happen. Trapped between the desert below and the wasteland of the woman's talk. They drank Seven-Up and were on their way to ten glorious days in Hawaii. She was well into the enjoyment they had received over the years from their subscription to *The National Geographic* when I noticed his greasy tie, her crocheted gloves limp in the gaping mouth of her purse. They were like, exactly like Mr.

and Mrs. —————, those people I whored after in my adolescent fancy, the parents of the nameless, faceless boy I loved with all my soul. A loss: the fine leather writing case I left behind in my rush to escape them. We suffer for our sins, don't forget it — "My child," I can hear the routine question of Father Lane in the confessional, "have you had any impure thoughts?" Yes, I have desired fools. I have defiled my dreams and for this I am heartily sorry.

Until this filthy girl came along, Jim Cogan played it cool: free of obsessions, skilled in reality: "I love basketball but I'm not good," he says. "I'm not natural enough. I used to work for hours on Saturday mornings just to keep in there, bouncing around the empty gym by myself, shooting hundreds of free throws, before the rest of the team was out of bed. You know it's a good thing to play a sport when you make out your application for college. In spring I was a long distance runner."

"How was that?"

"That was easy — willpower. I've got a lot of willpower. My mother always says that I'm smart but she's wrong."

"Did you run until you dropped? And shoot baskets until you were sick?" I asked.

"No I never went beyond my strength." He knew I was asking more than a simple question. "You shouldn't," he said, "a good athlete never should."

"When I was your age I danced until my feet had blisters the size of fifty-cent pieces and I practiced serving tennis balls into the sun until I vomited every day."

"How did you come out?"

"The dancing was always bad. I wasn't a natural either. But it was better with tennis: I managed to beat my brother, so it was worth it to me."

His fantasies, too, seem clean-cut, bland to me: Jimmy

16

has wanted only to strangle his mother, has imagined the suffocation of his brother and sister in an abandoned refrigerator, desired to drive a Porsche under the twinkling portico of the Plaza Hotel to pick up a mammarous movie star naked under her furs, to be swept away in a sea of beautiful (i.e., young) people on the high tide of primeval noise. Pretty straight stuff I say, compared to my term swollen with longing at the back end of the First National parking lot. Listen, I tried so hard on toe shoes, to belong to the world of people who could dance, that those blisters developed into erysipelas and I was weeks in the hospital for communicable disease with the sheet built up like a tent over the inflamed red ankles and puffy toes. I did not mean to draw up battle lines. I see that I have. Jim Cogan and I are not rivals, after all. It's so foolish of me to outplay him at every turn. Yet, what would I be without my defeats, without my defeats which I mock and transpose into victory. My story against his. It is only fair to see how Jim Cogan, given *his* first passion, will play it out.

The story can only begin with what I know of him. He is my cousin's boy — notorious now through events that were not of his making. Harry's right. We've all been through it — ordinary events, that's essential to my tale. The son of Millicent, my odd pretty cousin from Brooklyn, Jim seems to be doomed with the good looks and cleverness of his mother's people, all the unsuccessful Murrays. I have sent him five dollars for his birthday for the last ten years. A cold remembrance, indeed, but how did I know what he liked — and Jim was born, by coincidence, on my birthday so I could not forget him. His mother is my age, a cousin who came to visit once or twice a year during my childhood, bringing the fashion of the city to the bumpkins in New England. She was bright in her own manner, full of cosmopolitan gossip that she got out of the New York papers and which we took to be specially fresh as told to us in her assertive accent. Millie was like a foreigner to us, and our one trip to her house, a dark dowdy apartment in a building her father owned, might well have been to another land. The Brooklyn Murrays served us food from their favorite "deli" which my father did not touch and we were all invited down to the street to watch their spaniel deposit his turds in the gutter. In any case, Mill was a smartly dressed redhead working as a secretary in Manhattan when I was still hugging my knees with delight over "The Miller's Tale" in a dormitory that locked us in at ten o'clock each weekday night. She married early, a charming man named Cogan who never amounted to much, and had three children, Jim and a set of twins with silly Gaelic names. I never minded her airs in later years, for underneath the bristling urbanity she looked drained and bewildered, though the cause remained her secret. We were never close.

The few times her children were driven up to Massachusetts to see us they were well dressed and polite, in the past few years admiring my babies who must have bored them. City children — tentative with the trees and lawn as their mother had been years ago. Until he came to stay with us, Jim Cogan was fixed in my mind at fourteen, a boy thanking me for the five dollar bill that I'd sent him on our recent birthday. He blushed then, his skin still childlike and fine, his hair soft, the last of his innocence buried under flippancy — a beautiful boy. That's gone now: he will be eighteen next week — how can I forget, another year marked for the both of us — and the contours of his face are defined. His back talk is measured, probing and sincere — God knows, sincere. He is here with us until he is arraigned in court, because his picture was all over the papers and poor Millicent broke into tears every time she looked at his face. Out in the sun parlor he's building a village for the kids out of cardboard boxes and up in the guest room reading whatever he likes off the bookshelves. To have that again for the first time: *Dubliners* for the first time; to open to the first sentence of *Civilization and Its Discontents*; to catch the first superior chill from Mr. Emerson; to read the opening lines in my old marked text of Robert Frost — "Oh, give us pleasure in the flowers today;/ And give us not to think so far away/As the uncertain harvest." I never did tap dance along the pavements in the rain. I've drunk too little and now the good wine's gone to vinegar. Something was supposed to happen that was not prose. Right now I'm under contract for a book on women elected to public office — tape-recorded interviews with an introductory essay. It was an idea. . . .

Each morning Jim stands at the back window in the kitchen for a long while, silent, as though stunned by the small expanse of country in our yard. His eyes, calm, green eyes of the unfortunate Murrays, turn from the back meadow and fill with the hard questions that he puts to me. I would like to answer: tip of my hat to Yeats —

> Through all the lying days of my youth
> I swayed my leaves and flowers in the sun;
> Now I may wither into the truth.

But that toughness would only help me, not Jim Cogan.

Millie and Jack

In the morning the light fell first on the row of plants set on the window sill. Half dead now, they had been put there to keep the twins and the old cat away from the open window three floors above the highway. Millie Cogan, aware of all dangers, said she would hear a pot smash and come running before her children could kill themselves. But Cormac and Siobhan were outdoor kids who never played idly in the house. When they were in, they were in — shut off in their sullen closed-circuit rapport. The old cat had found its way nicely through the fronds and straggling vines to contemplate the dirty pigeons roosting in the drain pipe. "Courting death," said Millie Cogan without much fear, for the cat seemed to know what it was up to — a routine of twitching unfulfilled desire, pleasurable in some catlike way. "Courting death," was her refrain when the day was nice enough for air, but a short-lived phrase it turned out to be, for they'd only been in the flat a few months before the old cat was killed during rush hour on the road below. Somehow the plants survived in their exhausted condition, though Millie hardly ever gave them a look after the sun caught them for the first plausible moment in the morning. Though she no longer cared, she could not part with them.

Nearly two years ago they had moved in and the poor plants had survived about as well as his family, Jack Cogan thought. His wife and children had looked sooty, neglected, limp at the edges for months now. At Christmas he had replaced the dead cat with an elegant Siamese so out of keeping with the surroundings that it soon depressed him. After a short yowling romance with the twins, the new cat, who had no intention of going out into this neighborhood, withdrew into a preening narcissism. With a touch of her lost wit Mill had named it Oedi-puss. Now in the middle of the night, the Siamese came yowling, uncommunicative into the kitchen where Cogan stood drenching the plants with a tea pot. The water ran through the dry earth and out the bottom of the pots — "Damn," Cogan whispered, "Damn my luck." That night he had dropped two hundred dollars in a game that should have been a killing and Millicent would know the moment she set eyes on him in the morning.

A little sleep and he could face his wife's silent recriminations: her eyes averted, she would cook breakfast for her family as though it were a birthday. Bacon and french toast instead of the usual milk carton set out and the Kellogg's Variety Pack for the kids to fight over. A gracious and loving mom. The day ahead promised wonders of her making — the Planetarium after school and Jim could meet them at the Chinese restaurant if he could take the time from his studies. The twins, though confounded, were ready to take what came their way: Jim, a senior in high school, had known the score for years — the one happy day, the treats, but above all the attention that his mother lavished on her family when Cogan failed her again. It was all too familiar. Worse than open retaliation, it was her way of giving them a taste of what might have been. What might have been without the drawer full of unpaid bills, without the rotten flats and cast off furniture, without her guilty gin-scented smile, her air of terrible distraction — what might have been was this holiday *every* day: waffles, syrup, marshmallows plopped in the cocoa for morning fun. It never lasted more than one day and Jim hated his mother's indulgence. He knew it as a prelude to a long penitential season.

Jack Cogan knew, too, but was defenseless against Mill's real elation, her triumph over him when his loss was fresh. He also knew that nothing roused her in the night — that was his part in a ritual of shame, to fear that he might be confronted by an irate wife, his eyes the dull x's of a cartoon slob. Pure invention on Cogan's part, shushing the cat, pleasing itself now on a high castrato. "Shut it off," said Cogan, "you'll raise the dead." But the living breathing Mill, he was sure, would sleep till morning, take one look at his sleep-puffed face and know in a moment that last night there were losses. Years ago when Jim was a baby and Cogan was trying out law school she had asked, "Well, how much?" And "How much this time?" when they had been saving for a house out on the Island. For years now, she'd been silent, her only retort a hearty breakfast, a show of strength. On these mornings, which had dwindled to three or four in the past year (for Cogan was having a streak of luck) she would get up and put on a good dress, stockings, lipstick — one winter day there had been a sprig of rusty evergreen adorning the table from the bush down by the door. In time he would discover the worn envelopes hidden under the linen scarf on their dresser with her silent calculatons: orthodontist eight hundred dollars (for Siobhan and Cormac whose smiles were badly jammed), Jim's tuition at Fordham if they would take him, and most horrifying, the name of Dr. Sheer, the man who was supposed to tie off her varicose veins seven years ago when they were still in Brooklyn Heights.

"Shut up," said Cogan to the cat. His face was sunken with fatigue, the frail bones which preserved a youthfulness beyond belief seemed skeletal under the fluorescent ring above the kitchen table. Strong gray curls that showed as a full head of hair in the day were sparse under the merciless light. His frame was too young for him now, as though the years of ill-fated ventures had never touched Jack Cogan physically. He had the look of a boy who has not yet filled out. Here was promise still, a kinetic grace and he often used his body to advantage, displaying for the next employer an energy that seemed only to need direction. Successful men who should have known better were willing to give Cogan another chance.

A little sleep and he would be able to take the dose of Mill's nobility in the morning. But already he was rewound, tight. The big letdown had come on his way home from the Tivoli, an Italian steak house which sported red flocked wallpaper in the family dining room and a lot of wormy chestnut in the bar. This mafioso decor always excited Cogan at the beginning of the evening as he made his way to the game behind closed doors — the friendly elegance, the correctness of the linen and the waiters' dress which had been copied from a midtown restaurant, welcomed him with a showy prosperity. Tonight at the Tivoli he had tempted fate once again. He was known: *Mr.* Cogan to the waiters, Jack to the bartender who passed him into the private room with a professional nod. If he had a good night the glitter of the empty rooms still held an opulent warmth as he passed through, out to the parking lot where his secondhand Dodge looked possible among the Cadillacs and Continentals. Tonight the Tivoli had looked as pretentious as an old whore when he left, stained and tattered, one of those roadside places that would soon have a "kitchen fire" and lie charred and ugly behind its colonial brick shell for a bewildering length of time.

But the letdown, the familiar horror that he hoped never to face again had got him on the two mile stretch of Bruckner Boulevard. First, a recapitulation of the game, where he had luck enough but lost his nerve, where he was pure brass with no backing, and then the fear as he drove past the familiar turnoff to Korvettes at the soft ice-cream cone twirling in the sky, the fear that began as an acid rumbling in the stomach, ordinary for a while like indigestion. He popped a chalky mint tablet into his mouth at the next stop light, but the fear raged down into his bowels. Cogan's thighs trembled. He drove on. There were times in the past when he had been forced to pull to the side of the road and wait until the spasm passed, until his heart was calm and his hands steady on the wheel. The awful loss, but the loss was indefinable, his mind coated with blankness — a wipeout as though, he, Cogan, did not exist. Once he woke at dawn in front of a discount shoe palace, the mint taste gone sour in his mouth, and been comforted, truly pleased by the clear thought that Mill would bitch him with one of her happy days.

Fear had swept through him quickly tonight, absolved by a touch of spring air. There was already a spirit in him as he put the kettle on, a thrill of anticipation as he settled to the business of the racing news. On the kitchen table, direct center, there for some purpose, was a pink card, heavily scented:

Chateau du Chien
"New York's finest clip joint!"
Poodle Perfection
Featuring stud service — glamour togs!

The card was meaningless to Cogan. It wasn't until he was deep in the third race at Belmont and rushed to stop the kettle's shriek that he noticed he'd been sitting on a mimeographed sheet with a fat pigeon of peace roosting in the margin.

Resign now. The Peace that Passeth Understanding — understanding of the middle class schmucks who hear nothing but words, who understand HISTORY and are in total capitulation with the so-called "inherited and inevitable events" which have destroyed the moral fiber of our nation by involving us in a prolonged war with an enemy that does not exist. The Yellow Peril! The Red Menace! Cover-up cries in the night. The counteroffense against the basic truth of humanity which is to move towards CREATIVE RESIGNATION AND LOVE!

"That will be strong tea," said Millicent Cogan. She stood in her nightgown at the door of the kitchen. "I hoped it was Jimmy come home," she said.

"He's not in?"

"Apparently not. It's three-thirty in the morning . . ."

"Yes —" said Cogan dully.

". . . and a strange girl came looking for him." She handed him a spoon and the sugar bowl. "The tea's too strong. You'll want milk in that now. I thought she was an unhealthy looking thing, but Siobhan was taken with her . . . no color at all, hair straggling down her behind, pierced ears."

"They all look like that," said Cogan.

"No they don't," shouted his wife. A flush of anger rose to meet the brightness of her red hair. "They don't all look like this one and you weren't at home to see her. She wore no shoes and her dress was filthy — what there was of it. Colored beans on her neck — filthy. Her fingers were raw, bitten to the quick — and a nasty bell on her wrist. Cormac said it was strung on a blue cord, but I couldn't tell with the grease."

"Do you want a cup of tea?" he asked.

"No thanks." Her voice was sharp. She came, in any case, to the table and sat with him facing the clock.

"He'll be in soon. Why don't you put something over you," Cogan said.

"Don't start that one."

Yes, Cogan thought as he looked at her heavy white breasts displayed under a film of blue lace, that was one of their old arguments. Mill was remarkably free with her body around the house. He hated her semi-nudity in front of the children, yet she persisted with a simplicity that held no defiance. It was not like one of her fads — the isometrics, the health food, the weaving — which made her happy while they lasted. And it wasn't like her thwarted taste for fashion which distinguished her in the neighborhood. Somehow Mill in her old clothes could always manage to look better than the housewives she lived among. There was a difference about her that must have started with the red hair, the palest skin and high forehead. Though not beautiful, she was startling to begin with and had developed a dread of seeming common that led to Gaelic names for the twins and had recently transformed all the old furniture in the front room of their flat into a hard-edged experience with primary colors copied out of the *New York Times*. But the exposure of her body was perfectly natural, it had nothing to do with her challenge to a run-down neighborhood or dreams that could be abated by a can of paint. When the steam came knocking up through the pipes in winter she would strip to her underwear and carry on with the normal routine — checking Cormac's homework, peeling potatoes, feeding the cat.

"What's wrong?" she'd ask Cogan then. "We all have bodies."

"But you're their mother!"

"Exactly — I'm not some stranger exhibiting myself."

"It's indecent!" he'd cry.

"Well, if you don't like my peaches —" she'd say with a sly laugh, "don't shake my tree." An insinuation which proved to Cogan that she didn't get the message. Her children had become excessively modest which should have scored a point for him.

"Poor Cormac is so twisted he won't share a locker with me at Rye Beach."

"It's only a stage," said Mill. "I used to dress under the bed sheets when my breasts were coming on."

Cogan stirred his tea in an acid green mug, a color that spoiled the taste of everything but he could not complain since he'd ranted for months about the last set of kitchen mugs that read "Groovy," "Swinger," "Turn Me On." "Well," he said, "where do you think they went?"

"They! *They* went nowhere. Jim was out, thank God, when the girl came after him. I don't know how she got here — there's no one in the neighborhood of that sort. A knock at the door and there she is in her bean necklace and bare feet. Where's the Cog, she said, meaning your son, Where's the Cog? And she walked in and sat down flexing her toes, never looked down though they must have hurt from the city streets."

"The Cog!" Cogan laughed, but Mill was on the way now, her pale breasts shelved on folded arms. A mottled flush of excitement blossomed on her throat like the mark of a strangler.

"Get me some tea, Jack. Beans and bare feet! What's the date now? April — April Fool it should be still. Cormac and Siobhan giggling in the hall. She kept them off television for half an hour, I'll hand her that. 'Jimmy's gone to look for a summer job,' I said, 'out on the Boulevard' — but I wasn't about to say where. The carpet place needs men to lift those heavy rolls around. He's not strong enough, Jack. He'll strain himself."

"The Peace of Krishna Nuru is the Peace of Your Body," Cogan read aloud. "A whole and healthy body is the first Action of Love. The U.S. is swarming with a virus ridden people. Peace cannot dwell in diseased bodies."

"I can't believe he's with that filthy girl," said Mill. She lapsed for a while into silence, dwelling not on the strange unkempt girl, but her real concern — her son lugging carpets. Her son straining himself for the minimum wage. A rotten summer job to pay his way in college. Death of an old dream: in the summer her children should be playing ball in a mowed field, a tangle of inland woods behind, they

27

should, if all were right in the world, run free over ocean dunes to the safe tepid waves of Long Island Sound — a summerscape pieced together from the cheap excursions of her childhood which she'd been forced to repeat with her own kids.

"Lugging carpets," she complained: "He'll get a hernia. Give me some tea! I'll never sleep now. The hair! The hair! Down to her rump and wild. No underwear — she sat down uninvited and when Cormac came close to get a look I thought he'd die. Her breasts joggling in front of the boy."

Cogan laughed, "You're the one to give advice there."

"I'm covered enough," she cried, "I'm decent. I never set foot out of my own house like that." Mill's color flared in splotches on her fair skin. Twenty years ago it had been one of the neighborhood sports to get Millicent Murray's face to match her hair. Jack, with Tim Corrigan and Lou Falcone, would start on her as she came out of her house, prim as an illustration in the text on modern office etiquette that she carried back and forth on the subway to secretarial college. He had thought then that if her blood responded so to a few words it would be wonderful to touch her, and he'd been right. Mill Murray's famous blush rose against his face like a flame as he pressed her against the wall in her father's entryway. The blush of youth had gone but her blood still answered at a moment's notice to anxiety. She was worried, not angered, by Cogan's retort — worried to a state of red throbbing blotches, eyes fixed on the clock with a dreadful concentration. Cogan was not in it: only her son tonight and a terror sweeping through her that the boy had grown to a man.

"Never," she shouted at her husband, "I have never walked beyond the door without underclothes. The filthy creature was bending over a wool bag full of books and papers, not a stitch on — and she comes up with the Peace

28

That Passeth Understanding and hands it to the kids as though I can't read. Then she says, 'Cog's working?'

" 'Looking for work,' I said to her.

" 'We should work with the living,' she says. 'You should touch some living thing. Each day you should feel a breathing thing — touch, touch is important,' she says and reaches out to me with those nasty fingers chewed raw. So I gave her the card Jim left at dinner about the poodle parlor where they need a boy to help. 'That's not life. Not breathing things,' she says, 'that's all shit,' she says to herself. Cormac and Siobhan *died* — ran off giggling down the hall. They made for the front room but I wasn't so lucky. 'Dog sex,' she says. 'Cleaning out cages —' I can't recall the phrases — 'Poodle poop' — that's a choice one," Mill said, her eyes still on the clock. "Call the police, Jack, it's four o'clock."

He took off his jacket and put it around her shoulders. "He's seventeen and it's a Friday night. At his age —"

"At his age you were on Atlantic Avenue in the pool parlor all night. You and Falcone."

"What harm did it do us?"

"None. None at all." Her voice was soft, full of dreary resignation. "Will you call the police?" Millicent asked. She left him then with a last look at the clock. In the bedroom she threw his jacket on a chair and looked out to the highway that ran past the house; there the trucks raced by all night with a moaning she had absorbed into her life. There was nothing to see, the street lamp illuminating half the driveway, half the three-story house next door, a duplicate of the one in which they'd lived these past two years. Occasionally the light caught the side of a truck with blown-up letters — Yale, Esso — a mockery of the world her son would never gain. He'll be driving a truck, thought Mill, and I'll be sitting here with that man's losses.

29

There was nothing to be seen. She lay on the bed with eyes closed until Jack came into the room and lay beside her. Chilled, he reached for the spread and drew it over them. His hair, his skin all gray, a deathly pallor on the face of a boy. The nose blurred like the profile on a worn dime. A man forty-two years old. He seemed to her an intruder tonight after twenty years, lying on her bed with his head full of tricks. What had he lost? The down payment, beginning, possibility. She no longer itemized the washing machines, summer trips, piano lessons, winter coats. For years now she had lost the knack of wanting these small domestic treasures. Jim was safe from the draft now — their one stroke of luck — the bitter turn of it made her laugh — the lottery no less had come up with a winning number for her son. Send him to Fordham: her mind had settled on getting Jim to college. Train him for the world. He was not cursed with the charmed life of his father: all their days dependent on the smile of fortune, the condition of some crappy stretch of track. One horse slips in a load and it was a sure thing she'd be washing out sheets in the bathtub again. She knew that even now he was hardly thinking of Jim but figuring his foolish bets. Dreams of a stranger. She had never known what he wanted out of all the chances — something entirely private, that was it. The gambling was private, a solitary hope, exciting — away, far away from their home, the kids, their bed. After twenty years some nonsense she could not understand. She had her desire down pat now, one item, tuition at Fordham if Jimmy got in. Fat chance, lugging carpets on his poor shoulders, studying for Regents against the TV racket, sleeping in with Cormac, driven out of the living room by Siobhan on the fold-out couch. "Did you call the police?" she asked in anger.

"No —"

She turned to the window not to look at him. "It's getting light."

"Mill," said Jack Cogan reaching over to her. He drew his hand along the flesh of her upper arm. She felt him kick off his shoes under the spread, then he turned her round to him, in his clothes still, his whole body pressing her, as though that would always set things right. "Oh, Millie —" he pleaded, his mouth on her ear. The scene was too familiar, gone blank with repetition.

"The precinct number is on the cover of the phone book," she told him, "from the time that old man dropped in front of the house."

She turned her head away. Across the driveway the light switched on in the back bedroom, and Silvio, their young Italian neighbor, got himself up in the middle of the night to go off and work in a bakery. On her sleepless nights Mill had seen him moving around the side of the bed in his underwear, his thick body decapitated by the window shade. Later he would reappear in his white shirt and white cotton work pants, lean over, Mill imagined, to kiss his stupid bride who lay in bed half the day and then drove out with her girl friends in their cheap bright clothes and matching wiglets to the shops up in Bayshore.

Jack's hand traveled over Millie's stomach, her hips. She lay like a stone until he gave up, watching Silvio steal down the driveway in his floury shoes — a specter in the dull morning light — and then the little drama snapped. Voices called out: the heavy inflected bark of the Italian and a light response, "Cold as a blue fuck!" The voices of men.

"Thank God," cried Millie Cogan, "my Jimmy's home."

Harry Quinn

MY HUSBAND HARRY QUINN is a poor boy who's made good. That's important. I first appealed to him because I worked so hard all the summer that we met, and I didn't *have* to. He was shelving books in Widener Library: I stayed until they closed the place up and he presumed I was a serious person. It took us a long time to discover that I only wanted to get ahead of my brother and by the time that insight came my poor brother, Robert, was dead and Harry and I were set on our successful course. He's a lawyer, a very good lawyer, and will soon be a judge like my father. Unlike my father he's made a great difference to the Democratic party in this state. He cares about the law, honors it, likes to see it work — to manipulate it even, within reason. And to manipulate people, too — to let them know what they should have in mind.

Harry's father ruined his health on a WPA project, ripping out the old trolley line that ran out to Brockton. His mother washed curtains for the neighbors and his brother — a worldly, alcoholic priest — became a Jesuit because the priesthood is the only way they could get an education for him. There is so much anger and resentment in my husband — for the stupid way people's lives are forced and twisted by circumstance. It's the hardship that Harry's been through that makes him hold Jim Cogan at arm's length and to create a distance between himself and all the people he fights for. I understand this — he wants each case to be a clear decision, each bill to be passed as a reasonable request. He doesn't want handouts. Sympathy is beside the point. I sense that people are afraid of the public figure, Harry Quinn, but they respect him. I wish sometimes that he would open a little, just enough to get the advantage of an opponent or an old-line politician, or comfort a client with his own vulnerability. His rules are so hard. Hard on him most of all.

When he asks Jim Cogan, "Did you believe in this man Clauson?" the question is professional.

"I don't think so."

"Did you join anything," Harry asked, "go through any ritual to belong to these people?"

"No."

"Did you help to write or print any of their crackpot documents about the destruction of knowledge?"

"No. I only went there maybe a dozen times with this girl," Jimmy said.

"Then you didn't believe."

"Not exactly —"

"Did you know the intention of this group that day when you went down to meet them at Forty-second Street?"

"I knew all right! They were going to bomb the books and I went down to try and get her to come away with me so she wouldn't get in trouble."

"It was pure sex," Harry insists, "You didn't believe."

Harry scores. Later in the bedroom I complained that he's too hard on the boy.

"He's a good kid," Harry said. "Someone should tell him where he went wrong. No one ever told me."

He undressed. The good suit. The silk tie. The Italian belt. Each shoe looked successful on its own — together they are a partnership. But my husband sleeps in his underwear.

"Stalin slept in his underwear," I said.

"OK." Harry turned out the light. The cheapness of my remark had me wandering the house in shame half the night.

Yesterday I left the children with Frieda when she finished cleaning upstairs and drove Jim Cogan into Cambridge. I was on my way to Boston to interview a bigot I hate for the book on women in public office. She would not come to Cambridge, but insisted that I meet her on her turf in the heart of the city. It went badly — the venom

33

rose in my throat and I couldn't get a sense of what she was like outside of my preconceived notions. She is head of the school board and doesn't like children, fears education, flaunts her ignorance. Someone must have told her that when the enemy wants to sound you out you've really made it, for she sat there like a fat tabby cat, smiling and smacking down her lunch, playing up to my suppressed fury. I could not stand to watch her chew. The sound of her swallow was disgusting and I decided then and there that I would not write a balanced book. I saw exactly the kind of prig-faced disapproving mother that she represented to her constituents; if there was filth in the world she'd find it. To stand with her was to announce to the world that you know how to keep your bottom clean. To stand against her was to join in the licentious orgy, to wallow in sensual delight, to let the sores ooze on your children's eyes. Behind her careful conservative vocabulary she indicates a high-strutting life goes on here in Boston: doddering Commie professors in league with young health food emaciates, the off-season Portuguese cranberry pickers come from Cape Cod to enlarge the welfare rolls and despoil the city, a swarm of blacks gorge themselves on food stamps and squat in front of color TV. When she smiled under her slop-pot hat she looked like a woman in a George Grosz drawing. She kept referring to her program that will "protect our children," though the woman is barren herself. I would not report that about anyone else.

"You're Harry Quinn's wife," she said to me.

"Yes, I am. Surely you knew that."

"He grew up in my neighborhood," she said, gloating.

"Did he? Well he took speech lessons in law school to get rid of your accent." After I'd insulted her I still had to pay the check and get away so I told her that Harry was ashamed of it now, that he laughed and said it would have been a political advantage to keep the broad flat vowels of his Boston accent, but for the most part he was simply ashamed. The fat lady wasn't flustered at my confession and slyly watched me box myself in: I said we all had things in our past to be ashamed of.

When I picked up Jim Cogan in Harvard Square I still heard the enmity in the irrational pitch of my voice when I asked him what he'd done. He'd bought a bag of candy to share with the kids and two books — one a popular fairy tale about a land of little people that makes all our moral questions cute and belittles our humanity, and another escapist tract on hallucinogenics. "Did you believe? Did you really believe in that man Clauson?" I asked. "Did you think there was *truth* in the man?"

"It wasn't exactly P. J. Clauson I believed in."

"I think you're faking it," I said. "You just wanted to make out with the girl. What's so wrong with that? You're young."

"At first I went because of her," Jim Cogan looked straight ahead and his words were not meant for me. "I never believed in the incense and songs exactly. But the Indian stuff — it was peaceful there, so peaceful. I thought there might be another way — and the way that I knew didn't work."

Jim

HALFWAY DOWN THE BLOCK the Cog had stopped groaning a song he had listened to many times during the night. Stretched out naked on the big rug with Shelley, he had reached out to set the replay button: "Don't do it if you don't *want* to. I'd never do a thing like *that*." They had assumed the Leonardo position, arms and legs splayed as in the spokes of a wheel, only the soles of their feet touching. Their mentor, P. J. Clauson, had instructed them in the basic Leonardo figure, told them to fan out nude on the central design in his rug, to cleanse the mind, lose information, drain the system of useless facts which blocked Creative Love.

According to Clauson, a poorly paid librarian turned guru, there was an axis directly through Jimmy Cogan's central being forming a recharge circuit of energy and a further organic flow through the soles of his feet up into Shelley's which were tough because she had stopped wearing shoes. Shoes blocked the flow of ground energy that ran in loose currents and could be picked up anywhere by an experienced person. The IRT at Astor Place was a good spot. The Fifth Avenue stop at Central Park. The Children's Zoo. The Cloisters. Shelley was advanced — the basic Leonardo child's play to her. She had mystified Jim the first time they met by saying she had gone *beyond* sex. He had failed to understand then and had failed more miserably tonight in the heavily incensed air that hung above them on Clauson's fake oriental carpet.

"Uh — you *don't* do it if you don't *want* to." He'd drunk the dense beat into his body while the useless facts of a corrupt civilization had seeped out through his fingers. "Focus your mind," Shelley had instructed him, "on something that bugs you."

"Focus," Clauson intoned, "on a single aspect of your decadent knowledge. Push and focus. Push the burden from you. Focus: Feel! Feel the freedom begin to flow through your healing body."

He had focused: solid geometry rammed in for the Regents, early and late, ingested against the mechanical squabble of morning cartoons and the hollow taped laughter of the evening's comedy. The instant in which he had first

36

understood a proposition — the shudder of joy through him when he first saw its beauty. For weeks he had carried the geometry text with him, protected from the March rains and the twins' sticky paws by a cover of zebra vinyl. He was never happier than in those moments when he woke before the household's hostile morning din and reached down by the side of his bed to feel the book's smooth skin. Siobhan had left a half-eaten Hershey bar to melt on it while she and Cormac, creepy interchangeable kids, had popped their Bazooka bubble gum during "Divorce Court." He had washed the cover of his beloved book many times, in secret, not to be laughed at. Then in the exam he had defeated himself with a direct attack on each problem, forgetting the larger designs and the beautiful theorems. All that heartache to care about space and proportions, loving dead pages, only to find that under pressure his mind was bewildered, unretentive.

He had focused: at first with the record pounding, he had succumbed to the beat and thought a trickle of information was seeping out, mostly old Euclid and an octahedron, those crazy diagrams he had worshipped: the flat page that seemed to come out at you and instantly drew back into space. An optical illusion: a problem to which there need be no answer. His focus slipped: he was alone with a naked girl. His mind was not clear but cluttered with what Clauson termed "superficial images" — Shelley's legs spread out, a nest of honey brittle hair, her bright pink nipples (defying Leonardo's calculations) slanting cockeyed to the walls. "You have to be out of your mind!" he called out to her.

They were naked and *alone*. That at least had been established: he was not about to take his clothes off in front of that old fag Clauson. This was the first time Shelley had taken Jim to Clauson's, a storefront temple of the occult which she had described as a "beautiful free place." Patrick

James Clauson, a round-rumped queen, was like a chubby clean baby powdered with patchouli, emitting the sweet scent of pot further masked by a brisk lemon cologne. A "beautiful, purified person," Shelley claimed: true, his white embroidered shirt was as fresh as a surplice, an enameled Maltese cross his single ornament. At first sight of him Jim had stuck in the doorway of the shop, until Shelley who was shivering despite the ergs of organic energy pulsating from the beautiful Spanish-American pavement of East Thirteenth Street, literally pushed him into the roseate glow of tinted twenty-watt bulbs.

"We will help you," Clauson said, his voice was surprisingly deep, "to be free of the burden of knowledge. To free your energy for love. You must get rid of so much waste — it is hard, we here in Creative Love know it is hard work, but the satisfaction is great. You will be able to feel. You will re-create. That is seminal to our belief."

"That is seminal," Shelley echoed Clauson's incomprehensible words. "We can re-create this crappy world."

"Don't!" Clauson commanded, "Don't take two steps back, beautiful child." He held her tough young face close to his own.

"We will be able," Shelley murmured, "to re-create. That is seminal to our belief."

Together they drank jasmine tea and nibbled brownies baked by Clauson himself. Jim could just see him fussing in the little kitchen which lay behind draped Indian bedspreads. Clauson sprinkling in hashish and walnuts, tasting the batter with a delicate pinky. The pattern on the rug rose slowly, a tracing of spirals and stems — and he, the Cog, could see with a pressing clarity where their limbs would go in the basic Leonardo. He would focus when Clauson left — already the fat man was chasing the last delicious crumbs around the plate and sucking his fingers. Time went by.

They were alone in the room at least, naked, focusing. Parabaloids fell from Jim's fingers, still he was driven to a frenzy of desire. "You have to be out of your mind!" he shouted. "I'd rather be necking after a C.Y.O. dance."

"*Try*," Shelley said, not opening her eyes. Her hair was spread out above her head as though electrified in severe shock. "Try something that really bugs you."

But then Jim had broken their circuit and crawled to her, across the pattern in the carpet woven like a split cell with mirror halves. The girl was instructive and not totally reluctant during Jimmy Cogan's first attempt at making love. When Clauson returned they were sole to sole again.

"Progress," said Clauson as Jim grabbed for his clothes, "is painfully slow."

"He screwed me," Shelley reported in a tattling voice.

"Painfully slow —" Clauson sighed: "Your whole spirit is like a broken limb that has been in a cast, withered, deprived of light and air and exercise. Now we must build you up . . ."

Jimmy edged back from the man's clean, manicured hand which rested lightly on his shoulder.

"I'm afraid it will be a long while before you can approach the *sexual act*," Clauson scored the words with a belittling pity, "with anything like the spiritual forces necessary for Creative Love."

Shelley

SHELLEY WALTZ WORRIED on the way home that she would not get in before her mother who was on night duty at the Cross Bronx Medical Center. Her father had strayed many years ago and was to be reckoned with only as a memory of hazardous times, but her mother always showed up. Having spent herself on premature infants (Mrs. Waltz was in maternity this month — intensive care) she could really unload on Shelley after night duty. "Tramp," she called the girl if the kitchen was not cleaned up, if her white uniform wasn't drip-dried over the tub. Little enough to ask after eight hours in the hotbox, row upon row of frail new bodies breathing precariously in their simulated wombs. They were so cute, Shelley's mother said, you just wanted to love them all. Hearty appetites some of them had. One little fellow all the nurses were crazy about had been in five weeks and was scheduled for a kidney operation when his body could take it. Routine duty — still she'd rather be on a private case where you get a little more time to yourself. She was tired when she got home and liked a neat kitchen with the counter sponged off and a fresh uniform Luxed out, dry and clean over the tub. It was never too early, Shelley's mother said, to take on some of the burden. Broad and competent in her white support hose, Shelley's mother told her she could do worse than be an R.N. They always need you and you don't have to depend on a man. She was mad if the kitchen table wasn't set up for breakfast when she got off night duty — little enough to ask from a grown girl. "Tramp! Out — *always* out! You'd think you didn't have a home."

Shelley Waltz, daughter of Mary Waltz, née Mary (and in her heart always) Rowan, got home in time to hide her beans and Indian dress and do her chores, a dissolute Orphan Annie. Clauson had dropped enough grass into her Greek bag to keep the girls at Harding High happy for a week. Considering she only got a quarter of the take she would still clean up. The price was high this month. Her competition at school had been mysteriously rubbed out and Clauson set up the tab accordingly. He was a helpful, good person and tonight she had taken Jimmy Cogan to him for the first time — just as a beginning. But Clauson was right: Jimmy Cogan was all withered and rotted, clogged with knowledge and stupid information. When Jim broke their circuit she had been freaked out in a terrific vision of her mother's new uniform (Sanette Modes) billowing into a froth of Lux suds and rising stained with the stink of hospital and blood.

"Yes," she told Jimmy, "I've done *that* before." So why did he ask. No, she didn't *hate* it. Yes, she *liked* him. No, she wasn't angry. He was so out of it. Sex was unimportant in Creative Love. "I don't know," she said in her hard little voice, "why you can't get beyond sex."

Then at her door she had felt sorry. "It was ok — it's just that I don't like to be mauled. I don't want sex to be ordinary," she said, "and not mystic." She had taken off her bell of happiness and wound it round his wrist. He touched her face and touched her throat. "Touch is important," Shelley said. "You should touch a living, breathing thing every day."

Jim

IT WAS THE GRAY RIM OF DAWN when Jimmy Cogan ran down the block from Shelley's house. She lived in a long row of yellow-brick apartments built in the late twenties when it looked as though New York would go on forever with walled-in streets. But the city had stopped here on the edge of fields and used car lots, dwindled to a neighborhood with no future and an unremarkable past. It seemed to Jimmy like noplace as he ran through an empty lot behind billboards, much worse than his parents' flat on top of old man Grassi's house. The old man clipped the hedge himself in summer and had just installed aluminum screens. Their front window looked out on Bruckner Boulevard which was someplace, despite his mother's bitching. He had never been out this late before.

He ran along a street of little shops, a corner grocery, a cleaner's with faded crepe-paper streamers twisted in the window and a big picture of a couple of bleached-out college students greeting each other in their hard-surfaced clothes — he in a snappy sport coat down to his knees, she in a knife-pleated skirt and, up above, tits like cupcake mounds under an immaculate white sweater. He had never been out this late before. He felt that he would never get past this awful world, unpopulated and bleak in the half-light. A pile of morning papers thrown on the sidewalk still in metal bindings announced scandal in the city government. An unknown movie house with a Walt Disney feature (troubled boy with raccoon and beautiful-young-understanding parents). At the end of the street open space again. A few stars still in the sky and finally the railroad siding that ran some miles down into Hunt's Point Market where all the food for the city was sold and distributed at this hour. He could hear his mother's voice, gay, determined, overriding despair — how they *must* all get up and go to Hunt's Point and see the beautiful crates of fruit, the array of fresh vegetables from all parts of America. They must go to Hunt's Point — the aisles of leafy green lettuce, the smell of citrus fruit. They never went. They just listened to her talk about it when she had assembled her family for an inspirational session at the kitchen table.

At last, in the distance he could see the chain fence around the play yard of the parochial school the twins went to these past two years. Soon he would be home. He had never been out this late. An experienced long distance runner, he pushed on and began to sing: "Don't do it if you don't *want* to. Never do a thing like that." He had no real love for Shelley Waltz. She was cousin to a lively Irish girl in the Cogans' neighborhood who thrilled to the mention of a jazz Mass, a girl you could take to first run movies for a year and never get in — sweet and demanding. But Shelley was weird, foulmouthed, with her Greek shoulder bag full of pamphlets, astrological charts and, unknown to the good girl cousin, a steady supply of grass. Shelley was a Capricorn — turbulent, moody, but highly sexual with a desire for freedom like his. Supposedly her passions were dominant: that was all shit she talked and he told her it was foolish, finding out the *hour*, the *minute* he was born. Still it was odd, she was not torn asunder as he was, a home-loving Cancer, child of the moon. The first afternoon he had met Shelley, slumping around a record shop with her neat little cousin, he had known from the sullen wet-lipped way she looked at him that he could make out. He started calling her every day from a phone booth in Walgreen's. He did not like her, only the idea that she was easy and strange. Last night she was waiting for him when he came out of Kauffman carpets on the Boulevard, standing in the parking lot, barefoot, intense. Now in the chill light of dawn he wished, romantically, that the night could be outrun like her neighborhood: he didn't even like Shelley Waltz: he knew, sadly, that he would have to put up with P. J. Clauson's slimy lectures on the energy flow to get her again and the desire was already overwhelming.

"Uh — don't do it if you don't *want* to. I wouldn't do a thing like that." The sun was up by the time Jimmy Cogan got home. The morning cold as a blue fuck and Silvio was going out to work. Jim's father was waiting at the kitchen door, the racing form folded into a paddle as though he were about to whip a naughty dog.

"Look at the clock."

"Yes." (Shelley would be in bed now, asleep, not wanting him. The night closed on their experience.)

"What time do you think it is?"

43

"The time it says."

"Don't get fresh. Where have you been?"

"No place much." (He had heard voices laughing in the back room at Clauson's. At the time he did not think they were laughing at him. Now it seemed insidious, that queers were snickering while he lay naked with Shelley Waltz. Good for her — he didn't want creeps watching him.) His father was fully dressed — all but shoes and a jacket, his tie knotted, French cuffs crisp, linked with silver coins. He had never seen his father like this, fresh from the card table with the panic so thinly disguised. Jack Cogan covered for himself with spunk, a feisty little man, his anger forced, straining to get into the next round. Anything to wipe out the night.

"And where have you been?" Jimmy asked.

"Son of a bitch, since when have you the right to ask me?" Surprised by their bitterness they were quiet for a moment and then the inquisition went on. "Who were you with?" Jack Cogan asked.

"Some guys."

"Till this hour! Your mother's nearly crazy," Jack Cogan said and flapped a sheet of paper at his son. "What's this?"

"I don't know," the boy said, "I've never seen it. You tell me."

"The Peace that Passeth Understanding!" screamed Cogan. The fat, ill-drawn dove fluttered at Jim. The blown-up word CREATIVE rose from the page. "You smell of it — with some dirty, half-naked slut."

"I don't know any slut."

"The hell you don't," Cogan came at his son, his newspaper rolled into a weapon. The boy stood a head higher; his shoulders would be massive in another year. Infuriated, Jack Cogan beat the paper across his own palm. "You get in there! Get in there to your mother and apologize. You've driven her crazy tonight."

44

"Sure," Jimmy said, willing to trade this scene for his mother's hefty bare-bosomed sighs. "Sure —" As he shrugged, the bell of happiness tinkled, insolent and small.

"Take that off!" Cogan pulled insanely at the dirty blue cord until it broke and blood sprang in a ring on his son's wrist. "Take that off," he cried, holding the bell silent to his breast, "before you go in to your mother."

Blood is drawn to the surface with silk cord, that's to be expected. Jim didn't bleed — this confrontation between father and son is not so dramatic. His mother's heart was patched together. (It was my father who waited in the dark for me — forgiving my lips injured with the night's kisses, in order to claim me as a child once again.) "I'm all right now you're home," Mill Cogan said to her boy.

Or the dress my mother made for me, white organdy for the high school prom — white organdy with lace daisies over green taffeta. What in the world was I supposed to be? Pretty as a picture, struggling in the back seat of a two-door sedan with my beau. He was a few years older, back from occupied Japan where he had abandoned, he confessed that night, a wife and child, so that he didn't have much patience with all that organdy: I heard the silk tear and thought while his hand worked its way into my clothes that there was still a modern Butterfly singing "Un Bel Di," proving that nothing changes. Muffled through layers of crushed white organdy, I said something very like dirty little Shelley Waltz: That I didn't want it to be ordinary and not mystic. Ah, but my dress was torn over twenty years ago.

But I suffered. Let me tell you how I suffered. For weeks I sat in torture at each meal, at the right hand of my father, passing him vegetables and salt with an eagerness to please in any small way — at all other times avoiding him. Years later the vision would come upon me like a quick slap in the face of my father's grieving eyes as they looked at my swollen lips. Why are they so shameless now: Jim Cogan claims that, sitting on his mother's bed, he simply wanted her to get it over with so he could get some rest. She was glad to hear that Kauffman Carpets wouldn't take him on and didn't he think the poodle parlor would be more fun? It was midtown. The big world. Hadn't he always liked dogs? Sure, he *loved* dogs. Shamelessly making up to her — he had always wanted a dog. Back in the Brooklyn days. Remember? He might have strained himself with the carpets, he said — only wanting her to get it over with. A home-loving cusp of Cancer, Jim Cogan was born under my sign — predisposed to the domestic virtues. Why, in the name of God, has he no shame?

I have never acted so perversely in my life. From that first day when he came to us and I stood alone watching him play with the children, I have been like a hunted creature, like the ingenious moles I set traps for in the yard. Bold animals building new runs to escape me. When they are dead they are so weightless and insignificant on the trowel.

First: It is easy to like the boy, to be as charmed by him as the children, but before the first week was up I had come to love him — a gnawing adoration that I'd never felt at all for my own kids, plain Mary and Sam. He's central to my life and it's tainted, my feeling for Jim Cogan, with jealousy, guilt. I did once love my husband like this. I can't verify it. Not a drawer full of old notes or pressed flowers or dance cards to rummage through. We were green and happy together, clumsy in our love nest, a roach infested sublet in Cambridge. Harry never looks back, he'd never ask what happened to all that intensity we had and no chairs to sit on. The hot plate with one burner gone.

"Remember we used to have milk shakes for supper and not cook at all."

"I wouldn't try that now," Harry said.

"You were so thin."

"My weight hasn't changed in twenty years."

"But we are *different*," I said.

"Thank God for that."

"We didn't need much —"

"We are better now. We were ambitious and cruel," he said. "In law school we were vicious about the guys who couldn't keep up. You laughed at their wives. Memories are draining. They are false."

I stand corrected, but Harry as he comes home from work and eats and sleeps beside me is as shadowy in the last few days as a grand faultless hero out of the past.

It's suspect . . . all this desire for a seventeen-year-old boy — his body admittedly, his thick dark hair, his square Irish face that's sure to coarsen. His large neck will look like a sirloin roast by the time he's thirty, but it's now that I love him. I do not *want* his body, nothing I can take. Once before I envied someone like this — my brother, long ago. I wanted to be transposed, to be him. I wanted his presence in the world.

Presence? That's a laugh. Robert's dead and poor Jim Cogan is here with us in custody before standing trial in New York for possession of drugs — a minor charge. The explosives and intent to destroy public property — that's of a serious nature. His presence — oh, the particulars are always humiliating, like turning the contents of my pockets out — he's just a kid. *I want to be as he is now,* to crouch at the starting line and I'm furious that it can't be. It is his turn: that's all.

Second: I have grown thin and old. Not in years: Don't imagine it's that I care about: but only lately in my spirit. Lately, yes, the past few weeks or twenty years. I wait for Frieda to finish with the beds and laundry so she'll take over the children. She is so much better at it than I can ever be. She is *there* for them with all her spoiling of the boy and little life-quenching rules and the importance of the meaningless task at hand. Once I had the idea, the *idea* only, that I would turn from myself as turning from my image in the full-length mirror and discover another reflection — more depth, more shading, more than the simple flat image of myself, well-kept and sufficient. But the richer self eludes me. I am thin and old. It's best to cut my losses. What I do have left to me is experience. This is what Jim Cogan never guesses: that I can play from my strength — the small focus of self-knowledge, the sweep of history — that I am in control of my feelings as one is after years at a craft. That I am a professional.

Third: Wouldn't it be awful for me if he was really like my brother. The other night, Harry, on his way to a political meeting, was going to drop Jim Cogan off to hang around with the kids in Harvard Square. They were in the car, backing down the drive when Jim saw me with the children — the three of us left behind, forlorn — and he popped up through the open roof of the Mercedes. The resemblance to Robert overwhelmed me. A beautiful clown, hair flying, his arms raised to heaven in a salute of joy, a celebration. A gesture worthy of my brother who's been dead for over twenty years. A magnificent moment, blooming out of an automobile, but surely he can't replace Robert in my heart. He's just a kid, an ordinary kid. And why is all this put forth like strategy? The field freshly limed with bounds and goals? Why can't I just have my envy and my final self-denial about Jim Cogan's youth? We are not rivals. We are not lovers. Why don't I pick up my marbles and go home? There's this: I still have a great need to win.

"My mother never liked you." Typical prodding. Early in the day I can expect him to confront me, usually bare-

48

chested while I am scraping plates or putting cheese ends in plastic bags. This is not accurate but the sense I have that I am always engulfed in some menial task, drowning in warm applesauce while he, Jim Cogan, is clean — out there in a world of pure feeling (which is little feeling by my standards), sorting through ideas and people, people and ideas. A seventeen-year-old Montaigne in love beads, discarding whole areas of Western culture that do not serve him: The Reformation, the Industrial Revolution, most religions. Last week languages were approved of as an OK human game.

It is only my sense of it — stringy-throated old me, gasping for my life at forty, that he should not be allowed — this boy who has been bailed out by Harry when Harry doesn't owe him anything — that he should not be allowed to come down into the kitchen stroking the hair above his navel (which grows like a smooth feather to a fan on his chest) and say: "My mother never liked you." Or, "You don't dig your husband, do you," or, with book in hand half-read, "St. Augustine is hip." Or, "Freud is full of shit." I shouldn't allow it, but I'd sound a fool, arch, haughty, delivering my line from Oscar Wilde: "My dear, your dress is strangely simple and your hair is almost as nature might have intended it."

Certain proprieties. You don't come into my kitchen, sleep still in the corners of your beguiling green eyes and imply that I am not a soul mate (rolling in nuts and natural honey) to the man I have lived with for fifteen years. That I do not *dig* him after two difficult pregnancies, his nervous breakdown, my slipped disc, his unsuccessful congressional campaign resulting in financial disaster, my humiliating affair with a local painter, his mother's death by slow suffocation in our guest room, and our little girl with two winters of viral pneumonia. What the hell do you mean *dig*? You do not come into my kitchen, unshaven — where are your manners? — and tell me Freud is full of shit. How dare you! You with your charming reprobate father and cheery mother, the afternoon tippler. You know nothing of Freud. You don't know what shit is.

Of course, I don't say what I think. It's too late for me now. Jim Cogan is honest with me, open as he never was at home, as children cannot be with their parents. Nothing belligerent in his tone. We are supposed, in the straightest way, to bare our souls, to share, to love, love, love, to level with one another. Take my hand. I'm a stranger in paradise. I, who have cultivated sweet self-mockery, nurtured my children on gentle irony, because the world doesn't teach the simple moral tales you believe in, boy.

"My mother never liked you," he says.

"We didn't know each other well."

"She said once when she came up from Brooklyn, you and Robert put her up in a tree house and took the steps away."

"I don't remember that. Millie was different from us. She knew all the latest songs. She saw Sinatra at the Paramount and I'd never heard of him. She was way ahead of us always."

"You don't mean that," said Jim.

"We thought so then. That's all that matters. She had an autograph book before I did, high heels, an ankle bracelet. It seemed important. She grew up faster than we did. Later I felt foolish with her, when she was already working."

"She *had* to grow up," said Jim Cogan. "Her mother died."

"I know that now. The knowledge of hindsight is a wonderful thing. And at the same time your mother was buying her own clothes and saving for a two-week vacation I was protected, that's true, and sent off with a group of girls and a French teacher to Europe. But please don't accuse me of it."

"I didn't accuse you."

"Yes you did. You accused me of having been brought up with all the advantages. Believe me there's no advantage. Your mother never liked me. Well, I envied her because I didn't know any better. She came here with her shoulder strap bag and Deanna Durbin doll in an evening gown. How was I to know that was all she had."

Doesn't he see it's necessary to hold something back? What is the use of pouring ourselves like so much unbaked custard out of the mold? There I am, shapeless but true, every dribble of my being. The advantages did matter I suppose: the good high school, fresh air, English bike, quadrangle of Georgian brick dormitories. It must have seemed an idyll to Millicent Murray riding the subways, the ring of typewriter bells and mindless dictation racing in her clever head. I'm hurt that she didn't like me. It never occurred to me that I wasn't lovable — me and my snot-school girl friends. Me and Robert, the Judge's children, with our constant pranks, our privilege in the neighborhood, our immunity. All that to live down. In any case she didn't know me.

"Tell me about Robert," Jim Cogan asked.

I said no. No. That I never talked about Robert with anyone and there was no reason to break my silence. It is my story, the story of my dead brother, and the time hasn't come, not yet. "My stories against your stories," I said to him, "but let my brother rest in peace."

"My mother said he was pretty smart."

That's the only time I feel the boy is my enemy, when he pushes me about Robert. I do not want to talk about that . . . aspect of the past, how we were and why it was . . . aspect of myself, kernel of truth even, history, personal history with all its thick accumulations of detail, emotion — smell like rotten breath of the last white funereal chrysanthemums being thrown out of the house after the last bewildering prayer . . . the unhealed wound of his death. . . . There are other stories.

When he was arrested, Jim Cogan turned up with a galloping case of gonorrhea. "He's a good boy," his mother cried a dozen times when she phoned me. Each morning I remind him to take his medicine before he goes out with the children to play ball. He was apprehended with crazies of assorted ages, bound in some half-baked religious destiny. They were on their way to blow up the Main Branch of the New York Public Library. Your hearts will recoil, Mr. and Mrs. America, for this boy was brought up on the classics: *The Little Engine That Could, The House at Pooh Corner, Aesop's Fables* and La Fontaine. The Saturday morning trip to the children's room to choose a stack of sticky books in their heavy green and red bindings with the fat white titles, the smell and stains of other children on the porous pages . . . Babar, the noble elephant, enlightened despot, culminating figure of the humanistic tradition was Jim's favorite. His distraught parents do not know where they've failed — to destroy the library!

I blame that slut of a girl who deceived him. She is diseased in many ways, a pathetic child who got the short end of the stick all her life, still I can't forgive her planting the bomb on Jim. I refuse to see brutal Shelley Waltz — the name offends me — as a glorious rebel. What right had she to damn us all and embrace God-knows-what infantile pursuit of herself — Creative Love. Jim, for all his honesty, will not condemn her. There's a bad odor about a man who's been betrayed. He throws all the blame on his brother and sister as though their adventure at the time — running away — was to spite him. Hateful, nasty children to him now, the Cogan twins disappeared for a few days in the late spring and when the police searched through the crowded household they found a perfect diagram of the catalogue department, the main reading room and rare book collection of the Forty-second Street Library emblazoned with the date of the "Holy Day of Destruction," and the exact hour when truth would rise from the ashes, love flower from the dead rot of the past. But the twins, those poor lost children never thought of Jim at all — their running away was their business, to punish their parents who had abandoned them long ago. They were out to injure, I suppose, but then no one knows what they feel or think. Still Jim, my Jim, must have someone to blame since his parents are too easy a mark and he is not ready to turn on himself, so *they*, they are rats.

I have started to think, to feel that I want to touch him — not to have anything from him, but to stroke him. As I might an animal . . . pat him as I'd pat the flank of a good dog — a healing touch. He brings peacock feathers home and we're struck with the beauty of it. Frieda and the kids wonder for a moment in their prison of routine. Are we so impoverished that a kitschy item from the Square fills our souls with delight? But it is this: given the ticky-tacky junk of his world he can still make us notice. What are we seeing? His indiscriminate joy. It rubs off. We're his audience. Dance to that boring music for us. Go into a mood — the desperate young man in a sulk. Shave or don't shave, it will make our day. Read a predictable passage to me about depletion, lost love. (Seems like old times. It could be my brother Robert standing in the bedroom door.) "I grow old . . . I grow old . . . / I shall wear the bottoms of my trousers rolled." Such heartache to remember the dead. My imagination has not grown so slack that I can't see that I should have held my ground and snickered at Robert as I do at this kid now. But I never did.

53

Wouldn't a laugh serve us better than to battle it out with our mortal souls? Come into this reasonable world with me. You'll find it amusing. That's an order. Hold my arm at the elbow there, like an escort. You see how decorous my methods are. It's easier in the long run and in the long run there are many stories, not always your own story, your own questions. Let me touch you now with the cool hand of reason: (more than anything I want to save him, and yet the pure strength is his: I must hope his touch will save me).

The Twins

AN APPLE CLEFT IN TWO is not more like than these two creatures. They were always together. They had not chosen each other as lovers do, or were not welded together by fear — like an old couple waiting, watching for signs of death in the other. They were twins, born at once. Siobhan the girl; Cormac the boy. Mild freaks of nature. Statistically possible. They had been invited, while still nursing consecutively at their mother's breast, to join the Twin Association of America which proffered outings, a Gemini newsletter, prizes awarded annually — most alike in the boy-girl, fraternal category. The offer was never pursued by their parents, who, though outwardly hearty, were shocked and depressed by the prospect of feeding, clothing, schooling two adorable crowd-stoppers.

Not quite identical their cribs and blankets, bonnets and stuffed dogs. One pink, one blue in a pale monochromatic world their eyes did not distinguish. Their mother seemed to enjoy distinctions that they felt unnecessary from the earliest moment of half-formed comprehension. "See *he* knows, he knows it's his doggie," Mill would say. She seemed always to be redistributing sweaters and socks and toys, shoving things at one or the other of them in an effort to realize their dual existence. Cormac, the boy. Siobhan, the girl. It was all one to them. Identical their round button faces, staring up with tempered curiosity at the world outside. They were always together.

A society of two, they devised a life of watching, touching each other, endlessly swapping cookies, sweaters, socks, doggies in a world without confusion. Stripped to their colorless underwear, they sensed, as they grew in understanding, that their father, their brother couldn't tell who was who and didn't much care. They were they. Their expensive equipment — double carriage and stroller — had no resale value at the Women's Exchange. Their mother advertised in *Brooklyn Buy-lines* and finally gave it all away, including the matching high chairs and two little pots ("I'm a big boy," ditto big girl) to an exhausted Puerto Rican woman who showed up, desperate with the prediction of twins. They remembered it all for they were in kindergarten already and their mother was packing up the house, about to leave Brooklyn Heights for Park Slope. The Puerto Rican woman stood in the doorway, supporting her lower back with her hands, carrying nothing besides her great belly, her money folded in an envelope, pinned to the pocket of her maternity dress. They remembered her band of dirty black-eyed children who played noisily on the steps and then helped the woman wheel away the cumbersome apparatus that had belonged so specially to them. They would never forget the look the woman gave them, dark as a curse, *two*, Christ in heaven! There were two of them.

It was natural that they should confound their teachers though not by physical resemblance alone. Siobhan would be in plaid school dresses playing (not by choice) with girls — jump rope, circle games — while Cormac in his corduroys would be set to climbing monkey bars and whacking balls against his will. They preferred each other. And their teachers could not find the proper words in all their growing, learning, building terminology to describe what it was that made their efforts and the whole "classroom experience" seem remote to these two children. Teachers did not like the Cogan twins and though they reported them as "working well with the group" and "sufficient in basic skills" they could not stand their solidarity, their spooky habits of coughing, smiling, scratching at the same moment. Two bodies with one mind. There came a time, naturally, when it was suggested that they would discover themselves (himself and herself) to better advantage if separated and so Siobhan was put in one third grade, Cormac down the hall in another. They went on strike: silent and automatic as two wonderfully programmed machines, they opened and closed their books, they lifted their pencils but they did not add, subtract, or even write the date at the top of the paper. They did not read. Their passivity was mysteriously perfect, almost holy in its commitment to reunite them. At home they yowled — Cormac would begin a complaint, Siobhan finish it — or they would come out with the same objection in one instant, until at last Jack Cogan, to preserve his wife's sanity (*he* absented himself from the house every night for a week) insisted that the whole experiment be called off. There was no dealing with them.

Tested, they proved to be of average and identical intelligence. Siobhan no brighter than Cormac. Cormac held no edge on Siobhan. Their brother, Jim, was thought to be brilliant and lived in a world with their parents. Five years older, he had always defended them from the neighborhood bullies who found in their duplicate faces an eerie reflection of the unnatural and pelted them with stones and jibes. Jim at twelve had distinguished himself at school. He was tall, athletic, better than their father at pumping up bicycle tires and teaching them to throw a ball. But he stood alone: not even set against them in a family rivalry, leading his own life, somewhat bored and bothered by their games because after all they had each other. His gruff kindness at twelve screened a real distaste for them, a resentment that they were not one — one younger brother, even a sister would at least be a person. As he grew older he found less time for the twins, sufficient to themselves, and his loathing lost intensity. He could muster no easy case against them as he could against his father and mother. The kids were preposterous. At best their sameness seemed to Jim zany, far out. Like Eighth Street freaks who can't help it — they were they.

It never occurred to the Cogan twins that they had excluded their brother like the rest of the world. Now that they were twelve and Jim seventeen even the obligatory pranks were dropped. They no longer ribbed him about girls, swiped his razor, or discovered his copies of *Playboy* under the mattress. Their mother persisted, as she had throughout their childhood, in enforcing their separate identities. Siobhan was packed off to girls' parties and dragged to the ballet yearly, while Cormac was made to swim at the Y and fitted out with a lot of baseball equipment. Nothing took. Separated, they were like a slick surface to which nothing adheres: together they absorbed each other.

The Cogan twins had spent last summer on the back porch. From the heavy hot day school let out in June until the empty Monday of Labor Day weekend, sitting on the porch was their only occupation. They left their post for meals, trudging up the three flights to eat in silence, giving — in response to their mother's hysterical demands for their attention — compliance cool as a handshake. Would they want to go out to Shea Stadium, Millie asked. OK. To the beach? Fine. Van Cortlandt Park and bring a lunch? Sure. Her face blossomed with anger. What kind of life was it sitting down there on the porch? And she was three flights up over Bruckner Boulevard — what kind of life was that? If they wanted to go to day camp, St. Regis where Jimmy was a counselor that summer, she'd be happy to get a part-time job at her old office — better than sweating it out on the top floor. They *liked* staying home. Well, they shouldn't, said their mother, perspiring through her flimsy wrapper. It stuck to the small of her back: large half-moons soaked down from her armpits. It wasn't healthy sitting down there — they *must* go to camp. Play ball, swim, sing, breathe clean air. They pleaded with their mother to stay home, but the summer's drama had been set in motion. The two helpless ginger-haired children stood by and watched their mother, already taking up the hem of an old dress. She was about to resume her famous career.

Millicent Murray Cogan had been the top girl in her secretarial class. She could take eighty words a minute from her boss who was sharp enough to give them. After one week in the typing pool he had spotted her for a gem. President of his own small company, Mr. Spears was always glad to see Millicent over the years, sent her an impressive Christmas card, even to this dump. When things got bad at home she went back to work in his office and the twins were surprised by their mother's worldly beauty as she departed dressed for town. She left behind a sense of defeat: their father with a day's growth of beard had tied their shoes and combed their hair. One day he had forgotten to give them breakfast and they could not bear to tell him as he collected their schoolbooks and hurried them out the door: they sat through the morning class stunned with hunger and humiliation.

So now they insisted fervently that they were happy on the back porch. They promised to ride their bikes, play stickball in the driveway if she would only stay at home and save them from day camp. She retreated and for a week the kids had ridden their bikes around to a vacant lot and played gin rummy until it was safe to go home. Then they settled on the back porch again, thick as thieves. Whatever they had to say was a mystery to the world. Unhealthy, thought Mill and started in on them again. She would return to her illustrious office. Their father seemed to be passing his vacation at Aqueduct — an expensive resort — never mind summer camp, they'd be happy to get the rent money out of him. But when Millicent Murray called the legendary Mr. Spears at his small publishing company, she was told that he had suffered a fatal heart attack and the firm was sold to two young men she'd never heard of and what's more they had never heard of her.

After that the Cogan twins were left to sit the summer out on the porch undisturbed. No more activity than moving their tiny charms around the Monopoly board. In the afternoon Silvio came across the driveway home from work early, odd baker's hours that sent him out at dawn and left him free as a child in the afternoon. He wondered at them, the two fair children so alike. Their pale eyes, their round faces the mirror of each other — *gemelli*, the freckles across their noses reproduced with mechanical perfection. *Gemelli*, he named them every day, endowing the word with some of the magic he felt in their presence. And they talked. Millicent often caught them unaware — the three of them laughing and carrying on. She would hear them from the upper story window or find them in a state of rapture as she came up the drive with a bag of groceries. She couldn't understand a word Silvio said, but he was polite to her, carried her bags up three flights, calling her Missuz — "Thank you,

Missuz," he said, as though he were a delivery boy. Then they'd be at it again, laughing until it got on her nerves and she'd shut the back window. Lonely, cut out of her children's life while an illiterate wop, just off the boat . . . she was sorry then. He was a nice man. He was married to a bitch.

Though he had a last name, no one remembered it — Silvio married to that Grassi girl, the local whore. The Grassis, who owned the row of houses on the Boulevard, had sailed off with their brutish daughter on the *Cristoforo Colombo* and returned with Silvio, smiling, chunky in his Sunday suit. He wore a noticeably bright yellow wedding band. It was a scandal for a week. Then it became history as the Grassi girl settled into the flat opposite the Cogans' bedroom windows with her new suites of furniture, an enormous color TV and hi-fi in matching Renaissance consoles. Sometimes Jim kicked a ball around the driveway with Silvio in a friendly attempt at soccer. He was all right in Millie Cogan's book. She could hardly blame him for preferring the company of her kids to that of his wife. A childlike man in so many ways, who'd been bought like a piece of goods.

The camaraderie down on the back stoop was not quite innocent, neither was it intentionally corrupt. The twins had hit upon a subject of interest to them all, no less a matter than the record of their unfortunate lives — what had brought them to this backwater in the Bronx on the brink of their teens and joined them with this sweet Italian baker in mutual despair. The situation of good soap opera — misfits unite in a confessional mode — the duped foreigner, the powerless children in a brutal world. Ripe for the sentimentalist. Set on the back stoop of a fringe neighborhood during the endless hot days of a New York summer. Three unlikely friends, giving themselves to the suffocating heat, artificial soda pop and contaminated air that drifted to them from the highway out front. If only Silvio, instead of being able-bodied, had been in some way maimed or dim-witted, they would have made the perfect gothic trio, classic refutation of the healthy American scene. They passed the time together safe from the world — that was all — and by a precise calculation of the emotions, knowing that they were safe from each other, too, they told all.

Silvio of his marriage: how he had worked in the bakery in his city, Reggio di Calabria, since he was ten, two years younger than the Cogan kids now. He had swept up and run errands until he was old enough to learn how to make rolls for the morning customers.

"Who came to the shop?" one of the twins would ask. They became experts at prolonging Silvio's stories. The simplest question was reason enough for him to go on, finding his way slowly through the English sentences. Women came in the morning or sent the children to get little rosetti that were perfectly shaped, crusty, still warm in the center. He took what was left to his mother and sisters at noon.

"And everyone paid?"

"Yes." The poor lived on a coarse loaf dusted with flour from the dark little bakery in the old town. He would give his eyes to taste that bread now.

"Because our flour is bad," one of the Cogans prompted.

"Yes, is terrible flour," said their friend in a refrain that often ended one of Silvio's tales. And the oven is wrong, he told them a hundred times. The big stainless steel ovens down at Mercurio's "Bit o' Italy Bake Shop," with racks large and clean enough for surgery were a second best to the encrusted iron monster back home.

"And your sisters sewed?"

His three sisters and his mother. They sewed: taking turns at the machine, doing handwork by the window. They

61

sewed from breakfast to supper — from supper to bedtime, making dresses for the ladies in town.

It held romance for the twins — the continuity of daily life, the sameness of the passing hours. The noonday soup. The complete security of the spare household. Together they made a picture of it from Silvio's words: the near-sighted sisters, chunky like Silvio and dark — the youngest still with a heavy braid down her back. A streak of light upon the carefully sewn dresses, their colors and patterns the only changing aspect of the room. The rest was set for-ever: the photograph of their father and mother in wedding clothes on an empty radio cabinet adorned with plastic vio-lets, a large sepia tint of the Sacred Heart faded over the years until his eyes were scummed white, stoned like some hip religious beauty in a crown of thorns. A machine-made tapestry, bought at the market place, was displayed over the one fat armchair — the hopeful sheen of Pope John's peasant face. The scene fixed by poverty and yet, the limits of that room, the set schedule of Silvio's family in Reggio di Calabria — Thursday beef liver, Saturday baths, Sunday flowers to the father's grave — seemed beautiful to the twins. In their short lives they had moved so many times, each apartment was a come-down or so their mother said. Things were always different — they could never be sure when they came home from school that they would find the chairs and tables in the same place — there were constant improvements, incomplete, half-tacked, half-sewn. They hated the changing scene of their house as much as they hated their father's luck, whether good or bad. It was all too shaky, built of cardboard, full of thrills they'd never asked for. Silvio had eaten liver every Thursday of his life. Beauti-ful.

He told the truth: it was not so beautiful to him: the dragging sameness year after year. At ten he was working like a man, too exhausted to kick a ball back to his friends when he went home in the evening. At twelve he was trying to read at night. They had said he was quick in school, but that seemed long ago. He could not keep his eyes open. His mother would wake him, put a marker of thread in his book and send him off to bed. She was gruff, somewhat cruel — calling him professor. He'd be late at the bakery and they would get another boy. Once when he started from his nap he saw that his mother's eyes were flooded watching him and she had put aside her work quickly as the tears spilled down her cheeks and threatened the silk of a lady's blouse. But that was only once in his memory, and she had then embroidered a little bookmark for him out of scraps — an imitation of the ones she had seen in shop windows against an open prayer book. He had treasured it, but soon he gave up reading. They were cold in winter. There was one dim light over the table. His stomach was angry with hunger by the time he got home for supper and unsatisfied at the end of the meal. His sisters were stupid and sour.

"And then Angie came?"

Yes. Old Grassi and his wife and ugly daughter drove a big air-conditioned Cadillac into town. Whenever Silvio's story came to this point, a punctuation of giggles began that floated up to Millie in her isolation on the third floor. Sometimes a single word would rise in a high-pitched squeal from one of her children — "pigs," "toilet," "like pigs," and she stopped dead in the midst of her kitchen work, half-naked as usual, thinking that they were in league against her, those three. Yet she was powerless. There was nothing in the words themselves that gave her cause. When she asked, what were the pigs and toilets that were so funny — the twins had said, "Nothing," as a further addition to the nothing, nothing and more nothing that they had always given her.

63

"Matrimonial bed" was a further cry that alarmed Millicent Cogan one day as she looked out back to see if they
were still at it. It was close to suppertime. She thought she
heard the bus from Camp Regis letting Jim off and she liked
to be at the window and call down to him after his long day.
"Matrimonial bed" she heard first from Siobhan who was
bold. That was a shock to Mill and she wondered what
smut they were talking. Silvio was not a child after all.
Then Jimmy came up — not even puffing after the three
flights — and that made Millicent feel better. She resented
it when he stayed down there for a while, laughing and
talking. It was the only time he spent with his brother and
sister now. She should have been fair about it, but she
couldn't stand it. She was alone so much. The heat on the
top floor was awful. There was no place now for her to go
or even dream of going, since the old company was sold.
Mr. Spears had his fatal attack and a good part of her life
was dead and gone.

When Jim came upstairs she gave him a tall glass of iced
tea and asked excitedly who'd won. The camp he worked at
was divided into teams, the Reds and the Blues, and they
tallied up before taps at the end of the day — all the races
and games, the points for tent inspection and latrine duty.
Then the day was awarded. Open warfare and Mill Cogan
was caught up in it. She couldn't stop herself, though
Jimmy mocked her. It was neck and neck, the Blues being
better swimmers while the Reds had the baseball team.
Jimmy's boys at Regis were Blues, had a slight edge, but
they'd lost the day. "Damn Reds!" she cried and slammed
her fist on the table. Jim said, "It's only a game, Mother."
But she had found herself somedays at lunch hoping the
Blues had been first in place at table waiting for Father
Keene to say grace. There was an extra point. She felt fool-
ish about it, that she should care about the Blues more than

Jim who was out there all day with the boys. He was angry about the job which paid only twenty-five dollars a week. It was the job for some rich kid he'd told his mother. "Money isn't everything," she said and Jimmy said, to make her mad, "Since when?"

"Maybe your Dad will sell one of those machines," said Millicent, running for neutral ground. *She* could go on about Jack Cogan's sins all she wanted but her children were to stay off him as though her worthless husband were not identical to their disappointing father.

On this evening, when her Blues had lost, Mill said to her son, "What are they talking about down there?"

"Nothing," Jim said. He was already into the refrigerator, pulling out a chicken leg.

"Don't eat that," she said. "I've got your supper ready," and Mill went to call the twins. They came noisily up the back stairs, then settled in their unforgivable silence at the kitchen table. "And how's your baker friend?" their mother asked sharply.

"OK," said one child.

"OK," said the other. They shared a look. She had never found fault with Silvio.

"And do tell me," she said, laughing in a sham sophistication that they knew well, "about the matrimonial bed."

Cormac and Siobhan looked blankly into each other's eyes.

"I could hear you shrieking," her voice rose in perfect mimicry of their twelve-year-old cries. "The matrimonial bed!"

"Oh, that's just what you call a double bed in Italian."

She didn't catch which one gave her the answer that told her nothing, nothing that she wanted to know, but she would never get another word from them that was certain. God knows what these children might be listening to from that man, clean as he looked. She was bringing her family up alone, and she passed out their plates of macaroni and cheese, leaving a niggardly portion for Jack when he came in. Let it crust over and dry out.

He was held up in traffic, no doubt, over the Triborough Bridge, saying he made a late call — when the only customers he had out on the Island were nags, a losing proposition. She could smell where he'd been, not the smell of beer and cigar smoke for that was easily worn off, but the stench of his soul, rotten with guilt, only wanting her to ferret it out like the racing forms left in his pocket. She would not punish him. The rage which swelled in her throat against Jack Cogan was too good for him. Mill gasped as though for a cool breath of air in the silent, hot kitchen where she was alone — all alone with her children — Jim with his adolescent melancholy and those two, those queer quiet rubber stamps of each other. She smiled. She blotted the steaming red ringlets at her temples with a paper napkin. Once more she would call them to her and give them not the world three flights up, but the moon and the stars: "It's late," she said pleasantly, "Your Dad's probably sold one of those marvelous machines."

Silvio

THE STORY OF THE TWINS, their family. An interlude, what they learned from an immigrant, Silvio, a man unaccustomed to his surroundings who told them about their world though they never suspected it. The kids thought they were listening to tales of another land, like the children's stories they'd recently abandoned. Silvio was everything they wanted in a prince, in a father who was not their father, a brother of their blood by the machinations of wacky cartoon comedy that whisked away Jim as a pretender and gave them Silvio, solid as the wages he earned, an adult, yet tender, open as they were to pain. A man for whom they were real. The twins seemed to hold back from growth, to wait longer than other children for the next step up the receding fun-house ladder towards maturity. They didn't understand that it was an interlude: the long summer that consigned them (as though by another of their stubborn fancies) to the back porch, the empty afternoons of a man who came home from work at lunchtime and who lived with his wife in an American city (shopping, visiting, riding the highways) though he had not spiritually moved in. He didn't understand the ball games on TV or fit with the lax beer drinking company at the neighborhood bar. He believed in a nap after lunch and his wife did not understand that.

Some days she would lie with him until he made love to her then telephone to her mother or a friend. He would fall asleep with the interminable English chatter in his ear and wake to find she had gone out. More often she was not home at all when he returned from work. It was after his nap that Silvio dressed in one of the up-to-the-minute outfits Angie had bought for him — up-to-the-minute trousers, flapping at the bottom, binding in the crotch, shirts meant for a fairy — and crossed over the driveway to sit with the Cogan kids. All dressed up and no place to go. He did not even have a driver's license. He seemed stunned as much by his marriage as by the entire world around him. Within ·a year he would zoom round the corner in his Pontiac to watch the Mets at the Italian soccer club up on Fordham Road. It was only this season that he had with the kids. Friendship flared like first love. The twins taught him to ride a bike. They played softball until they broke a window in the downstairs flat. They kept up the endless words for each other like unending gifts, stories within stories. They had time for the leisurely narrative of their lives.

The matrimonial bed came at the end of a story. Old Grassi had driven into Reggio di Calabria, to the town of his youth, in his air-conditioned Cadillac with his wife and daughter sealed in the back seat. The tinted windows concealed Mrs. Grassi's obesity and Angie's fixed nose, her capped teeth and irremediable skin. The word got around that the girl was breathtaking, blond, tall. The legend of Angelina blossomed for one night to wither before noon the next day when she walked out in her sleazy bright slacks, her unexceptional breasts poking her gay jersey in a futile attempt at sensuality. She spoke to no one. Boys made sucking, popping noises with their mouths. She was haughty and grim, withstood the flack as she passed the town café like a pro. Before evening the word was out — Grassi's daughter was a pig, fat-assed, breasts like little lemons. By the next morning she was bald, wore a wig, her nose had shrunk to a wart. Angelina was, in fact, only a high school whore, the ugly girl, too friendly, who can only make it on her back.

Grassi's hopes of a young doctor who might be willing to take on Angelina if staked to a couple of years to qualify him in the States, collapsed within hours. As the days of dry heat wore on his daughter seemed more repulsive to him. Her expensive face pouted behind large sunglasses. She constantly changed from one gaudy outfit to another and was thought pathetic by her poor cousins in their simple, well-made clothes. His wife bursting with weeks of pasta, fought with him instead of her relatives whom she had not seen in thirty years. Having wept and embraced them, she hated them all — their nasty little kitchens, their washboards and old-fashioned laundry soaps, their piety. Above all, she was resentful about two green toilets which she had sent ahead — one for Grassi's brother, one for her old mother. They sat, clean, beautiful, inviting and useless, like works of art in the hall of each house. No one could install them. The pipes were different here. The toilets were not even admired — better ones were to be had from Milan.

Day after day Grassi woke to the groans of his wife suffering with constipation. At noon he gagged watching her consume more spaghetti and macaroni, ziti, fettuccine, loading herself like a cart in the supermarket. They must leave: his love for his sisters and brothers was disintegrating under the daily exposure of his wife and daughter. This was his success then — after years of work as a mason, president of his local, delegate to the Labor Council, AFL–CIO — this family, this car, a few cheap rents in the Bronx. He ordered Angie to pack the suitcases. She was delighted and at once became as sweet as the stamped plastic doll she resembled. For the first time she offered to help, went out to the bread shop where she met Silvio and fell in love.

Angelina was the sort of girl who had always known as she wriggled out of her underclothes in the back seat of a car that it did not really hurt her to be bad, for she thought it *was* bad to pass herself around as casually as a shared can of beer, but there was some part of her, she believed, that was not touched, that was saved and pure. In her neighborhood the great sexual revolution of the sixties had not established itself beyond the newsstand. Startling and grotesque to her as the mores of some naked African tribe was the idea of love reduced to a catchword, scattered as promiscuously in life as it was on every manufactured article of the day. She was too dim to realize that she was not one bad girl but part of a cultural trend, absolved by the times, *her* times. She thought of herself as fallen but only in some public part of herself. Her telephone number she knew to be scrawled over urinals in high school while the private Angie, essentially innocent, was ripe for redemption.

Fumbling, she counted out the Italian money on Silvio's

bread counter. Their fingers met in the coins. Shyly she drew her hand away and waited for him to sort his payment from the change spilled between them. He was young and black-haired, natural behind his loaves, unconscious of her sharp colors and porcelain smile. When he looked at her, Silvio saw her eyes were as honest in response to his good nature as the eyes of an animal — eyes like flecked marble of Italy, eyes like the prettiest girl in this town that she might have come from, the only thing left to her, set in the bizarre construction devised by the plastic surgeon, the orthodontist, the dermatologist and beautician. She was a nice enough girl. Flustered by his straight look she walked to the door, left her purse, came back unbelieving to his smile once again.

Grassi's daughter bought a lot of bread and before the suitcases were ever packed she presented him with Silvio — broad-boned, undernourished, smiling, always smiling with perfect peasant teeth, a boy radiating honesty through his cardboard Sunday suit. Good and plain as his bread, a twenty-two-year-old virgin. (This was put to the Cogan twins as never having loved a woman and translated back to its plain meaning as they had all of Silvio's groping words that skirted the details of Angie's past.) At their first interview old man Grassi knew he could not get a better bargain than the baker's boy: for his part Silvio wanted a job in America, free apartment *and* a matrimonial bed.

Laughter on the back porch — uncontrollable giggles. Matrimonial bed! Twelve-year-old spasms of the urethra. The Cogan kids were convulsed, as though in laughing at the odd foreign phrase they were laughing at adults' closed doors, lowered voices, contradictions and quarrels. Laughing at their parents' big bed which they hated. It had only lately occurred to them to fear what might happen there upon the double stretch of space, but nothing — they could believe that nothing happened between their father and mother. Once, in some time before the memory of man, perhaps, but nothing on the matrimonial bed.

Silvio had his own reasons for laughing: the courage it had taken to throw in a demand for the bed. Why not? Grassi knew his daughter was no bargain. He had staked his manhood on that extra. If he didn't get the bed — what then? Return to the bakery for life — the drag of three sisters and his mother squinting over their stitches year after year. No delights and little meat. Silvio smiled on Angelina's father: this was his one chance to be bought with honor. The bed became an important demand.

He would laugh at himself for the rest of his life. How could he have imagined the showrooms of furniture that Angie and her mother had been lusting after — the baronial suites, the Spanish credenza, the ceramic leopard blooming three-way light bulbs, the coffin-size freezer and the king-size bed with velvet headboard concealing the massage controls. They had haunted the furniture stores desiring all of it, wanting tables and chairs with a shared passion more consuming than their passion for clothes. They had put out a lot on Angie's face, her closets were stuffed but all of this still lay ahead. The fantasy of one of Grassi's flats being turned over to them like a gigantic dollhouse ate at the mother and unmarried daughter as they wandered through the furniture displays desperate with wanting: Angie excitedly pacing off a sofa's length, trying the feel of it on her butt, stroking the fabric — her heart set on cut velvet — deep blood velvet with a pattern of flowers rising from a rust background, the color of an old fender. Angie paced through love seats and lounges, never settling long — like a bitch in heat, while her mother, fat and spayed, would collapse into an easy chair, spread-legged, sighing, her large unopened purse held to her stomach like a poultice.

71

So much for Silvio's manly ultimatum. The matrimonial bed indeed! He could not conceive of the delivery vans that would back into the narrow old-fashioned driveway to unload the monstrous suites of furniture that now made up his home. The Grassi women bought and bought and bought — but he was the first essential item. He wondered one afternoon sitting out a heat wave with the Cogan twins, if he were to disappear or meet a violent death on the subway at night would the furniture go away too. He felt so bound with it, his destiny shared with all the wood and foam rubber and springs. A van would draw up and carry it away, piece by glamorous piece, and old Mamma Grassi would scream and throw the money out of her purse at the moving men but her dollars would be useless as the play money that went with the game the children played. Angelina would cry behind a blank window, stripped of its ball-fringed valance with an antique satin swag. Angelina would cry in her ravaged apartment and he, Silvio, still unsure of the English word for bread, for milk, for bitterness, would be gone too.

The Cogan kids looked up at the back-side of the drapes, drawn to keep the light off the new carpets and furniture. Their mother had cursed every piece that had been hauled into Angie's apartment. She had laughed at the starlight Formica. The story was a mystery to the kids, their mother's mockery and the dream-like desire of Angie and fat Mrs. Grassi. For what? Scraps of wallpaper the twins had rescued from the trash can for an afternoon game. Dazzling stripes, mottled flowers. Who cares? And their friend Silvio, his sad story. The first months of his marriage: he would go to work and come home at noon and lie down alone on his matrimonial bed. Toward evening he would hear Angelina's car drive in. She dragged herself upstairs — her father had given them the top flat in the house, a daily reminder of his charity. Silvio would lie on the bed and wait for the sound of her key in the lock, her shoes kicked off, the pad of her weary feet to the door of their bedroom. Haggard and sallow, her reconstructed face fallen under the strain of a day's buying. She looked terrible, terrible, Silvio thought, frightening too, haunted by her knowledge and sorrow as a man come back from war who has seen too much to tell. Often she held samples in her hand — bits of cloth, paint chips, a chain hung with floor tiles. He would pat the bed for her to come and lie beside him and let him smooth her stiff bleached hair. In his deft hands her ruined forehead and cheeks and nose would shape again like dough into the untroubled doll's face she had purchased at such cost. He looked into her eyes: wounded, dazed, dumb. She was a nice girl and he loved her.

Here was the secret of the matrimonial bed, not to be believed by the Cogan kids: Silvio loved his awful wife. They laughed no more. The eyes of a princess in the face of a toad. The baker's wish was to cure Angelina, to lie with her, to hold her until one day she would be at peace. There would be no need for her to buy, to buy anything at all, and she would be waiting for him when he came home, smiling, at rest. He saw her laid out as though in death on their vast vibrating bed and when he kissed her he would see from her wakening eyes that she was no longer possessed, the insatiable craving was gone forever. The twins turned sulky when Silvio, by one route or another arrived at the princess on the bed. They did not understand. For the first time Siobhan averted her eyes, not to meet her brother's look. There was something here that they could not understand together.

Stories: Upstairs their mother poured gin into her ginger ale. An old story that. Millie Cogan's drinking had regis-

73

tered with her children years ago. It was controlled and steady. Jimmy knew but was silent. He looked hard at the twins one day as they carried a glass which seemed to be full of water out of the bathroom to the back of the stove where their mother could reach it easily. They knew never to tag along when their mother went out in the afternoon. That improbable errand every other day at the drugstore always to return empty-handed, the half-pint in her purse. Cheerful and false, Mill had no complaint about the stairs then. With grim pleasure she climbed to her tower. Millicent Cogan was never drunk. The most that her children held against her was a scorched shirt or that some nights they were served both potatoes and rice. At five she made a pot of coffee — her movements were perceptibly slow, overly precise — and began coming out of the afternoon haze. Each day her children felt the strain — would she make it back to her corner, ready to come out swinging when their father came home? Her recovery was a miracle to the twins. They spoke of it once to Jim, but he managed only a grunt, a slight tribute to their mother's resilience. If it came out in the open, he would be the first to cry.

Their mother had a rotten time last summer when the Cogan kids spent so much time talking to Silvio. They sensed it coming on: Siobhan eyeing Cormac — that crazy fix on Jim's Blue team. Calling down to them from the back window the few times it rained — "The baseball game will be off this afternoon!" Not that they should come in and keep dry, but that some silly kids unknown to her would not be fighting it out in their ridiculous camp war. Silvio understood nothing of this. Her daily bout with the bottle overwhelmed him. He asked after their mother each day as though Millie were in the throes of a terminal disease.

When the terrible moment came for Mill *not* to get a job, to be turned down by fate, the passage of time, the death of a now legendary character, old Mr. Spears, Silvio was at a

74

loss to comfort his friends. Had the man been her patron? Her lover? No, the children said, but found it too difficult to explain—the years they had suffered Mr. Spears. Mr. Spears for years — his auto — Chrysler Imperial, his office —red leather and mahogany. His home — Spanish revival abutting an Eden-like golf course. His wife, a paste-up of good labels. His children embossed with the seals of fine schools. Where to begin with the glory of it all? Mr. Spears was her one and only boss. Oh, the trips that she had made to Sherry Wines and Spirits when he was stocking his cellar for the season. Little Miss Murray with an incomprehensible list of vintages and chateaux in her hand. For Thanksgiving and Christmas she still bought a bottle of wine off that list, or what she thought approximated that list of long ago.

Their mother's language always took an elegant turn when she recounted her years with Mr. Spears. The time she had "assisted" him in selecting an incomparable brooch for Mrs. Spears at Cartier's or the sumptuous peignoir she had advised him upon in Saks for the Spearses' anniversary. The weekends that young Millicent Murray had spent at the Spearses' home to take dictation and type long catalogue listings were replete with eggs benedict, soufflés, crab quiche and linzer torte. The kids wondered, really, how there was time to stuff it all down. Whenever their mother ripped a recipe out of the *Times* with flair it was accompanied by a cheer for the good old days: "Oh, this looks like that simple apple charlotte that Mrs. Spears made one Sunday night!" That simple apple charlotte must soon be served to the Cogans and they all must love it, though it was only at their kitchen table and not set out on little trays with a plate of *fantastic* sandwiches so that they all might draw round the fire in what their mother recalled as "the utmost informality."

Now Mr. Spears had had his heart attack. Never again

would Millicent Cogan become the heroine of her stories — planning her triumphant return to the publishing house, setting out clothes that still suited her, colors that complemented her brilliant hair. She would never again roam through the shoes and handbags at Altman's during a luxurious lunch hour as she had done twenty years ago and ever after in her dreams.

Millie had spent those weekends in the grandeur of Mr. Spears's home as his secretary, but truly, she told her children, "I was more like a daughter to them, and your father was desolate." She had to leave her suitor, Jack Cogan, to fend for himself. But after two years with Mr. Spears (the twins sang in private: "Mr. Spears for two years! Three cheers for Mr. Spears!") she did, in fact, marry Cogan and though she worked till Jim was born it was never the same in the office, nor was she so special. Her wedding present from the Spearses was a decanter of Waterford crystal, never used. Mill Cogan carried it in her lap whenever they moved and placed it behind locked doors of the china closet where it was now, three flights up, catching the smogged sunlight off Bruckner Boulevard. What her children could never understand was *why*. Why, if it was all so grand had she ever married their father and brought an end to the tale. It was a tale, of course, and reality claimed her as it must all sensible grown-ups: Jack Cogan was in her neighborhood, of her world. To believe another of their mother's stories — that their father was a romantic figure, a rival to her glamorous career — was as much beyond the Cogan twins as the mystery of the matrimonial bed.

So with the news of Mr. Spears's heart attack, their mother, Millicent Murray Cogan, became unknown, another mop-up call handled by a girl on the switchboard. That day Siobhan, coming up from the back porch to go to the bathroom, found that her mother had burnt her hand on the kettle. Long blisters were struck down the back of each finger. Millicent cried and gave herself readily into her daughter's care. Easy enough for the child to steer her mother into bed for she was half-clothed, her globular breasts heaving with sobs: "You've been a good girl," said Mill in drunken final judgment.

Then again, their father was a gambler. During the summer he was losing his spring gains at the track and returned home each evening too late to have been at his job. Waiting for dinner, Cormac clutched his transistor to his ear: The ABC helicopter announced a five-car collision on the Van Wyck Expressway. F.D.R. Drive leading to the Triborough was moderate to heavy. The WPAT top tunes were interrupted to report a trailer truck jackknifed on the Major Deegan. Gosh! Poor Dad. As his son well knew, Jack Cogan's trip from the track was clear sailing. At La Guardia he joined the Grand Central Parkway coming into town against the traffic.

Still, it was something grisly for the twins to pursue — all those streams of cars choking the arteries of the city. They read in the *Post* about a retired schoolteacher in Yorkville who had lost two dachshunds within the year walking them down by the river — lung cancer. Carbon monoxide . . . sulfuric waste. And here was Jack Cogan courageously driving home. "A team of research scientists at Manhattan's Rockefeller Institute has computed that during the peak traffic hours the air on the major highways in and around the city comprises a solid mass of lethal materials equal to the cubic feet in the standard apartment house elevator." Cormac clipped this from the *Reader's Digest* and read it to his mother when it looked as though she needed help to pull out of the afternoon booze. "Poor Daddy!" moaned Siobhan.

"Oh, I imagine he'll make it!" Mill said sarcastically, but she did have another cup of coffee to bring herself round.

77

"Perhaps he's sold one of those marvelous machines." They were always glad to hear that from her. Even Jim felt that the old domestic ship, creaking and unseaworthy as it might be, was launched for another few days.

Silvio believed all this against his will: the mother of these miraculous children was a drunk: the father a gambler. Right now the Cogans were living on the end of a big commission that Jack had earned nine months ago. As a salesman for Merganthaller he need only sell one computer-linotype to carry him for the year. The price of a complete installation (with yearly servicing for a five-year period) was anywhere from ninety to one hundred and fifty thousand dollars. He had been lucky and sold a deluxe model with an extended memory bank on one of his first calls, cashing in on months of work done by a salesman who'd been bought by IBM. It was the perfect job for Cogan — he spent only a few hours each day bringing round Merganthaller's new brochure to the customers in his territory and the rest of the time was his. The sales meetings were a challenge to his love of invention. Once a month he would rise from his chair at the conference table and report on calls he had never made, whole conversations with an executive officer at the research division of Standard Oil would be brilliantly fabricated. Cogan, the fourflusher, was more convincing than the men who had dutifully gone their rounds each day, played golf, eaten lunches, sent Christmas greetings to prospective customers, indeed performed well in their friendly but slightly subservient roles.

The job at Merganthaller came to have an excitement equal to an open challenge to fate. He had promised Mill that if things went well and he sold another machine they would look for a house — somewhere in Rye perhaps, or New Rochelle. Having promised, he avoided any serious

78

pursuit of selling the wonderful machines. It frightened and thrilled him as the weeks went by. His days at the track were busy and taut: his life at home a cheerful avoidance of any honesty with his wife and children. In the fall, after Labor Day, say . . . there was nothing doing now . . . luck would run with him. He'd make a sale.

Stories within stories: One of their tales Silvio refused to believe. It was true what the kids described as their life of crime. They did steal and cheat in all the local stores. This is where Jimmy, their brother who had grown so peripheral, came back into their lives, saying, "You kids stay out of the shops up on Conner Street or I'll beat the hell out of you." The threat was idle, but he might tell their father — just when the horses were running against Cogan. It would kill their mother. Jim would never say a word.

Their brother had paid the manager of the Rivoli ten dollars out of his own savings, after it became known that they had worked out a racket passing two Cogans into the theater for the price of one. They would never forget the scene — this big bald guy yelling at Jim about turning them over to the juvenile authorities. The carpeted warmth of the movie-house lobby became a high-ceilinged nightmare. The lights were up. The popcorn machine shut off between performances. The cold reality now of this familiar place, usually more inviting than the front room at home, this dim foyer to darkness and dreams, the enchanted self.

"A couple of gangsters. Twelve years old. How many times you been in here kids?" the manager asked.

"Five times," they lied. Jimmy took out ten dollars.

"I'm glad they're your problem," the man said. "I wouldn't of known, I hadn't seen the boy there," pointing at both of them, "coming out of the ladies' room."

So they were ordered by Jim to the back porch and dared

79

not leave. Even when they gave Silvio the details — how Cormac passed his ticket stub out the rest room window — he did not believe them. Such pretty children. They said life was a prison and continued to serve out their term. They never convinced Silvio that they did actually steal and cheat and lie. It started with them as a game, to trick the sharp-tongued fatty in the drug store, a two hundred pounder with access to cosmetic samples, made-up like a show girl. She hated kids. The neighborhood toughs snickered, called her names, stared at the garnet dinner ring grown into the rolls of blubber on her hand. Her voice was broken and hoarse, "Don't touch. You gonna buy? Buy already." It was too easy: Siobhan, in a sweat shirt and jeans, a perfect replica of Cormac. A rusty-haired, blue-eyed child would pay for a package of gum and by the time fatty looked up from the register, the same child with the same gum would smile at her, lingering, not gone yet on his way. They progressed to candy bars, combs, notebooks, ball-point pens. They worked Grant's, the stationery store for greeting cards and comics, the delicatessen for Devil Dogs and Eskimo Pies.

When they were caught at the Rivoli the thrill had worn off anyway. They wanted something bigger, something they could figure out that would transport them beyond the next illicit afternoon movie and stolen Hershey bar and this time it would not depend on the simple trick of their being like one.

Whoever compares the present and the past will soon perceive that there prevail and always have prevailed the same desires and passions.

I stole, though Jim Cogan hardly believes it. He would save his own from the juvenile authorities. Save his parents from the bitter truth, but I — I was dragged before my father by evil Mr. Nakurian. Match that with the idle threat of "authorities" from some half-baked social agency. I stole a watermelon. For weeks my brother had been after me to do it — to run across the street while Nakurian was turning the tomatoes to their good side, and steal an enormous watermelon.

The Story of the Enormous Watermelon. It wasn't funny. I was supposed to prove I hated the Nakurians as much as my father and Robert did.

Nakurian had rented the empty lots across the street for a fruit-stand. Sneaky Syrian bastard, his son was a lawyer and got the variance. In our neighborhood — a fruit-stand! My father, a judge of probate then, had disgraced young Nakurian in court, calling him on his misuse of every legal term. All night the trucks drew up by the side of our house. Derelicts unloaded crates of fruits and vegetables under lights bright enough for a ball park. It was claimed that rats and cockroaches were about to take over the neighborhood, though I never saw any. The stand was huge — three lots on the corner of Main Street. The whole North End loved it. Strange kids ran on our lawn while their parents shopped on Sunday. My father put up a fence, lacy wrought iron, but spiked on top. We constantly injured ourselves on it and all because of Nakurian's Open Air Market. He thrived and our family withdrew behind drawn shades. Bums slept under our Rothschild "estate" rhododendrons, waiting for Nakurian's night shipment and a possible job unloading the trucks. My father called the police. More accurately, he called his friend the chief. *No Parking* signs were posted all along the side of our house. It was open warfare: Nakurian simply paid off the patrol car and rolled the signs away when my father's car drove off in the morning.

The inspiration belonged to Robert, naturally. I was to cross the street, looking dreamy, loiter by the mountain of watermelons. When Nakurian was busy, hopefully short-changing a customer or in his absolutely illegal (no plumbing) toilet, I was to snatch a melon and make off to our back porch. Snatch I could not, but finally I managed to get

81

one in my arms. It slipped from me with a splat heard round the world. "Dirty rich kid!" yelled Nakurian. The seeds had splattered up on my shoes and legs. He dragged me across the street up the stairs into our kitchen. Robert, the rat, was found calmly reading *Boy's Life* upside down. My father appeared in the doorway, overweight, immensely dignified in his white linen suit. "Get out of my house," he said to Nakurian who still held me in front of him like a hostage and then in a scene from foolish melodrama pushed me at my father's feet.

"Your daughter is a thief!"

"Get out of my house," my father said again, with god-like control, reserved for his pronouncements from the bench.

"You pay for the melon!" Nakurian screamed. "I call the police!" But, of course, he couldn't call the police to come get my father and compounding his folly he shouted, "My son gonna take you in court."

"I doubt that," my father laughed and raising his voice for the first time, his face scarlet, his neck straining furiously against his collar, he commanded: "Now get out of my house!"

"I hope you get a heart attack," were Nakurian's last hateful words.

And he did. Within an hour the ambulance was flashing impatiently at the front door and my father was carried out on a stretcher, the first attack of angina pectoris. He had just set our punishment, a punishment so severe that I thought I would never forget, and lay down on the couch when the pain began. By the time my father died ten years later young Nakurian held complete control of the Democratic party in our district and the old man presided in a cinder-block market across the street which was rezoned for commerce and light industry.

"I never got it straight," Jim Cogan says, "why my mother didn't like you."

"I'm tired of confrontations. I've never been good at them." I have the feeling now that he's not awaiting trial but that we are on probation with each other. I lose ground.

Bare-chested or flaunting his white tunic like an ersatz pajama with its cheap matted machine embroidery, Jim trails me around the house with his nagging honesty. "My mother *still* doesn't like you."

I've never written about myself or those close to me. I am a hack — three books of surface value to our time. One on capital punishment, another on the robber barons of industry, and a slick novel based on the Lindbergh kidnapping. All of it palatable — even my peek at death row has the gloss of good journalism, my words chosen to get me quickly in and out of ugly places — there along the "clean gray corridor that smells of Lysol, the walls with a single ornament, the fire extinguisher so essential to public places. Yet there is something different here in the heart of the prison, something like a macabre sanctity that doesn't exist in the hospital ward or school basement that it resembles, something ominous." Something my book never gets around to saying in the welter of legal arguments and coolly written scenes that find me "happy to join the mayhem on the highway heading back into Kansas City, to be free of the gray corridor with its beacon of hope, the fire extinguisher, there where the final conflagration would matter least of all."

Terrible. In all my carefully documented visits to the condemned men, it is death I never speak of —

I've said to Jim Cogan, "Look at my work. I skim safely over the top of things. There's no place to get at me. I'm just not there."

"You must have felt something. I mean those guys had raped and murdered."

"Yes, I was afraid. That's all — afraid every minute that I spent with them. I don't know why. I sat behind my tape recorder across from the men. A guard present, of course. They, the murderers, were all very different. One man was blond and delicate with glasses. He looked like our milkman in his gray convict's shirt and matching pants. He was so amiable — while the others all had passion left, pleas — and I thought the friendly murderer would ask me if I wanted a pint of cottage cheese today. The milkman was without hope. I feared him most of all."

"Why? He didn't want anything from you."

"That's right. He wanted nothing. It was frightening. Smiling his milkman smile in his milk-toast way. He knew something that I couldn't know. The others at Leavenworth, at San Quentin, asked for help, for life — it was understandable their hanging on. I could imagine their crimes, the moment in which they lost themselves to kill, if they killed in fact, but he was resigned, beyond all legal and moral arguments. There was no use putting him to death. He was already there."

"What had he done?"

"Shot the man he worked for. He had embezzled — an insurance claims office. He was passive, yet his answers to me were so articulate with pauses, long silences, interminable empty spaces on the tape when I played it back in my motel room. Silence that spoke really of his boredom: he had no interest in my cause. And the milkman's eyes were clear blue behind steel rim glasses. My depressions were awful after I'd seen him."

"Why didn't you write about that?"

"It was not the purpose of my book." Stuffy. Closed-off — the book made its points, sold well to libraries but disappointed me in the long run. Arguments in themselves are not moving. They must be staged; but I want nothing so demanding or so exalted as the artist's role. So I tell myself. Lively reportage is enough. I must be out of it. Now that I have an adversary I can say that. Listen, I don't want to be the center of every scrap of work. I don't want to be the principal. The drone of my own voice, to see myself performing like a clown, an exhibitionist.

"But if you told about that guy, the milkman who scared you, people might have cared about you and read your book."

"He didn't scare me."

"That's not what you said."

"Something *in* him frightened me."

"Because that guy had resigned. Had given up the show we're in. Like a holy man!"

"He was a little freak. A killer."

But the boy is right. I never cared to write a good book, to confront myself to say that the frail prisoner's not begging for his life was an assault upon me and all my logic and liberal goodwill. I surely knew that as I stood alone looking out of the picture window of my motel in Kansas City upon the drained swimming pool with its crazed blue paint and rust dribbles. As I waited to put through the evening call to my husband I understood the hopeless milkman perfectly and wondered about all the days of my made-up life.

"I think my mother liked Robert better than you." That again: not so much an accusation as an inquiry — why? Why didn't Mill Murray, that saucy redhead from Brooklyn adore her country cousin, that plump show-off on roller skates, ice skates and toy-shop skis. I must have seemed like a performing monkey, rich and spoiled, princess of a two-block span. Why didn't she love me?

Her father and my mother were brother and sister, but my mother, through no great effort of her own, had escaped the Murray clan by marriage. Pictures show my mother to be an impressive beauty with a worldly air and my father must have fallen hard for he defied his family and married her — a Catholic girl with a handsome face who he'd met while he was clerking with a big law firm in New York. The worldly air my mother sported soon proved to be no deeper than her closet full of flapper's costumes. She was a simple woman, but I do remember when an occasion came for my parents to dress up she was awesome, like no one else in their set. How odd it must have been for her dinner partner at a political meeting to find that this Juno, the Judge's wife, had no conversation beyond the banalities of her kitchen and children. But my parents suited each other and laughed a lot together when we were young and played golf and bridge and went to Florida each winter when court was not in session. My mother was quick to imitate her new Yankee relatives and tried all the flower arranging, antique collecting nonsense but failed and then stayed home a great deal by herself during the day hooking lumpy rugs, painting wastebaskets and card tables with sticky tole bouquets. She could not after all go to the Monday Club or to the Wellesley Alumnae meetings with my aunts. I think she was happy about that, at least while we were growing up. On my father's part it was more than satisfactory to have steered clear of the stone-face and husky aristocratic voice he should have married.

My mother was magnificent when she was all dressed up, dramatic even, and in that way very like Mill Cogan. Mill, too, always looks impressive and just to tell this to her son gives me pleasure, to be able to reveal something that I have learned about the world. One woman reminding me of another. You see, my mother had no more idea how to cope with me as we grew into people than Mill Cogan has now in dealing with Jim. The façade of beauty and style almost fooled us into believing that they were sophisticated women, but it is skin deep and underneath their limitations and fears are shared with frumpy souls, dowdy spirits. Checking what has sagged and died on them each day, berating their children with memories of how things were when they were better, when they were right, when the time was their time. Praying, for they remained, my mother and Mill, simple Catholic girls — praying through a haze for those (and there are plenty in an endless bookkeeping that is to save their souls) who have trespassed against them.

I am sorry that Mill never liked me. It must have been early on that Robert and I outgrew our admiration for her bunny-fur coat and swing bands. Later, her bebop bored us and seemed, played loud on our Stromberg-Carlson, somewhat vulgar midst the Sarouks and antiques gently lighted by cloisonné lamps that were early Sloane. We were kiddy snobs, my brother and I, with our collection of Beethoven Symphonies, "Rhapsody in Blue," "Malagueña," Iturbi at Hollywood Bowl. How awful we must have been to a girl who had already begun to take her life from fashion magazines. The one time we did get on: when I was out of college working in New York at my first miserable office job and Mill Murray took me on many a lunch hour to Lord & Taylor, her favorite store, there to indoctrinate me into the mysteries of padded bras, Capezio shoes, the smart budget dresses worn by glamorous hordes of working girls in the city.

"God no," she'd say, as I took a dress off the rack, "everyone in New York had that last spring."

I can see that she got her own back as I trailed her through the store, for I had abandoned the life of the mind as soon as I left college and was in a hurry for high heels and hairdos, gummy red nail polish which would help me to look like one of those beautiful New York girls, like my

87

cousin Mill. It was all sex, though I hardly recognized it. I was so immediately concerned with the particulars. And she was commanding, pulling me past racks of cocktail dresses intended for suburban matrons. She already wore Cogan's little diamond on her left hand. I don't think she hated me then, but later when things went from bad to worse and the Cogans had to move from her beloved Brooklyn Heights with gas lamps flickering down the charming street and when I wore those overdesigned cocktail dresses in my suburb of Boston, married to Harry Quinn now, secure in my bad taste, arrogant, unchallenged as we were in the late fifties. We went to Europe often and I wrote my books and Harry was the defeated darling of the reform Democrats, finally rewarded by the handout of a few golden years in Washington. She must have wept when we sent greetings in a gray February from the Caribbean — childless, glittery people in the presidential entourage. Gone forever. It was fool's gold. I do think she must have hated me as a child. Now that it's out in the open I can tell her son of our cruelty in detail, as though I were the artist I never wanted to be.

Harry is fed up with the whole thing.

"Send him home," he said last night. "Our lives have come to a stop. When did you last pay attention to your own children?"

I said, "There are times when our lives *have* to stop." And then angrily, that the time had come for me.

Harry cried, "For pity's sake . . ." but caught himself and switched to a lower key, "It's a hell of a strain."

"Yes."

"Are you getting any work done?"

"No."

"I thought part of the rationale in having the kid here was that you would get some work done on your book."

"I listened to the tapes of those women going on about their political careers and fell asleep."

Harry didn't dignify this at once with a reply, but came across the room rather heavily as though he didn't want this encounter, but as a man of principle he must take hold. "You signed a contract for the book." His voice thickened in his throat, near to rage. "It was a *good* idea."

"It was another public idea."

"What's that supposed to mean?"

I said: "That we always do public works."

"Yes?"

"And I want to do something personal this time."

"You have the children. You have me . . ."

"That's our *private* life," I cried.

"That's boring for the best of us, isn't it?" Harry asked with a little smile.

"No —"

"Well, what the hell is it then? Private and personal — the distinctions are too fine for me. Your book is worthwhile: it matters. You were going to Washington next week."

"I cancelled. Another public cause. It's ineffectual . . . oh, let me be."

"And this kid . . . this kid is enough to make you give up the world?" He suggested that it was sex, I don't know. His argument came at me with such force . . . that if there was a girl in the house I would simply be envious of her body and contemptuous of the naiveté that thinks it will inherit the earth. That's not true. That's not so, I said. "But a young man," Harry said.

"That's not true!"

"I don't think you know what you're into," he said. "Isn't the boy tired dragging around the house after you? Send him back."

89

"I will not. For once can't we do something outside of ourselves."

"Something *personal*," Harry said with a sharp laugh. "He's not particularly interesting or bright: it's common as rat cheese all that Krishna guru stuff."

I said: "You have such limited sympathies." His anger failed him then.

"I'll stay free of it," he said.

Cold days for June. Like England, another country, not home. And yet I've lived all my life here. Always come back after going in to the world. Forty years. No one but the old Walker Aunts still on Beacon Hill. Same napkins I remember from childhood, mended now, frayed edges of the tea cloth. Lemon, sugar, plain store-bought cookies like brown cardboard. White sandwiches with pale cucumber, S. S. Pierce mayonnaise. No airs ever. For as long as I remember this tête-à-tête for my birthday. Trying to make a lady of me, peel off the Irish or the New York I'd picked up from my mother, one as bad as the other to them. I took Mary this year who felt cheated as I did when I was her age — sitting through that whole damn thing staring at the stains in the ceiling. No money, I suppose, to keep it up or so much money they don't have to. My children will get their money and that house — there is no one else. Wellesley, Harvard, perhaps, the tradition of giving to institutions in the Walker blood. The world depends on them — on us. I don't feel part of them. Narrow, self-assured.

We talked about my advanced age — some banter about the family aging well. *They* have — two excellent old ladies in their linen dresses and white shoes, straight backs, voices like queens. The stronger of the two, with carefully colored hair, had held an administrative post at Radcliffe: the weaker sister at home these seventy-five years, trustee of the

90

Symphony, Fogg, Gardner and all that. This year I don't bristle when it's suggested that I take my place on some committee that I've heard about since 1935. Foundling home, great "interest" of theirs, childless old women, never held a baby in their arms. Service to the community. Why not? Why the hell not at my age? I'm not doing anything better.

They inquire about my book on women in politics. Frightfully interesting to them. Words they use, still the enthusiasm, the hope. They are absorbed in the world, in so many things, in nothing, really, bright-eyed long-beaked birds, carrying the burden of their intelligence and education like proud crests. I see so much of the Walkers in me at times like this: I talk with genteel gusto — how compelling it is — my subject that I've lost sight of. After dry kisses we part until the fall. They will be in Duxbury all summer. Mary found the cucumber sandwiches repulsive and they commented separately and together on her poor appetite.

Afterwards I did exactly what my mother used to do with me — took Mary off to Howard Johnson's for a hot fudge sundae. Laugh at those tea biscuits, the whole Yankee scene. A thin slice of bread they give. What a treat! That lemon they slice must last all month.

Then we went to pick up Jim Cogan who'd been invited to see Harry's office, spend the day in town.

"It was neat. Great lunch."

"Did you like the office?"

"Sure. That kind of thing is swell."

"But it's not *your* kind of thing?"

"No," he said, "and Harry made me feel I was supposed to like it a lot. I was supposed to want to be that — a lawyer or something."

"It's his *life*."

"Yes," he said sullenly.

"He likes the Democratic party. The court house gang. His office. Elizabeth."

"She's nice."

"Elizabeth's in love with my husband."

"She's kind of old."

"In the way secretaries are in love with their bosses. Like your mother and that man she worked for."

"It's really nice," he said, changing the subject, yawning, "this whole new center of Boston. There's a fountain and everything."

"Yes, it's *successful*, if you can understand that. People worked hard for it. Harry's the lawyer for the Urban League and on the redevelopment commission." Now every time I speak to the boy I feel like I'm fighting with a lover, terrible edge to my voice, ready to burst into tears.

"He gave me some money to buy records and stuff. He was really nice."

"Really nice. The money from Harry is for your birthday. I think it's rude and impersonal to say *he* like that."

"I thanked him, but I didn't go buy any records. It's best to travel light."

I drove home and on the way Mary fell asleep in the back seat. A deep loneliness with the two presences in the car. The boy draws off to a safe distance, the alternative to his open, soul-baring posture. I don't honestly know why he bothers to stay with us. The whole thing a sham. My pleading for the old cause, the dead beat banner of reason. Words lost in the atmosphere. Like the intelligence that has guided those two well-bred old ladies in Boston all their lives. Admirable and tough.

It came to me as we sat in the driveway on the brink of a lovely June evening, that he didn't intend to listen to any of it. Not to be heard is death. Not to be loved, not to have the feel of a man with you, not to have children or a home or a purpose for your days is tragic, but not to be heard is final and it is death. See how I punish myself with rhetoric and it will no longer serve. I am like an old fool on the bus with schoolchildren telling them above the noise that I *walked* three miles to school. I'm not quite ready for the condominium without stairs, easy ramps for mature living. But I know that I've always asked too little of myself, been content with contrived ideas turned into delicate tales and though it takes me where I don't want to go, to places in my own heart that I fear, I will be heard.

"You're not going back to New York to stand trial, are you?"

"No way."

"You're saving your birthday money to take off, aren't you? And that money that your grandfather and my husband put up for your bail will be lost. What holds you back? Do you have some conscience about us? Is that why you're still here?"

"I thought I'd wait till I was supposed to go back to New York."

"And become a fugitive? Be lost to us forever. Turn your back on everything we've given you. Your parents, no matter what you think and what they seem, have loved you. They won't know where you are or whether you're alive."

Jim said: "Suppose I don't get off like you say. Like Harry and the lawyer he's got for me in New York say. Suppose all the defense and truth and all that doesn't work and I get it for a couple of felonies. What good is it then to say I've done it the right way, your way. Suppose I honor your system and it doesn't honor me."

"Don't run. Please listen this once. My brother ran away. I've never been able to see it this way. It's too hard . . . but when things got tough, Robert ran. He wanted to become a nameless man without a history."

93

"What about him anyway? What's the mystery?"

"What do you care? Your mother and why she hated me and Robert. All that's in the past. You think you're so free. Why do you care?"

"I don't care," Jim Cogan said. "That was all before my time."

Mary watched us from the back seat, intent upon our every gesture, the pitch of our voices, a little student of the passions. "I'll answer your question anyway," I said. "I've made up the mystery about my brother. It's only a story and I guess it's time."

Robert

"IN WAR THERE IS NO SUBSTITUTE FOR VICTORY." These the words of Douglas MacArthur. They were well-worn by the time he used them in his famous pomposity delivered before the Joint Session of Congress in 1952. I have never hated anyone so much. After my brother was killed in the glorious invasion of Inchon early in the Korean "Conflict," I became obsessed with General MacArthur and knew enough about him and his long spectacular career — a fourth oak-leaf cluster to his Distinguished Service Medal — to easily turn out a book about "the old warhorse," but I did not. I write, instead, of fabricated concerns and I never spoke of Robert. I knew even then that my loathing for MacArthur was the only way I had to abate my terrible sorrow. Any book of mine on the General would have been filled with emotion and I was afraid of that. The hatred that accrued like layers of bitter tarnish over the precious center of my love for Robert, was for every aspect of the General's person, his skillfully dyed hair as much as his sacrifice of young men to his bloated ego, his ascot to hide the aging throat, the affected slop-ass uniform, the scrambled eggs on his cap — all made him the most absurd operetta figure of an officer, a Macaroni who would have been parodied in any other century but the heavy one we're doomed to survive. Rouged and corseted like a Restoration fop, toddling out of the Waldorf Towers to his Cadillac limousine to address the screaming rabble. In New York alone he was welcomed with three thousand, two hundred and forty-nine tons of ticker tape — better than Ike did back in 'forty-five. Welcome! Welcome! Welcome! There are no more Caesars, no more Wellingtons, no more saviors. One last agony of adoration for the great Romantic who in the age of nuclear weapons fashioned his great opening play of the Korean War upon Montcalm's surprise attack on Quebec. We should have known then that there was something terribly wrong. We gave our greatest tribute, the tribute meant for conquerors to a man who came home in defeat.

Meanwhile my brother had died in the early weeks of the war, stuck in the mud off the island of Inchon, a five-thousand-to-one chance which the great General had pulled off. It was not called a war until 1958 when the army officially struck the word conflict from its records. I like that. I like people to be particular with words, to adjust their meanings as the truth unfolds. I am glad my brother did not die in a conflict.

For General of the Army Douglas MacArthur it was never anything but a war, though I like best this description (by his admiring adjutant) that Korea was "Mars' last gift to an old warrior." Beware of Greeks, my General, lest they give you a conflict, a substitute for victory and not a brave soldier's death, but a long complicated fading, monkey glands, catheter up the leg of your three-hundred-dollar suit, and the spectacle of your young wife yellowing with age.

My brother was high in my Olympus. These household gods are always with us. We make our first and best myths of their battles, their rages and good fortune. The love affairs, the disaffections in our early rooms take on such heroic proportions with the years. My father, Zeus-like in his downstairs study, the essays of Mr. Emerson, *Harvard Law Review*, golf trophies, embodiment of fear-love-justice-success. My mother, Diana of the pressure cooker, eternal giving of soft meat, flaky crust — love, love, love and guilt, love and sadness, love and art — ah, I remember a coconut cake in the shape of a newborn lamb sacrificed to us on Easter. Family life is like the classics played in modern dress by an amateur troop. Vulgarized version of the old tales.

My brother was born two years before me and his spirit dominated me all of his life. I say his spirit because he didn't bully me, never a threat or the shoving and pushing other kids complained of. But I do remember from my earliest days the aura of specialness about him. I always tried to keep up with him and never made it. To survive I turned to girlish pursuits, jump rope, embroidery, endless batches of Toll House cookies at which I excelled, but I was always second best. As is often the case in marriages where the man and woman come from different worlds, this child, their first born, became the focus of their life together. Robert was a fiercely bright, naughty little boy: I was a good, complaisant girl who followed in his wake. We all loved him to excess.

My husband is annoyed that I keep a picture of Robert in the little room where I write. Robert, not as he was in his last formal portrait at graduation from Harvard — handsome, brooding poseur, air-brushed to a waxy perfection — but a picture of a three-year-old boy, a high intelligent forehead, wide open eyes, his little smile like a secret kept from me that was to plague me all my life. This photo stood on the mantel all our childhood half-blocking a fine primitive of Walker Farm, Concord, done by an itinerant painter, circa 1845. My mother was not an educated woman. (Later we were to find a Childe Hassam that she had stuck under the eaves in order to display a tin tray she had stenciled at the Art League.) My mother did not know that Robert in his sailor suit should not be front and center. How offensive this must have been to the Walker Aunts whose "personal photographs and treasures" were stuck in some out-of-the-way corner where their friends need not be troubled by their private lives.

So Robbie was set up like an icon and it was perfectly proper that he should be three years old for he must have been memorably awful at that age. My mother kept a little book and wrote down the grand events of his life (even I entered the picture for a few years) — his vaccination, first words, first steps, first sentence, mumps, tonsillitis, etc. It is all of it dull yet intriguing to me. The little book ends when he entered kindergarten. Robert, age five: "Reads all rhymes in *Up One Flight of Stairs*, all cereal boxes and Dad's *Boston Globe*. Adds well, subtracts with help of fingers."

What a treat he must have been for the teacher ready to point out the big bold letters of the alphabet. The Judge's son, old family, smiling wryly on his tiny kindergarten chair, his immense forehead full of brains. They shoved him into the first grade and from that day on he was the smallest boy in his class. Weak wristed, bored to death, he became the bad boy of the school. How else was he to prove himself. Play the fool, of course. First, in the elegant clothes from the Lilliputian Bazaar, and later, because my mother was a New Yorker, from the boy's shop at Brooks. Robbie had too much spending money. His school bag was English leather, his lunch box was from the sporting goods counter

97

at Shreve, Crump & Low where the Walkers had run an account for the last hundred years, a perfectly handsome box with silverware buttoned in and a round pocket for an infamous collapsible cup. The lunch box survived grammar school and was still in his room when I went home to clear it out after he died. I must have had a dozen tin boxes, Donald Duck, Snow White, Jane Withers, that rusted and came unhinged. It was considered chic to carry a brown paper bag by the time I got to the upper grades, but Robert's superior box outlasted all fads. It is beautiful: I had forgotten the mother-of-pearl handles on the knife and fork, the leather lining, and at last with Robbie in his grave I discovered the trick by which he pressed the collapsible cup to spill his milk or hot cocoa in the lap of the enemy. The cup is an exquisite device made in telescopic rings of German nickel. Why had they done this to him? My father was not a stupid man, and yet there was some Yankee grit in him, an arrogant pride that insisted upon his standards in the face of all the odds. We must have well-tailored winter coats, good shoes, pigskin gloves, the eleventh edition of the *Encyclopaedia Britannica* while the world around us grew cheesier every day. The professional people in our neighborhood moved out to the newer suburbs. The larger houses were broken into apartments and one became a nursing home before our unsuspecting eyes. But we hung on, the first family in the finest house.

I never stopped to notice the injury to me for the damage to Robert was soon obvious. The big boys in the neighborhood stuck pins into him one day as though he were a doll, to see if anything so clever and privileged, so different than themselves would bleed. He bled all right and could not conceal the stain on whatever sweet costume my mother had dressed him in that day and then had to endure the shame of the big boys getting it from my father. Perhaps my father *was* a stupid man, even then. Robert would have played tennis well, softball, in another neighborhood, but he couldn't compete with the fullblooded Irish and Italians who had invaded ours. It was selfish of my father not to see what was happening to his son. He had freed *himself* from the bonds of correctness imposed by the Walker family, had married an Irish girl and embraced the Democratic party, but what of us. It was easy for my parents to swank the neighbors with their good rugs and established rose garden. It was easy for my father to star, with Harvard and the family money behind him, in the midst of uneducated politicians and young lawyers out of Boston College. It was easy to belong to the old clubs — he always stayed on the lists and I still get notices from the Athenaeum — as something of a maverick, but what of us. We were "bused" to social dancing classes in the best neighborhood to be ignored by snotty kids who couldn't believe our address. I was happy with my girlfriends on the street but Robert turned odd. School was a drag. At nine he was a successful dilettante, best as a magician, but a good watercolorist, botanist, poet, printer. Clarinet was his instrument. Given the fact that we were outsiders Robert had chosen to be a character rather than a hopeless misfit.

I'd say that he was envied more than admired. His classmates stood in awe of his talents and though he was still the smallest boy he had at least grown into his big forehead. He whipped the principal in a chess match. He did not bother to do his homework, instigated marvelous crimes against the teachers and, in general, did not become a creep. By careful calculation he managed to rank third or fourth in the class every report card. I was always first. Forthright and staunch, I was torn between the idea that I must emulate Robert (my attempts were so pitiful) — ballet for which I had no talent, dramatic readings I recall with em-

99

barrassment — or, be ordinary and "fit in." Fit I did, with a vengeance. When the girls in school jumped rope I jumped. I skated, crocheted, joined Girl Scouts (boring), collected a shelf full of simpering costume dolls. There was nothing left to me at all. Except for the painful hours when I would hide from my friends under the kneehole of the big desk in my father's study to listen to the thump of my own heart alive with the guilt and excitement of being different and alone. The story is not about me and the riches of my hours in the kneehole desk. Let this account of Robert be my first expedition into the *personal*, the first opening of my "work" (the quotes emphatically mine), but not of myself.

I believed Robert was a genius. I am sure this is why *Doctor Faustus* was my favorite book in college, tracing somewhat obsessively, the career of the gifted, the special Leverkuhn. Now I would argue with the narrator whose role I had perhaps assumed as my own: he insists that the artist's childhood is infinitely finer, more fully endowed with possibilities, that it yields more to the imagination. No, I think that my childhood was as full and terrible as my brother's but he could have mined the experience while I must always let it rest — for fear. He died young. How can I say what he might have done. Already he had fashioned himself through the sleepy, passive years of high school and college. He was formed. He was *about* something. His pursuits were not idle. Because he didn't have a chance at the real thing, his life was his art — that is how I've seen it since his death.

That son of a bitch MacArthur was not looked for and Robert's death was not a romantic gesture. It was a foul way to die. By military miscalculation the tide had gone out leaving the troops that were to form the second wave of the Inchon invasion stuck in the mud. There they sat off the worthless island like so many dumb boy scouts waiting out the hours till the water would set them afloat and on their way to victory. The long hot hours of a low tide. Meanwhile the enemy had recovered from the surprise landing of the first wave and took pot shots at the little row of boats as though they were set up in an amusement park. The casualties were low but Robert got it from a bullet that ricocheted off their landing gear and into his heart, to die nowhere, some obscure mudflat in the Yellow Sea. One of his men wrote to my parents that he had made the ace of spades spring out of their packets while they waited for the tide.

In his last hour a performance that made Robert a fool to my father and a saint to me: "Fool to the last," I read in my father's sigh. The breach between him and his son which had been widening for years was now final and unalterable and that must have killed the old man. Indeed, my father died soon after Robert, never having forgiven him, never having quite defined their quarrel. He was different, that's all, not the son he was supposed to be, unbearable really in his charm and perverse intelligence.

At four he had taken apart a good watch. Legend has it that he sat surrounded by the tiny gears and shafts, bemused by the irate adults, and put them all together so that the watch kept perfect time. He never displayed any mechanical ability again. The private, quirky use to which he put his discoveries must have been infuriating. Nothing to show for your money. Having refused to go away to Groton, he took up with all the oddballs in the local high school — a ham radio operator, a threadbare Italian violinist with hysterical eyes, a slick article named Wally, I remember, who ran a bookie joint at the back of the candy store. He effortlessly ticked off the necessary A's to get into Harvard, but his valedictory was an affront, a slap at the proud parents who had come to see their children step into life, who were expecting the immature idealism of fresh-faced youth. They got instead Robert, neat, small, distinguished as a little European professor spinning off some tough thoughts on the violation of peace treaties.

I pleaded with him the week before graduation: what's the point of insulting a whole lot of people who want to hear about peace and the bright future. We had just celebrated the allied victory in Europe. Peace in Our Time. A few quotes from Churchill, and a sober attitude towards the responsibilities that our generation would have to bear. . . . I could have written that speech for him so easily and what's more believed in it: "Though we did not fight on foreign soil, our hearts and our minds were striving for victory at home."

"You're right," Robert said, "but I can't do what they want this time. I want to be honest, no tricks, no sleight of hand and besides if I delivered your oration I might yawn in the middle."

"You're making a big mistake."

"We'll see," Robert said. "We'll wait and see."

Many of our arguments ended in a draw. We were friends at this time, having come through a period of total revulsion. I wanted him to play an impossible role. I wanted to praise him without reserve. In the way we always want the people we love to be mended, flawless, I wanted Robert to be a regular guy.

The valedictory was simply a disaster, the beginning of my father's break with Robert. The old story, no — of the son tearing himself away from the father's tacky values. On that sweaty June night in our high school auditorium it was my father who could not keep the faith with Robert. He had already gone up in his cap and gown, baby-faced, younger than all the others, to receive the Latin prize, the Physics prize and the Harriet Beecher Stowe medal for English Rhetoric, so a proud expectant hush fell on the audience of parents and students as Robert Lyman Walker came to the podium. His voice was low and manly, surprising in one of his age, and would have been perfect for the sentimental summing up we yearned for, but my brother launched into a long attack on Wilsonian idealism and the lesson we must learn from our diplomatic failures after the First World War. For all his integrity and moral vision Wilson had failed in the world of real politics. He could not estimate his support. He could not control his forces. The time was past for naiveté in America. It would do no good to wallow in our victory.

The speech was seven minutes long. He had timed it in his bedroom, but it seemed endless in the heat and hostility that pervaded the auditorium. Mothers in dressy hats and tight set curls, fathers in their best suits — was it for this negative harangue and unseemly warning that they came? The war was over, or nearly so. It was the June that fell between V-E and V-J days. These were their golden boys and girls ready for the challenge of another golden age. Yalta, my brother Robert said, had its treachery built in. The sacred photo of Stalin and Churchill and a withered FDR came to everyone's mind. Was this why we gathered with presents and flowers? To watch a quiz-kid cast his meager shadow on the great? Next to me my father's face was rigid, drained of life, without moving his head he spoke to my mother who reached in her purse for the little bottle of digitalis. Her white gloves, the tilt of her smart panama were intact, but tears of confusion came to her eyes which she patted away as though they were no more unusual than the beads of sweat that gathered on her pretty upper lip. Proud and ignorant, she would see her son through. "Nothing is more useful to the nations of the world than lies, nothing more harmful than the truth." Robert ended with this cynical twist from Diderot. Soon we were mercifully joining in the school song — "And gladly singing to you always/ Our loyal hearts with joy shall fill/ O, dearest, dearest Alma Mater/ We will love and praise you still," swept into a final prayer for our comrades from Bradford High who were still serving the cause of freedom overseas.

"Pomp and Circumstance" and we were out in the lobby, making a quick getaway through the crowd who mumbled their congratulations to my parents like condolences. On the way home no one said a word until my mother, looking straight at the green pigeon-stained statue of Colonel Philo T. Walker that graced the square, said in a trembling voice and in spite of my father's heart attack: "I think it was wonderful that you spoke right out, Robert. I could hear every word just as clear." We were silent again until Robert threw his rented cap and gown over a diningroom chair and said with the old razzmatazz: "In any case, folks, it will soon be forgotten." And we sat down to a good supper that Beatrice our colored girl had laid out for us with both chocolate cake and lemon meringue pie and soon the phone rang and it was some kids who had a swimming party going for the graduating class and Robert was to pick up some girls in the car and bring his clarinet.

From that day they were set against each other, my father and Robert. All the promise of the bright three-year-old was still there, all the spirit, but he was not what my father intended. I hadn't known that my father was a narrow man whose one act of imagination was to marry my mother and defect to the seedy world of Massachusetts politics, a big fish in our little pond. Robert's career at Harvard never lacked invention. He played Sir Andrew Aguecheek in *Twelfth Night* as a start, mincing about the stage and delivering himself of a piping falsetto, switching to his true actor's timbre for *Man and Superman* in the spring season. He wrote poems, sang madrigals, studied Russian to read Tolstoy and, after a short romance with tennis, never played any sport more strenuous than Ping-Pong after dinner. I supposed then that my father was ashamed of Robert, but I'll change that now and say that he found his son impertinent and outrageous. Though he never said it, I'm sure Robert's achievements in poetry and theater seemed to my father the sort of thing that was all right for the bright New York types (and we knew what *that* meant) who came to Harvard, but not for his son.

My mother and I loved our Rob more fiercely. Like star struck fans we knew every delicious detail of his career and nothing really about his private life. I think now that I knew only two or three projections of him for he was what we'd call now a protean figure. Poor mother kept a scrapbook with all his poems and stories from the Literary Magazine and clippings of his triumphs on the stage. He had grown to be quite handsome in the style of a soft matinee idol and bleached his hair to play Billy Budd at the Brattle Theater — our father cursing and having another famous attack. I saw him as the Handsome Sailor and he appeared to be no ordinary mortal. Robert died young and my father lingered on in a gray bewilderment at his bereft wife and daughter, his feeble heart pounding on for two years after his son was killed in Korea. I know that bastard thought his boy better-off dead than a disgrace to the family. He knew *nothing*, nothing about Robert. His mind was cheap and conventional, and when I found out about my brother I could not even knock on the door of the fake "study" downstairs where Emerson and "The Law" moulded on the shelves for fear the old man would drop his crummy detective story, have an attack, and die. Now then, Jim Cogan, listen: you are not the only kid to find your father a fraud. The son is, the son was — the better man.

His room was exactly as he left it — the cartoon of Oscar

Wilde ("Strike me with a Sunflower"), the photo of Ezra Pound in a peacock chair, a top hat he had worn in an Edwardian production of *Midsummer Night's Dream,* books stacked everywhere in some mad arrangement he had known about. My mother in the useless sickness of sorrow had washed and ironed all of his underwear and shirts and placed them back in the drawers "so they wouldn't get musty." His room was like another living presence in the house, oppressive, unstated like my father's guilt that he had not loved his son and my mother's dazed, tight-lipped nursing of my father. I decided to clear out Robert's room for them, to break the silent angry thoughts they'd started to live off. It would take me half a day to take the books I wanted to my room and pack the rest for the Salvation Army. It took me three long days because I was no further than the first desk drawer when I discovered under the term papers for "Proust, Joyce, and Mann" the first of twelve speckled notebooks filled with the story of his life.

Huddled under the quilt on his bed, the door bolted, I began to read with a queasy fear that I would discover secrets about Robert that would destroy not my love, but my sense of him. It seemed a violation and yet once I had started I read on and on, committed now to knowing everything. I say that it took me three days to read my brother's notebooks, but much of that time was spent in a trance, my sense of wonder at coming to know him, to find what I had always hoped, that Robert was a serious person. I remember trailing off into the heavy-breathing distant sleep of emotional exhaustion to wake fresh and ready for the next pages written in his queer, quick-printed hand, a defiance, I knew, to the pages of humps and circles and chicken fences we were forced to practice in the Palmer Method.

All this for Jim Cogan, for my running battle with him. It's my history against his and my life against his. I respect

my adversary, but I will give him only what I want of
Robert and even that is difficult for me. It's been a long
silence. I have never spoken of him since his death and
made it out that it was too painful. For my mother and my
husband it was a morbid silence with the three-year-old
bright boy looking down at me in my workroom, the only
remnant of Robert's life. There's no mystery, Jim Cogan,
but the brother I discovered in the speckled copybooks I
kept for myself and I have always measured myself against
him. So my adult life goes on as my childhood began — trying to keep up with Robert, trying by any means to get
those who I love to love me as much as they loved that
weird bright little prince in the sailor suit.

Entries about his courses and roommates make up the
first of the notebooks which runs through his freshman year
in Wigglesworth B. Not interesting, except to a sister. He
shared my amazement at rich midwestern kids who were in
full possession of their world, not troubled as *we* were by
the burden of our bodies, our clothes, our movements, our
strange heritage from a "mixed marriage." "I am not
natural," he writes, "but must develop manners, strike atti-
tudes, ways of being to get me through. I am self-conscious
and suffer deeply from being *wrong*. Again tonight I chose
the wrong things to eat in the Commons, no one else from
entry B accepted the ladle of à la king or the cherry pudding.
My supper was delicious, but my shame ruined every bite.
Caldwell and Mason left at once for another of their parties
instead of coming back to the room for a while and farting
and pretending to read. They know everyone who matters to
them. I don't like them and yet I lie when I'm going to
Widener and tell them that I have a date as though suing
for their favor. My best moments with them by far are
when I imitate my Latin teacher who is wildly fey or when
I explicate sonnets from Donne which we are all doing in

English. They, Mason in particular, never suffer or feel suffering in others. Only last night I ate my hateful tray of déclassé meat loaf and wrong tapioca and smoked two of Caldwell's Lucky Strikes and had to throw up. They heard me retching, I know, though I ran the tap water at full blast. When I came back to our room they had gone out, thank God. They do not take the trouble to know me. Later I got very excited launching into Dante — a few Cantos being assigned for the history survey. I stayed up till four reading. *They* came in at two, but I did not greet them to get the rundown on how many bottles of beer, etc., but kept to my book and my own awesome joy." He copies out several passages from the early Cantos and makes the highly literary observation, laughable in a boy, "The way up is indeed the way down. To transcend sin the sinner must pass through sin." His final remark is a cry from the heart: "The loneliness continues."

Sensitive, yes. Bright, but freshman material. Nothing is ever truly remarkable in his scribblings, except the boy who reveals, finally, a degree of self-awareness which is the mark of a man. Soon the loneliness dried up with undergraduate friendships, intense and whole as love — full of self-discovery and a lordly evaluation of his pals. He found his own among the poets and actors, most of them older than Robert, veterans of the Second World War. "Healy is remarkable in rehearsal. His talent for farce is beyond what any of us can achieve. Goldoni seems like an academic exercise when we are on stage, but his timing is thrilling, delicacy of movement, a mobility of facial muscles down to the tip of his nose which sniffs complicity. Unlike the rest of us, he never confuses the nature of his role with insignificance. This funny, moving man was on the beach at Anzio and fought his way down to Naples, house to house. Burns on his back the size of dinner plates, the skin stretched shining and smooth, and a pin in his hip that is painful in the cold. I'm a twirp sitting next to him in class and walking home at night from Hayes-Bick where we both realize I imitate his order like a puppy, "Make that two apple pies!"

A late entry in spring finds Healy preparing for a philosophy exam with Robert and an older man named Marks who fought in the Philippines and found his best friend by the stench of his body days after a bombing, trapped behind a wall that had fallen without a crack, the corpse kneeling in a final prayer. "We were all quiet and gave Marks our respect and then he talked of his nightmares. He is ashamed that he wakes screaming in the night at the sound of a commercial plane circling into Boston airport. We didn't go back to *The Critique of Pure Reason*, we'd had enough of Kant and the rest. I am without experience, a life without real events. When my mother was trying to make Catholics of us . . . the drawing on the blackboard of measuring cups, the nun's sleeve powdered with chalk as she pointed to the smallest vessel, our little bodies, vessels of grace capable of expanding by religious mathematics to the gallon size. My time stopped then, or so it seems, a seven-year-old, one cup measure leaking the thin days of the past."

In the last entry of that year he is waiting for us to pick him up with his footlocker and trophies of the year. "Healy left last night for his home in Akron where he will work in a tire factory for the summer. I am not so lucky — next year we will be in Eliot House together, but before that all the humiliating days of being at home with my father."

It came as a shock to me huddled up on the bed in Robert's room, that he was conscious of my father's disapproval so early on. There's nothing else in the copybooks to hold me — nothing to give Jim Cogan. My brother's years at Harvard are perfectly ordinary. The enthusiasms changed, after Italian it was Russian. The theater always. His friend

Healy, whom he obviously adored, came back from Akron after his sophomore year with a wife and settled in a Quonset hut that was soon strung with diapers. Robert felt alone and betrayed, but visited often at first, looking at the friend he had idolized across the "abyss of squalor and family concerns, straining for our intimacy that was ruined forever by a pretty, plodding Ohio girl who says that she would die happy with a big new refrigerator. Gone Nietzsche and Schopenhauer and Byzantium and *The Education of Henry Adams*. Healy will never act again. There is no room for play. The second-hand marriage bed is impossible as a couch. Hollowed with their loving it lies in front of the three of us littered with gay pillows while the baby cries in the partitioned room."

Friends more fashionable than Healy came on the scene — witty, my God they were a flock of little aesthetes in training, utterly insubstantial, clever men. He loved to display them at home. When there were any girls they were such bedraggled artsy types, graceless buddies to the literary set. The battle with my father flourished. They taunted each other. Robert with his extremes of dress, straw hats for Christmas, Byronic collars, uncut hair (you don't know a damn thing about long hair, baby, unless you tried it back in forty-nine).

Entry: Mom will be waiting with strawberry shortcake, worried that there is not enough cream to please me. The Judge will look at my scarf, so inappropriate for June, hold his hand to the heart so that she runs for the pills. My sister will sit speechless, the witness to our folly, ignored, taking it all down and dying to get out of the house. Another vacation is launched! Luncheon at the old man's club was designed to pay the upstart back: a talk "Man to Man," i.e., what the hell do you propose to do with your life? Have you met my son, the queer?

Sept.: Much weighty talk tonight at supper about "The Law." My bags are packed for the ride to Cambridge, my last year.

Serious family moment. Sister smoking constantly, picking at her cuticles with shame for us both. "The Law." It is thought that government or history are a better preparation for IT than flower arranging or whatever he thinks I'm doing. Question: What did he ever do for "The Law" besides put petty thieves in the county jail and more recently collect his cut as probate judge. "The Law" *re* domestic squabbles and the few switchblade hoodlums from Lynn and Dorchester. When we were little and he lectured us on Sacco-Vanzetti and justice and The Hague and Roosevelt's ill-fated attempt at packing the Supreme Court, he led me to believe that he, too, was a man of the Law. To have done the one adventurous thing — marry the Irish beauty and maintain himself in his old neighborhood, not follow the nervous hordes to the suburbs, led me to believe that he was an independent spirit, but it is not so. He hasn't lied. The Law was once contingent to his life, but he has failed. Now a pomposity covers all. I love him. I wish that I could tell him to stop. I want him to care about me again, but instead I grow more the monkey in his presence. My sister scratched the top off a mosquito bite and let it bleed into a good linen napkin. Even this fuss can't shut him up — "The Law was well known to Alger Hiss. How can a man — my era from Harvard, when the law was still . . ." — baiting me. The gates of my fury open slyly. "I think actually, I'll do a senior thesis on Virginia Woolf, though I'm still rather drawn to the Rossettis."
De Profundis —

Then there is nothing Jim Cogan needs to know until the end. That winter was the triumph of his Billy Budd. Rob with blond locks, and entries about the difficulty in getting "into an innocence that is plausible, to show a 'face never deformed by a sneer or subtler vile freak of the heart within.' " But in spring his last great role and this last story.

I followed her after rehearsal to the Radcliffe Library where I knew she was to pick up a book from the reserve shelf. I waited just outside the gate near a large forsythia already in bloom. To

111

follow her tonight was the only thing. Dream-like movements that were sinful and dark. She came down the steps with her book, anxious, defenseless, not pretty at all as she is on the stage, plain and rather sallow under the campus lights, not the Alice who I play to, hopeful star of stage and screen. I've wished since we first met at the reading that the play was anything other than *Taming of the Shrew*.

She cut through the grass to the steps of her dormitory where she read under the lamplight for no more than a minute and looked to see if her lover was coming. The danger of being there flashed through me, my degradation, too, but I could not leave. He came finally, the famous Kenny, like a truck driver stomping up to her. Alice's smile one of sickly yearning. She touched his wooden shoulders, his fat neck first, before he laid a hand on her. Girls went up the steps but no one spoke to them, as though their conversation, a fake lover's yearning, were sacred. I could hear nothing . . . only once a forced laugh from Alice along with a coy tossing of hair. Awful for her, the mincing movement, the small pleading gesture. Kenny reached inside her raincoat and massaged her left breast without the least ardor and as an after-thought kissed her, kissing her more thoroughly as the lights dimmed in warning that there were five minutes left to them. Then I realized they would find me out. The guards had shut all but the main gate and if I watched them any longer we would meet, Kenny and I, squeezing out at the last moment together in an unbearable coincidence. I stole through the shadows out to the street where I lingered until he came. The guard knew him, of course, one of the great studs of our day. Then, in a quick, reckless move I went towards him, but he checked his watch by the bell tower's first ring and looked past me, not quite remembering who I was, someone in his house, perhaps, or the man who made love to Alice on the stage.

No more voyeur sessions recorded. Robert worshipped from afar, kept busy — his days were full of meetings at the Literary Magazine, poems written, rehearsals of *The Shrew* and the usual term papers due. I felt deprived never having known he loved this girl. I felt his loss before the story ended. It had a doomed air from the start.

When we are together I am almost hysterically clever. She knows that I am in love with her. This week we have been with each other a great deal; things are not going well with Kenny. She calls me with a note of panic in her voice. We are incredibly gay, whipping off our lines like Noel Coward and Bea Lillie. But Alice makes a lousy fag's moll. She is too soft, fades into a distracted silence, then revives and we carry on. I love her without any hope. Our roles are assigned.

Went to motel in New Hampshire with Alice. All evening she projected what is referred to as "grim determination," that we should be close to each other in front of Murray and Alfred and the gang, all the "kids" in the cast, like lovers playing our last scene: "I am ashamed that women are so simple/To offer war where they should kneel for peace,/Or seek for rule, supremacy, and sway,/When they are bound to serve, love, and obey." As though the poem had become my personal triumph. We were a great success. The wonderful exaltation after. Embracing. Kissing. I had wanted my parents to come but my father's health does not permit him to see me on the stage. Mother called and I could hear the longing in her voice, the longing to come to see me, to be free of the gray eminence who holds her there with threats of his fluttering heart.

Something had been wrong with Alice all week, clinging to me as though she were searching for something in my pocket, as though she could will something into being in me which is not there. "Oh, Robert, my Bobby," she says. "Why have they never called you Bobby?" It was a seduction. I knew that from the start. Sweet, searching looks — then a hot insistence that we go somewhere in my car and in the car her fondling of my ear and hair as we drove north out of town was belied by her moody look at the dark road. She said that she had signed out to her aunt's in Lincoln, that she didn't have to "go home." We stopped at the Blue Spruce across the border. The word cabins had been painted out and a red neon sign "Motel" stuck below, but the cheap trellised breezeway between the little buildings was no disguise. They were cabins of the thirties. Ours as clean and poor as any room I've ever seen, so respectable it led Alice in her supposed passion to fold the worn cotton bedspread like a housewife and put it dutifully aside. She then commenced a scene in which I was to be passive, unbuttoning my shirt —

"I love you," she said.

"No."

"Yes. I do love you. That's the pity."

"Let's not push it," I said to her. "When our voices come together on the stage, sometimes we seem inspired. You know that."

"Our *voices*, oh yes, our voices," she replied, and then — "Oh, I can't go on with this. I can't," and at last left the rest to me. The night was longer than others. We slept and woke and made love and slept for a while again and woke to our impatient discovery of each other. We were not content — as though the quest for each other would never end, as though this idyll were just that, a time that as we lived it was assuming its past. A film: brave wartime movies, romances, where you know from the London haze, the softness of the rain, the sweetness of the heroine's smile as she stands waving goodbye in Waterloo Station, that it is all to be some perfect memory, not life. To hell with that. I don't want one night at the Blue Spruce.

On the way back we couldn't find a way to be with each other and she cried more than once, "Now I've really ruined everything."

She had ruined a couple of lives, that's all. When I read the outcome of their affair I tried to picture her — tall, blond, dull WASP blond, with a better figure than she ever knew, the sort of pretty, well-bred Radcliffe girl who seemed to me self-assured, but terribly afraid of sex, overly delighted and surprised that she could do it at all. I don't know. It's conjecture on my part. I don't even know Alice's last name. But she was quite pregnant the night she took Robert to the Blue Spruce Motel and after a week Kenny returned with the honorable proposition that he would marry her and Robert was through. The story has dated quickly. I don't imagine you would play it this way now, but in those days Ivy League kids from good families accepted the rules. Only a piece of blue notepaper stuck into my brother's last copybook lent poignance to the end of the affair.

Dearest R,
Never feel that I used you, for if I did it backfired. We should have left the inspiration to our voices.

He came home after graduation, having turned down a Fulbright to Oxford: mammoth heart-attack fight with my father. Perverse, bitter, but I remember Robert as immensely entertaining in those weeks. Like a desperate stand-up comic, another convention of those years — keep talking for the people, pouring his ineffectual, battered heart out to us at every meal. He played the clarinet up in his room for hours, listened to my father talk about "The Law" and by July Fourth had enlisted in the army.

Final page:

I can only think of punishing myself. I cannot breathe in this house. My chest is tight. Hard knot of pressure bearing down. I play the clarinet till my lungs give out. My father slams the doors — "the noise up there will kill me" — cannot stand Harry James or Erroll Garner or Haydn or my life. My mother and sister laugh at everything I say. Mom still beautiful and trim, careful about herself, so simple to amuse, but worried, worried that my father will die, that she will grow old, that I will not be happy? Happy is the word she uses: "Are you happy? Are you unhappy?" No, Mom, I've had a real life not so happy love affair. What can she do for me, her baby boy? My sister, poor little Laura, is embarrassed by the whole show at home. She is closed off, unwilling to try alternatives to the good girl, fine family stuff. She is on the dean's list at Wellesley and has been elected to the student council and furthermore will work in Uncle Lyman's law office for the summer as I should have done. She is trying to be what I am not, to be what they want and still they don't love her or lust after her soul as they do mine. I want to shake her sometimes in her boring little round collar blouse and bermudas and tell her that the competition is over, over. She is not second and under all the correctness of her life there is a fury to escape the whole rotten show. Why did they name her Laura — oh, if she continues to button all the little buttons on her sweaters and wash her sneakers clean I fear no one will ever write a sonnet to her, Petrarchan or other.

One thing I understand: her desire to be ordinary, not strange like me. God, how I want to be ordinary, a faceless enlisted man in uniform, kept busy with senseless routines. I think, among other things, that going into the Army will show my father that I am a man. I have begun to care again — to woo him, to eat at his feeble heart. Even Alice fades in the strong beam of this one old story: I love you, you rotten old fradulent grandee, you cheap politician, you mother fucker. I know that if I'd gone to Oxford I would come home an Anglo-phile fop. That's too easy for me, and I want him to love me as he did long ago, to love me before he dies.

Months go by when I don't think about the speckled ten-cent store notebooks that I keep in the drawer of my desk. Years, even, when my first child was born and when we were living at court in Washington in the golden years of the early sixties. But they are my burden as history must be, and just to think lightly of Robert always brings tears. That's his story or what you'll need of his story and mine, too. I'm not sure it even has the energy of pulp fiction. I am still the unloved little sibling and every day I work at being better than my brother, to get my father to smile at me from the grave. Twenty years ago Robert was gunned down at Inchon. Fifty thousand deaths in the Korean War and so at last he proved himself an ordinary man.

Ordinary is a word I've used against Jim Cogan, used to my advantage. But the loss is so final; the admission is, my friend, that I've been self-deceived and that my brother's life was less than grand opera. It is just ordinary, after all, predictable to be a doomed young man. You are so like him. Don't make your life into a perfect little study like his.

Don't pretend, Jim Cogan, that you are in disdain of history. You are the one who provoked me — "My mother never liked you." You are the one who asked, "What's the mystery?" You more than half want to know what made us — your mother, your father and my own glamorous life that's a sham. Think when I was a kid like you I did not know my own brother, who was the only one I loved. Think that I am a good child-woman whom no one can fault — loyal to my husband though given recently to flirting at cocktail parties, devoted to my children (who will be better off for my career), true to the enlightened journalese that will justify my days and do nothing whatever to improve our lot. Think that during my youth I was flaccid, passive, joining that first great audience who sat and watched the McCarthy hearings until our bottoms were numb, who let the days wash over us while General Douglas MacArthur sent out his troops from occupied Japan to the Yellow Sea. (Robert sent me a kimono from Tokyo for Christmas signed "Pinkerton." I knew for certain it was all chopsticks and cherry blossoms over there.) Think that when I look at myself "I spit in the face of time that has transfigured me," and that we were once like you, ignorant and beautiful and young. Think that this story is your answer: Robert and all my honesty and self-knowledge are here for you at last. Think before you run.

II

FOUR MORAL TALES

1

The Pigs of Krishna Nuru

THE DAY THAT JIMMY COGAN was accepted at Fordham
was a happy one for his family. The notice came in the
morning mail on a Saturday before he left for work. He
whistled as he ran downstairs even though he had missed
the express that would get him to the *Chateau du Chien* by
eleven o'clock. On Conner Street the cement sparkled with
a thousand flickering specks of mica he had never seen before. He was not usually a cheerful boy but this morning
the world was filled with promises which he never believed
would be for him. His mother and father had smiled until
he thought their faces would break.

At the kiosk he bought a copy of *Time* determined
to attack the problems of the day with a keen mind. The
picture on the cover was of a young Democratic senator, a
bright hope, handsome as an actor. Jim had never heard the
man's name, a fact that wouldn't have troubled him in
the past; though he had read every word from the mouth of

Ché Guevara, politics had always seemed too remote and meaningless. The war was still on — his peace button thrown in a drawer with paper clips and cuff links. His peace poster over the bed had popped its tacks and now lay in a roll on the closet shelf. Today he felt that he must know something beyond his blind acceptance of a cause. Beginning now, with this magazine on the subway. There was not a moment to be lost.

For weeks he had done nothing but stare into space, thinking of the bare body of the girl he slept with — Shelley Waltz. He had tried calling her his girl but that was wrong: there was no way in which he possessed her. She was somewhat crazy, a wandering, angry girl. Though she had a home she seemed more a child of the streets. Days went by when he did not see her, then she would be mysteriously available again, waiting for him outside school or sitting on the curbstone near his house. When they made love he felt drawn into *her* defiance of the world (operation total crap), so they touched and felt and were finally bound together in her fierce beliefs. Often when he thought of her nakedness it was to see her still arguing, arms thrown up in exasperation at one of his middle-class notions, breasts jiggling as she stamped her foot in protest. Only in fantasy could he have Shelley as he wanted her — naked still, but smooth, compliant, free of all the mimeographed texts that proclaimed her free. Sometimes he would dress her in his mind — in short skirts and a clean blouse like other girls wore, stockings and shoes. She looked up at him and listened for once: in this impossible vision he found that he could love Shelley Waltz.

Today, as a sacred vow, he would not think of her. He had left his family in a state of exultation. His victory was theirs. The twins were loud and high spirited for a change, asking if he could get them tickets for the Fordham basketball season now. After a powerful hug his mother had stood back against his father's chest in a conscious pose — looking as parents are supposed to look, solid and self-congratulatory. It was a happy day. "I am on the right course at last," thought Jim, ignorant as Percival and confident that there was still a quest for the chosen: "I am ready now. There is no time to be lost." The young senator, he read, often worked an eighteen-hour day, slept in his office, was capable of working all night as he had recently on his proposed amendment to a disarmament bill. When defeated in committee the next day he had started to redraft the amendment at once, dictating on his way home into a little Japanese tape recorder his children had given him for Christmas. Years ago as a junior congressman he had cried openly in front of his staff upon hearing of the execution of Caryl Chessman (a footnote in the magazine identified Chessman for Jim Cogan as a convicted rapist, murderer, pervert, sentenced to death who after an arduous, inspired and inspiring battle, etc. . . .). "I cry," the young statesman said, "not for the dead, but for the terrible limits upon the minds of men. That will have me in tears for the rest of my life."

Sitting next to Jim was a Puerto Rican girl in tight pants and a white sweater cut low like a man's undershirt. Her breasts were dark. A miraculous medal hung on a thin gold chain around her neck. She was meticulous in her movements, looking at Jim with the expert blank eyes of an experienced subway rider, opening her purse with fussy delicate fingers, extracting a folded Kleenex from an orderliness that bordered on stupidity. He had gone out with a girl like that when he was fifteen, in the first throes of calling up girls and going to dances. She had gyrated as though her whole body was filled with sex, in a trance smiling her clean smile at him out of her private sensual world and had turned to stone when the music stopped, like this one whose

123

heavy thigh touched his. *Her* little gold chain had dangled a cross, and her father's name was Jesus. That had always killed him. She had looked good out there with him in the lights and for months he was the envy of his friends. He was never allowed to touch her — she was saving it. She carried movie magazines inside her notebook and had nothing to say to him. He was her foreigner. Some girl friend, *chocha*; she had quit school the day she turned sixteen and married some guy who had probably been into her for months.

"Hot," Jim said to the girl next to him who was carefully blotting her upper lip. When he spoke she got up at once and moved to the door. "*Chocha*," he said to himself — cunt, one of his few Spanish words. Shelley was something else, indifferently willing and ready at all times. He thought about this for a while, seeing her bedraggled hair like tangled honey, her narrow naked body, wondering when she would show up next and in a moment the wonder turned to desire. At Fifty-ninth Street Jim got off, full of sorrow — already his resolution had weakened. Knowing that he was late for work he stood on a windy island facing the Coliseum and read to the end of the article:

Last week, facing an audience of today's youth, the Senator insisted we keep our eye on the historical process. Quoting Louis Brandeis, he said: "Like the course of the heavenly bodies, harmony in national life is a resultant of the struggle between contending forces. In frank expression of conflicting opinion lies the greatest promise of wisdom in governmental action; and in suppression lies ordinarily the greatest peril." The Brandeis decision, he pointed out, was written in 1920.

Across the street at the Coliseum the Northeastern Gifts and Greeting Card Show was announced on the marquee:

clusters of what Jim Cogan now saw to be disgusting people were trailing in through the big glass doors. Old ladies mostly in pale spring coats and foolish hats, a few hopeless slope-shouldered men with their wives. He was filled with a loathing as much for their bodies as for their purposeless day. He marched through them swiftly, when suddenly he came to a woman laughing uncontrollably, her cheeks like withered dumplings, her weak eyes ringed hideously with bright jeweled glasses. Her hand was full of dollar bills which she pressed upon her friend in some private dispute, and turning she slapped her hand into Jim's face and the bills fluttered away. "Cunt," he said to her in the moment before she chased her money across the broad sidewalk and into the gutter. It was a triumph that died by the time he got to the next corner: he would soon be at work and there lay his betrayal.

At the *Chateau du Chien* he clipped, combed, perfumed and polished the nails of quivering pedigreed poodles. He had been quick to learn. The money was good. His boss, Mimi Devereux, large bones, deep voice, wrists and hips of a tennis champ, had wanted a young man. Jimmy Cogan was a sweetheart, tall, slim, polite — crew neck sweater and sport coat. Ah, where had they gone, these college-type boys. Mimi, thirty-five and unmarriageable, fell in love with him at once. Her customers were ecstatic. If they had a son — instead of a poodle, presumably — he would be like this. The dogs were handed to him with confidence. Jim Cogan was gentle, calm — such a boy. He remembered Belinda, Amie, Serge and Watteau — and hated them all. Hated his job, and above all hated his part in the twisted love of these idle, neurotic women for their pets. Their admiration showered on him like slime, a perversion of the elements.

He did it for money, for money, he said, because there was no money to educate him and he would have to do that himself. Because he had listened to the pleadings of his mother for the last time: in some way the *Chateau du Chien* touched upon a world she had seen once — an Irish secretary's view of the parlor. The job was *nice*, the big world and one step up from being a camp counselor. It was wacky. It was experience. Couldn't he look at it that way, his mother asked. For three weeks he had — grist for the mill, a fund of funny stories. And when he handed a dog back, washed, poufed, beribboned, rhinestone collar in place, sweet as a farting rose, he smiled and always remembered the owner's name. Last week he had passed Hi-Marx Llewellyn into the loving arms of his mistress, "Looks like you're all done up too, Mrs. Schlotzer!" That was worth a five dollar tip and though he murmured the obligatory "Screw you" as she strutted out the door, it had not saved him. In three weeks he had made three hundred dollars: it was fantastic for a boy of seventeen. What did the world expect of him anyway? He had not wanted the truth for himself: coupled with the money there was sex, the grinning American two-headed eagle. By working midtown he could easily meet Shelley, go with her on her travels in the city, appease the final obsession. Now that he was making so much money his parents had shut up about his late hours.

The minute he walked in the door he told Mimi Devereux that he was accepted at Fordham. She was relieved, thinking that something had happened to him on the way downtown. Now he could go right on working during college — "Great," she said, "That's too great!" Mimi had an accent that Jim could not place, a plain direct speech full of buoyant tones as different from anything he knew as an actress in an English movie. For reasons beyond him she was not supposed to be running a poodle parlor. "I'm something of a rebel," she told Jim. He loved that — Mimi in her neat skirts and sweaters, loafers and a man's wrist watch. Something of a rebel. As if it were a school regulation, she never wore slacks, though it would have been easier with the dogs. When the shop closed she split a beer with Jim. She told him that the customers didn't know a good animal when they saw one. They cared nothing for breeding. Last year there was a standard black from Central Park West, clipped in a show-cut with the conformation of a winner, bred out of Champion Pierrot Prime, and last week when he came in he looked like a flabby, slouching child. It was criminal. Together, they made fun of the customers and Jim felt that he and Mimi were of one age, one mind, "You're a natural," she said to Jim Cogan as he swept up the clippings. High praise, indeed.

"Yes, I'm something of a rebel," Mimi said, "I've just got to work with dogs." He wondered what it was she should be doing, what she had left or put aside for the *Chateau du Chien*. Her program was to clean up on these well-heeled floozies with their pathetic ruined poodles and get hold of a kennel — Kerry blue terriers were her passion — to breed and show real dogs. Despite her awkward size Mimi handled the dogs gracefully, with an economy of movement Jim had never quite attained even with his best shots on the basketball court. She had a singleness of purpose, a dedication that was pure and appealing. Jim found he could not belittle her to his mother or explain what seemed so right about his boss to Shelley Waltz.

"What a sellout," Shelley said, "smiling at those dead people and that dyke."

"She's not," he said. "Mimi is something of a rebel."

Now Jim saw himself on the straight and narrow, going to college. He must look at things honestly: his mother and father had stood together this morning content and happy, like they never had through all the years. *He* was going to college. *Their* dreams were fulfilled. They had done everything in their power to defeat him: moved him from school to school, each time the neighborhood getting tougher and the teachers more like keepers patrolling the aisles, then plunging him into Bronx Science where he could barely make the grade. His parents had sold themselves into captivity — his mother for a gin bottle, his father for a stack of poker chips — and then overlaid the whole picture with a trip to Sunday Mass. All of them pulled together, washed and dressed as though this could absolve the sins of the week. Ordinary sins that they had all settled into — moody silence, dishonesty, private solace. At Mass and after when they drove over to Brooklyn to visit relatives they looked like a family instead of a bunch of small-time gangsters. This morning his brother and sister, those two delinquents, presented themselves as normal happy children — happy, happy, happy — that hollow word. He was going to college — the rest was a lie. Fordham because he could live at home and save money and because he had listened to them for years. Father-this-one and Father-that-one who had taught his old man — a splendid product there of Catholic education. His mother and father stood for nothing but the Sunday morning mock-up, nothing more than muddling through. He was infected. Already he felt their dishonesty had seeped through him — insulting an old lady on the street to set himself up, sucking up to fools with fat purses, fussing over silly animals, making it (one more time, one last time — already the lie was born) with a girl he did not love.

Jim Cogan worked hard during the afternoon. Taking in poodles from the front waiting room, following Mimi Devereux's directions. He was allowed to do only the simplest and cheapest clips. After a shampoo he dried their ears and topknots with a little electric hair dryer meant for a person. If they nipped at his hands he put on gloves. The miniatures trembled, their hearts thumping heavily in their tiny chests. In the late afternoon a CBS newscaster came in with a brace of gray standards for a shampoo and comb-out. The man's face was a mask of prominence, betraying nothing beyond the measured warmth with which he announced our national disasters. Jimmy Cogan stood in awe of his haircut, his polished fingernails, his clothes — things he did not notice on the women who came in the shop, though his mother had said, having stopped to see him at work — "Those ladies! The money on their backs." He saw the customers of *Chateau du Chien* with soft bellies, tortoise-like, laboring under a hump of greenbacks, being walked by their poodles at the curb. At five Shelley called to say that she would be in Union Square at nine-thirty. After a long pause he said, all right, wanting to tell her he was accepted at college as though she were an ordinary girl friend. "What's the matter?" she asked, "You sound funny."

You bet I sound funny, Jim Cogan thought, and I'm going to sound funnier, because you are a weird sad girl and I don't need it. Hanging around street corners by yourself. It had been a month now since he'd seen any of his friends. He had not even called them this morning when he got the news. That's how far he was into Shelley's world — like he had dropped out of life. No more (just one irresolute bang tonight) and then no more. At five-thirty Mrs. Schlotzer who had no appointment showed up with Hi-Marx Llewellyn. She was hysterical. The dog would not walk for her. She took him downstairs and he would not budge. She carried him to the curb. He urinated and stood there. Up in the apartment he sat on the couch, was lifted to his meal of chopped steak for three days now. Same for Mr. Schlotzer. Same for the doorman. She knew Hi-Marx was faking — had caught him romping with his rubber porcupine in the middle of the night. What had she done to deserve this? Her couch was slubbed silk, getting a large oily spot from the one place he sat. Lifting her drained face to Jim, she pleaded, "Give him everything."

"Yes, Mrs. Schlotzer." The dog, an apricot toy, went readily to Jim.

"What have I done?" the woman cried jealously, and, answering her own question, said, "I should have bred him, but I couldn't bring myself. Give him polish, cream rinse, clip and comb."

"He was clipped last week."

"*Pretend*," said Mrs. Schlotzer, "make a buzzing. I never should have let you people do the utility cut. From the moment the pompoms went he's been strange."

"Yes, Mrs. Schlotzer." I hope the stones fall out of your rings. I hope your credit cards are stolen. I hope Mr. Schlotzer is making it with his secretary.

"He likes you —" she said gloomily, "Pick out something for him — a rain coat. Two weeks ago I got him one of those Italian baskets — he sits on the couch. My God," she cried, "what have I done?"

Hi-Marx Llewellyn walked pertly into the back room with Jimmy Cogan and leapt up on the counter to be serviced, a quivering small beast, panting with excitement.

"That poor soul," Mimi said, popping a tranquilizer down his tiny throat. "This is the third dog that bitch has ruined. I don't know what she expects of them, but they feel destroyed by her, broken."

Hi-Marx Llewellyn raised his anxious face to Jim, his delicate muzzle dwarfed by a monstrous ruff of hair, his heart slowed to a heavy throb as the tranquilizer set in. He pawed Jim's sweater, he scurried around the counter, his nails clicking on the slick surface. Poor little bastard — he was having fun. Coyly dashing at Jim he had an erection: the pale pink crayon of his defeated masculinity. He was brave to sit in his oily spot on the Schlotzer silk couch, to pee and sit at the curb, not to be paraded up to the shops on Fifth Avenue in absurd costumes and a showy ruff. Jim grabbed a set of clippers and worked fast (the dog was so small he could conceal him with his body) shaving Hi-Marx Llewellyn down until he was bare as a rat. Gone the tuft at the end of his tail. Gone the ornamental rings of fur on his spindly legs. His head unnaturally exposed with the topknot gone was flat and narrow: otherwise he looked the miniature of any normal self-respecting mutt. With the dog hidden under his sweater, Jim waited for Mrs. Schlotzer to return and wrote this note:

Mimi,

I take full responsibility for my act. There comes a moment when we must stand up and be counted. Today that moment came for me.

James Cogan

P.S. I am sorry we must sever what has been one of the most meaningful relationships of my life.

Hi-Marx Llewellyn growled when he heard his mistress's voice and ran into the front room to nip at her ankles. With his rolled, tattered copy of *Time* Jim waited until Mrs. Schlotzer's screams reached operatic proportions and ran past her out of the shop. Bring them down, Jim thought. Bring them down. Mimi Devereux nursed a broken heart like an abandoned woman, she was that sorry to see the end of him.

It was only when he was slouched in a movie seat wasting the two hours between his exit from the *Chateau du Chien* and the encounter with Shelley Waltz in Union Square that he realized he had not been paid for the week. He felt enormously proud: Life had begun after all. The battle was launched. On the screen a girl with fantastic legs but a plain face made love with an artist, an older guy. They ran down the streets of a blue-hazed New York doing beautiful free things, eating ice-cream cones, lying out in Central Park. Then the artist's wife showed up and it was over — he had faked it with the girl and gave this feeble speech, in a business suit and tie now, about how much it had meant, truly. Bring them down. Bring them down. Bravely the girl rode off on her bike in the final scene, her honesty and integrity intact in the full light of day. Wearing blue jeans and a fatigue jacket she pedaled off across Brooklyn Bridge.

Shelley Waltz waited at the top of the subway stairs in Union Square. Her round childish face looked less sullen than usual, more actively annoyed. This evening she wore a new Indian robe, diaphanous and white, and looked like a child who has lost its role in the Christmas play. Her first words to Jim Cogan were not encouraging: "This is all a big mistake."

Jim looked down at her filthy bare feet.

"I have to go to Clauson's place," she said defiantly.

"So?"

"*I* have to go there," Shelley said. "There's something on."

They argued for a while in front of May's and she started to walk east on the long block toward Third Avenue with Jim at her heels. Having seen her, he wanted her. A soft breeze billowed the white stuff of her garment and he saw, or thought he saw, that she was naked underneath. One more time to be with her in a dim back room at Clauson's or in the dirty forgotten park near her house and then no more. To impress her Jim told the story of Hi-Marx Llewellyn: in one manly act he had finished with the poodle parlor that she hated.

"You're so involved with all that," Shelley said.

"I'm *through* with it!"

"It's the same thing," she turned on him, "look at you — just look!"

It was true, he did look a sight in his chinos and neat sweater when he finally trailed her into Clauson's place where a crowd of squatting white-robed figures murmured in the candlelight. From a dark corner a woman with gray hair and big pearl earrings came forth twanging finger cymbals while she sang a song without words. The man next to Jim passed him a joint and they shared while Jim heard his long story, this man with orange sideburns and extremely yellow teeth, how he had done something holy that day. As participation in Creative Love he had felt the entire side of the office building he worked in with his eyes closed. He felt the oppressive regularity of the cement and the hard cold surface of the aluminium panels, the inhuman scale of the whole, the mass, the enormity of structure that made him into a wincing midget each day as he went through the great arcaded entrance. Now that he had felt, the man said, it could never frighten him again. Now that he had charged himself with negative power from the monster he could meet the beast in battle every day and stand like a giant in his new power. He could re-create the touch of cement and glass. If you know with your body you do not fear, the guy said. After a while Jim felt obligated to say he had felt the flesh of a dog that day, the soft close curls, the nearly hairless underbelly. Some people sang together. Patrick James Clauson, their leader sat by himself facing the group on a leather hassock, wrapped in white, of course. A plump faggy Irishman, he might have been a priest in the Diocese of New York. From time to time his voice rang out in maxims: "We will feel and breathe our way back into the world. The world will not change us. We will re-create the world."

Jimmy Cogan emptied his wallet into a brass box that

was passed to him and began to chant. He felt again that life had truly started. He was free. His words seemed to him inspired as he told a girl with long snarled hair that he had felt the underbelly of a dog. Having experienced that soft flesh with the heart pounding he would always feel kin to the animal, feel one with its small anxious body. Girls danced, Shelley among them, rotating her head in a frenzy of relaxation. He thanked God, the old man with the beard, the God whose cross he drew on his body before each quarter in basketball, each fifty-yard dash — that he had not told Shelley Waltz he was accepted at college.

"The daughters danced in the desert, their bodies like fountains," P. J. Clauson rose from his hassock in glory, "and the desert was the city. With their tongues they licked the foul air and breathed forth their purity. With their hair they watered the stone and flowers grew. With their fresh bodies dancing they brought forth a garden until the city was no more."

Quiet descended as though a signal were given. All the white-robed people read in thin green books which reminded Jim Cogan of his bankbook. He alone was empty-handed, apart from their feelings. His legs were sprawled out while they, he noted, they had magically tucked their limbs neatly away like nesting birds. Trying to be one with their mood he took *Time* from his pocket, his only text: "Last week," he read, "in Los Angeles Superior Court, curvaceous Sherrill Lang (39-23-35), space-wife in TV's popular *Stardust Lane,* defended herself against accusations of ex-husband Mike Dougherty that she had undergone breast surgery in El Paso, Texas, in 1962 to obtain the remarkable proportions which launched her Hollywood career. Surprising Judge David Marcus, braless Sherrill bared her bosom for the jury who awarded her the five dollars plus legal fees she was seeking for defamation of character: "Money means nothing," said Sherrill buttoning up her simple dress. "I want to be a serious actress and I'm sorry if my breasts stand in the way!" Even in this story, Jim saw the terrible deceit. It was supposed to be funny, he knew, but that was too easy. Fraud everywhere. Lies. Had Sherrill Lang *wanted* to play that scene in court? Yes, in the photo, "Space-wife with Agent," he discerned her cheap smile of victory. Priceless, this coverage in the national media. Oh, bring them down. All around him these crazies, Shelley's white-robed people, were striving for honesty and it seemed that he alone wore a sweater of dissent. What did the world expect of him? It was too hard, the pieces too various — as though there were a thousand scattered bits of glass and he was asked to assemble them into a mirror. The folly of Clauson's storefront temple bewildered him: incense and Indian bells you could buy in any gift shop. Yet there was no disputing the fact: The room was still and full of peace. Tears streamed down Jim Cogan's face.

Shelley was beside him, holding him, begging his forgiveness. He could come with her always to Clauson's. Jim told her that his whole soul seemed to laugh and cry in torment. He was torn between visions of freedom and the dutiful years ahead. "I'm going to college," he confessed.

"You're so involved in that," Shelley said.

His mother had planned a celebration he knew. He knew her ways — given hope once more, he knew all the little embellishments that she would foist upon his triumph to make it her own. Now she would put away the uncut cake at home, rejected by her wandering son. She had not boozed all the long afternoon. The children were washed and dressed. Their father was home, but now he would go out to find a card game. At Jim's own place on the kitchen table a large present gaily wrapped awaited him and he could not guess what lay inside. His tears were blotted by Shelley's hair.

"Cry," she said, "Go on — cry."

It was a real breakthrough he knew, to cry with this weird girl. In her white robe, in the candlelight a beauty flared in her and in a torrent of words he confessed it — that he had wanted her one more time.

"Sex," she murmured to him soothingly, "is unimportant."

"My friends! Because of you," he cried in final confusion, "I haven't seen my friends in months."

The voice of Clauson rose as though out of Jim Cogan's own emotion: "My friends, let us observe the lesson. Upon his feast day Krishna Nuru received from the sly Prince Dhrahman a farm which was old and in great disrepair. Thinking that the god Krishna would list the property among his dominions but would not care to see the farm, Dhrahman was well pleased with himself. Immediately Krishna Nuru rode to the place and saw that it was on the north side of the mountain where the village ends. Here lived the poor in their shacks, the farm no more than a pitiful collection of these buildings leaning one into another."

The story rang true for all the squatting figures on Clauson's floor. Holding Shelley to him Jim Cogan wondered at the man's cleverness for the last time — he was a pure spirit, an instrument of god. P. J. Clauson, pudgy, pink as an angel, was lost in his own performance: "The fields of the farm were bare as dunes 'and the well was dry. A few chickens and three thin pigs were the only creatures on the land. At once the god Krishna sent a letter to the prince thanking him for the tribute of this beautiful farm. The prince raged and rode out to make sure he had not given the wrong property away, but upon coming to the old farm he met Krishna Nuru sitting on the broken gate in a robe of gold cloth celebrating his good fortune with wine and song.

" 'Come see,' he said to the prince with godlike demeanor, 'come see my lovely pigs, for they are surely the wisest animals in the land.' Though Dhrahman saw three pigs who had been fed and washed but looked no better than they should, still he worried at the delight of Krishna Nuru. He returned to the palace to say that the god's powers were sorely depleted when he thought he had riches in three thin pigs. Still it troubled him and he sent spies to watch the farm. The god Krishna lavished great care upon this land. A new well was found and wheat planted. An orchard of wonderful fruit trees which had been thought dead blossomed in the spring. All the little buildings were set straight and painted. The gate was put back on its hinges and the mysterious pigs grew fat and beautiful. When Dhrahman heard these stories he was devoured with jealousy and rode out to the farm where Krishna Nuru himself was throwing grain out of a basket at the merriest chickens ever seen.

"'Come see,' said the god, 'come see my lovely pigs, but be quiet for they are hard at work.' 'Surely,' said the prince to himself, 'he is demented,' and thought with what relish he would describe the great god feeding chickens in the barnyard."

Shelley Waltz swept her arms up around Jim Cogan's neck. Lovers at last, they were enfolded in the same white robe of belief. The silence in Clauson's presence was perfect. A last shallow flame of life flickered from the candles upon the faces of his audience — his congregation.

"But strange to say the three pigs were truly busy feeding on corn that was bright as gold and when they had finished they turned to the prince that he might see their marvelous girth and it seemed to him that the pigs smiled. Now the prince rode off in a terrible fury, humiliated by the cleverness of Krishna Nuru's pigs.

"Each day for a hundred days he returned and each day it seemed to the prince that the pigs grew more beautiful and that they mocked him, for he could not believe that they merely ate and slept and grunted in the mud and that the god Krishna had not performed some magic upon the animals. His cheek grew pale and his body wasted with envy until at last one day the prince cried out to them: 'Why are you so happy?' and Krishna smiled with his pigs.

" 'Why are you so happy?' cried out the prince in anguish.

"And Krishna Nuru answered: 'What your eyes see, your heart will believe.' "

Jim Cogan was enchanted by Clauson's tale and listened with full respect as the prince met his just and terrible fate. Dhrahman was outwitted by pigs. Bring them down — the empty, the deceitful of the world, the devouring parents who would feed on his heart. *He* was going to college, driven by their years of desire. Sure, he would do their bidding, but the triumph would be his — already he could see himself in the garment of a simpler time and place they could not understand, a lamb in a murky difficult landscape. Fuck their sold-out world. He would torment them with his peace. Tracings of flowers, birds, vines adorned the white, white shirt he would buy tomorrow in some heavy-scented Indian shop.

Clauson stood in the dim light with arms outspread, a fat hovering Holy Ghost above them:

"Krishna Nuru has written: 'Dhrahman, who valued appearances, attempted to cheat the god Krishna but cheated only himself. For Krishna by honest work transfigures the commonplace into beauty. Thus he would instruct us all to live with effort and grace.' "

2

Three Cheers for Mr. Spears

MILL WAS WELL AWARE that her own children made fun of her, laughed together at the stories of her past — not all of her past life but the time that she had spent as secretary to Dawson Spears. Mr. Spears was president of a publishing firm with offices in a slim bay-windowed brownstone in Murray Hill. The operation was small but prestigious. So many, many visitors to the Minotaur Press — authors, editors from abroad — had said that the cluttered homey atmosphere seemed more English to them than American: more the way things used to be. "A human scale," cried a bearded poet from the West Coast who had looked so original in the early fifties. Mill clipped the poet's reviews: they said his verse was a lacing of commonplace observations that made him accessible and odd epiphanies that made him obscure.

It was one of the moments Millicent Cogan remembered fully: the great hairy poet in a lumber jacket being greeted by Spears in his Savile Row suit before lunch at the National Book Awards, crying out "a human scale" when he saw Mill at her little desk with the geraniums and Spears's office like an old sitting room with the worn Kazak. The wallpaper was stained, but the pictures! There was a Jack Yeats portrait, a Moholy-Nagy design for a book jacket and a stunning Blake, a picture of Satan smiting Job with sore boils.

Millicent was not literary. That wasn't the point. She was clever and quick. She would have picked up real estate or ladies' ready-to-wear, so it was pure luck, the grace of God, she sometimes implied to her children, that she had those years with Mr. Spears. It wasn't merely that she read every book published by the Minotaur Press — she really learned the business: she knew what slot a book filled on the spring list, how it was to be promoted and how it was received, the number of copies run off in the first printing, and when, alas, a book was remaindered, the pink slip with the great man's initials was sent out from her desk to the warehouse like a death warrant. When she resigned after five years in the office, her girlish figure blooming with her first child, it was the end of an era. Mill's education was complete and Dawson Spears presented her with a fine gold watch like a graduation present. The problem for Mill was that she did not enter the big world but left it behind. She went home in a taxi that day laden with baby presents — one of the memories she did not repeat to her children — the beautiful watch ticked on her wrist while she wept bitter tears for her confinement and the long marriage ahead.

"What's gone is gone," Millicent said. "Here we are now. There's no point in dwelling on the past." Though these were her words the Cogan kids grew up with the idea that her past at the Press stood for better times. It belittled their life. It made their father's efforts more paltry, this time that she claimed was gone. All they could do was laugh, after all what was it to them — the first distinguished paperback editions of Dickens, of Howells, of James. The sherry and hors d'oeuvres at Christmas, not the usual office brawl. The well-cut skirts their mother had worn just below her knee, the cashmere sweater sets dyed to match, the Audrey Hepburn look and the Pulitzer prize biography of Franklin Delano Roosevelt. *She'd* read it in proof. Eleanor Roosevelt had attended the publication party — "and carried herself like a queen. She was, yes, the most beautiful woman I have ever seen." It wasn't just the stories over and over again. It was their mother turned into someone else, her voice altered to a fluting richness. She was absorbed as she never was in the stuff of their daily life. If they didn't laugh, they'd cry, Jim said. All this Millie knew.

She was a survivor, frail, helpless, but a survivor: the past was one prop, the bottle another. Her children must see what she had been, that there was strength and purpose in her still as there had been long ago. To cut these years out of her life, the stories of these years, was to give way to a silence like death or resignation. Let them laugh.

One day in spring, Mill got up early and was dressed in her best suit before the children were at the breakfast table. They wrangled and ate everything in sight. The twins splitting the last banana between them to spite Jim. And Jim to spite them won her favor telling her the events of his day — a chemistry test, track meet after school.

"You have your keys?" she asked the children. This was in case she was not there when they got home from school. They could see that she was dressed for a visit to Grandpa in Brooklyn though she never said so anymore. "Your Dad has a sales meeting at the office," she told them instead. "I'll go into town with him." And go on over to Brooklyn they knew. Their father and Old Man Murray were no longer on speaking terms.

She fussed over her hair while Jack was shaving and

reached into the drawer for her alligator purse. It looked as elegant to Mill as it had years ago when she was working and laid out the money for it. Then, when she was about to push the drawer closed she saw the troublesome small book — a pebbled black calf binding worn smooth with a gold cross in the center. The Book of Common Prayer which she took up and examined. The fly leaf was inscribed in a bold boy's hand — Dawson Spears, III, Easter 1916. It had been on her mind since he died.

"Are you coming?" Jack called to her. She stuffed the things from her everyday purse into the alligator bag along with the prayer book and ran out to meet him.

The day was beautiful as they drove out on Bruckner Boulevard and over to the East River Drive. No smog, just a clear spring sky. The man on the radio announced that the air was acceptable.

Mill took the prayer book out and leafed through its thin gilt-edged pages. "I've been thinking," she said to Jack, "that I should send this to Mr. Spears's wife, now that he's dead. She might like to have it for her children or the grandchildren."

"I wouldn't bother. They probably don't know it exists. It means something to you."

"Yes, it does," she replied. It was the token, or the tribute, of her one serious and personal conversation with Mr. Spears. She had come into the office with the unmistakable smudge on her forehead on an Ash Wednesday and distracted him from his work.

"*Remember, Man —*" he said.

"That's right," Mill answered politely, "*that thou art dust and unto dust thou shalt return.*"

He asked her to sit down for a while, told her that he'd been a choir boy with a lovely voice, a devout youngster. Pushed in that direction by his parents. From an early age he had his heart set on the ministry. "The process of losing my faith was so gradual," said Mr. Spears. "I didn't seem to notice it. I've thought since that it was a counterpart to attaining my physical growth which I never noticed either. One day it was complete — my loss of faith and my height and it was easy, painless. I wish that I had suffered."

"Why?" Mill asked.

"Because I'm afraid I might have to do the suffering now," said Dawson Spears. He was a tall, muscular man who played tennis and squash. When she first came to work for him before she fell in love with the business, she thought that it was dreadful for a powerful man like that to sit behind a desk reading most of the day. He reminded her of some movie actor she could not place exactly — one with crisp gray hair and a smooth daddy voice. Joseph Cotten, but not quite. Fredric March a little.

Mr. Spears said: "I think your people are right. You're better off to have the ashes now while you're young."

"But, I'll have them every year," said Mill. Her hand went up to the grit on her forehead.

"Don't rub it off! It's blessed isn't it?" He said that life was treacherous, which Millicent Murray found hard to believe from him. Then he took the prayer book from his top desk drawer and gave it to her, showed her the inscription: the week before his confirmation, Easter, 1916.

"The date didn't mean a thing," he laughed. "That's a hell of a time to record in a Protestant prayer book."

"The Easter Rebellion," Mill said with pride.

"There's a good Irish girl!"

"We're Catholic," she said, "but we're not Irish in that way. I know about that from the book we published last fall on the Abbey Theater."

"You are a sweet girl," was all he said. Then the Book of Common Prayer was put into her hands and she understood she was to take it.

"Thank you. I'll read this, too." She was somewhat flustered by his gift, but Mill had a natural dignity and said directly to Mr. Spears: "I hope some day you'll ask for it back."

"Not a chance," he coughed pleasantly and sat behind his desk. They were ready to resume the business of the day.

When she and Jack got to midtown Manhattan everything conspired to bring the old days back. The morning traffic. The streets full of people on their way to work. It was the young office girls who held her attention, so many of them, freshly done up, as pretty as they could make themselves, hurrying towards the adventures of the day. Glamorous little birds from plain homes or half-furnished apartments — "Oh, Jack," she cried, her voice thick with emotion, "what's your meeting about today?"

"The usual sales meeting. Nothing more." He looked at her queerly. "Are you all right?"

"I'm fine." She brightened as he drew to the curb in front of the dazzling new building on Park Avenue. "How is it going?" she asked her husband. It was absurd that they should have to leave home and come all this way to sit in the car and talk to each other at last.

"Not good," Jack said, though he looked like a winner this morning in a new pinstripe suit, a polish on his Sunday shoes. "I haven't made a significant sale in months and I have to bullshit my way through the meeting."

"Why?"

"Everything's slow right now. They *know* that. The industrial park out in Westchester that was to be my salvation is all screwed up with zoning laws. . . . It's not too bad . . . I have something on the line . . . I have a half-dozen promises on the new file system."

"What's that?" Mill asked.

144

"One cabinet contains a five year correspondence — very neat, a cheap microfilm process."

"How marvelous!" she exclaimed as though she were talking to the children.

"It's obvious," Jack said flatly. "I told you about it months ago. You don't listen."

"I can't listen anymore. The last time I listened was in 1961 — the restaurant business. Jack, I'm sorry that I can't."

They sat quietly together, both quick to recall the old enthusiasm that Mill used to have for every job he tried — the expertise she would acquire in a few weeks. The ghost of a smart hopeful girl spoke in Mill's vague pumped-up enthusiasm for "the marvelous machines."

"I'm so hard on you," Jack said.

"Never mind me. It's Jimmy's college that I have on my mind. That's so expensive and we've no guarantee he'll get a scholarship."

"I won't let you down," Cogan said.

She smiled at him and edged over to the driver's seat. "I'm sorry." She kissed him on the cheek and stayed behind the wheel after he had gone into the high glass lobby of Merganthaller. Sorry, indeed, that she aided their bad luck in recent years with her afternoon drinks: it was a question now of who let down who. The neighborhood they lived in was a disaster for the twins and she was sorry about that too, about the cramped flat that was supposed to have been a short stop on their way to suburbia — New Rochelle or Rye. It had turned out to be mighty convenient for Jack to go to the trotters up at Yonkers Raceway. The network of card games in the city pursued him, though she was certain the loan shark had been cleared out of their lives. It was as though they had been in hiding these last two years. She was sorry that she was not going to some clean carpeted office to face the comprehensible tasks of the day. Next, the taste of lies in her mouth as she drove back to the highway and headed for the Williamsburg Bridge. Jack would kill her if he thought she was going to see her father rather than stop at Macy's to buy underwear for the kids.

Old Man Murray was a terrible bastard with tobacco stains on his teeth, slowly suffocating from emphysema. He smoked a pack a day in defiance of the doctor's orders and his daughter's pleading. His apartment was littered with the dainty Haviland ashtrays that Mill's mother had thought sweet, all of them piled high with butt ends and the overflow of ashes everywhere — on tables and carpets, strewn in the kitchen sink. The armchair across from the television was burnt in a half-dozen places. Since the death of his wife twenty-five years ago he had left everything in place, just as she had set it on the last day of her housekeeping — not out of reverence but because he was a tight penny-pinching bastard who had not bought himself a man-sized ashtray or a decent cover for the old chair in all those years.

"Not dead yet!" Old Man Murray shouted to Mill when he heard her key in the lock. "I'm still here!" He wheezed and laughed when he saw her standing in the doorway dressed to kill.

"Hello, Daddy," sighed Millicent.

"How's the redhead," Murray asked nicely enough and accepted her kiss. "I see you're still wearing the suit I bought you. Good things last — I always told you that."

The suit, was she ever allowed to forget it, was bought at Saks when the twins were small. After a lecture from her father on how awful she looked — dragged out, shabby, down at heel, like a sick cat — he had come through with a check for a hundred dollars and Mill had combed through the sales racks at the good stores. Now that her father was sick she shut up and didn't argue. What was the use of feeding him the lines.

"Reach me the matches over there," said Old Man Murray, and collapsed into his chair, "and don't give me any story. If I want to die that's my business."

"You'll never learn," Mill said and in spite of herself she pleaded with him once again to stop drenching his lungs with poison. "Please, please, Daddy," like a little disappointed girl. Her voice choked. Her skin blotched with strawberry patches. The more she loved him the more he taunted, and the more perverse his ways the more it wrenched her heart. Underneath was the unstated fear that she might hate him really, her own father. She could never believe it of herself. "Have you been taking the pills?" she asked.

"The green ones for the blood pressure, yes," he said hacking into a soiled gray handkerchief, "but not those others. They make me urinate and I'm running to the toilet all day."

"But you breathe better!" Mill cried. Well, what was the use. She went out to the kitchen and put on the kettle for tea. Everything there was neat and worn. Her father was a fastidious man — only the filth of his smoking habits was left about for her. The cups and saucers were clean and neatly stacked, the same blue willowware her mother had left behind when she went off for the exploratory operation twenty-five years ago — never to return. She checked the refrigerator and threw out the spoiled food that she had cooked for him on her last visit. He lived on frozen packages and orders sent up from the neighborhood delicatessen. The waste was nauseating, a sure sign to her that the efforts of her visit were wasted too.

In the bedroom an air conditioner in the window and an air purifier which the doctor had prescribed and Mill had bought were the only changes. Her mother, a quiet, self-effacing woman had bought a new bedspread and carpet, hung fresh curtains at the window knowing she would not be there. Mill dusted the tarnished dresser set and the dead woman's bottles of evaporated cologne, checked the sheets and pillowcases to see that he had changed them. One wall of the bedroom was covered with photos in plain black frames — all of her father in different stages of his athletic career. Skip Murray up at bat, with the rookies in Fort Lauderdale, with the Babe at a dinner behind a baseball of white chrysanthemums. Skip because of an odd little hesitation step in his run that made the fans hold their breath and then laugh with relief when he made it. Skip Murray with mayors and cardinals, Eddie Cantor and Pat O'Brien.

Millicent was thirty before she realized he sure loved to get his picture taken: her father was only with the Yankees three years before his knees gave out. They played a hard game then, the old man said, and hit the damn ball. Today it was all a pitchers' show and he'd stopped going over to Shea Stadium and sat glumly in front of his television set. He shouldn't complain, Mill thought, the sport had been good to him. He'd spent the rest of his life living off those three years in the majors — coaching, speaking at Rotary and Kiwanis Clubs, selling sports equipment. He was always a favorite with the men and boys. The only sensible thing her father had done was to marry a plain girl who would bask in his glory and cater to his childish demands, a narrow-hipped sexless woman with little imagination who had produced Millicent as the dutiful fruit of a spare marriage.

It was through her mother's frugality that the Murrays owned this small brick apartment house — four floors, a creaking elevator, a corroded furnace, twenty rents in all — and while she was alive the halls were clean and painted out biannually in dull grayish green. She had left the scene when blackout shades were on the windows, long before the first Puerto Rican came into their neighborhood. The memory of her mother's goodness and self-sacrifice annoyed Mill. She had saved so carefully while Skip Murray was off around the country displaying himself in a major's uniform, recruiting for the U.S. Army as though it were no more than a large ball team — the poor woman had lived like a nun, mending Mill's stockings, eating tough cuts of meat to get together the down payment for this property. There was not one picture of that good lady here in her bedroom. She had been too shy to pose even for a family group. The smells in her apartment house had changed from boiled lamb and cabbage to rice and beans and plantains fried in heavy oil. The garbage out back was full of Goya cans, arroz con pollo, asopao, guava, calamares. Inside, the apartments were painted pink and lavender. Some windows that faced on the street were covered by sheets and torn pillowcases. The noise was terrific. In the first floor apartment by the entrance, there was a fat bachelor, Gonzalez, a notary who had put up a sign *se habla ingles*. What would her mother have thought — that thin woman who had faded out of sight. Not much. Mill imagined a passionless ghost — she would have taken one sniff of the enemy and silent, unprotesting, removed her family to some other clean gray-green sanctuary with the smell of boiled lamb.

One thing was certain to Mill: she was not like her mother at all. She was said to be like her aunt, the Murray girl, a beautiful Brooklyn secretary who years ago had married into a good Boston family — left them all behind and run off with a Protestant who had at least become a judge and a high mucky-muck in the Democratic party. She was like that aunt, down to the red hair and fair skin, the flair for clothes and the desire that still rose in her to run away. But she didn't leave. Mill stayed with what was set before her because she was like that old bastard, Skip Murray, too — full of hot air. Her drinking was like his smoking and she was an expert at trading on her past. It sickened her to hear him go on about the World Series of 1927–1928, the incredible four-to-nothing sweeps against Pittsburgh and the Cards and the apartment building *he'd* decided to buy right here in his native Brooklyn, in the parish where he was born. "I'm like him," she thought. "Full of self-deceit," and then she would say to herself, "Oh, no — it can't be that I'm like him."

In the living room he was searching for another ashtray he could start to fill with butts. He was a sad sight to behold: bald, gray-skinned, hunched up hard over his chest as though the disease were sucking him in. He found his chair but he had forgotten to turn on the TV set while he was up. The effort to speak was too great so he directed Mill to turn the button with a gesture of his hand. Mill did not obey.

"I need some money," she said quickly. "It's not like the other times, Dad. It's not to bail us out. This is for the children. Jim is ready for college. The twins should be sent to camp and have a summer like decent kids."

"I don't have it," the old man wheezed.

"You do. I know you do." She stopped short. She had never been so direct with him. The approach had always been through some disaster: sickness, Jack out of a job, the children in rags just before school opened. She would plead, a figure of pity and her father would rescue her again. The last time was the worst. Mill was in tears: Jack had borrowed money from the wrong sort of man. The one and only time he'd gone to a loan shark, by mistake, by mistake, she cried. Skip Murray had written out a check for his little girl — gagging, cough, cough, falling onto the couch, death's door anyway. An academy award performance.

"Don't bring him around anymore," her father had said.

"He was a punk deal, but you were *young, young,*" Old Man Murray said with contempt, "goin' at it hot and heavy." Jack was furious with her, said he'd rather die than take that money but take it he did and never said thanks, never went, as he was supposed to, out to Brooklyn to say that he was sorry, it would never happen again.

"I'm not asking for myself and I'm not asking for Jack. He has a good job."

"I'll believe that —" he coughed and couldn't finish.

"Why punish the kids because of us anyway?" Mill was begging as usual and she had determined not to. Her voice lightened: "I'll make out a check and you sign it. It'll be painless, believe me."

"The taxes," her father complained.

"I know the taxes and I know rent control and that whole story, but you haven't spent a cent on this place in years. You have *not*. This place is free and clear."

"You're very smart! I've got a mortage, Millicent."

"For tax purposes, Daddy, I know. I'm not dumb. You were the one who always said how clever I was." She went to the desk drawer and got out the checkbook, wrote the amount and left to buy the groceries she felt were needed. When she returned with two heavy brown bags she saw that his name was on the check and he was smoking, watching the midday news. She made lunch and put it before him on a tray. "Thank you," she said as she picked up the check. "It won't be necessary again. I'll get a job." Tears stung her eyes.

"Tears, idle tears," intoned Skip Murray in something of the old manner of the grand raconteur, before he coughed and reached for the napkin she'd set out with his lunch.

In haste, a quick dust mop here and there, water on a discouraged philodendron, Mill put the last touches to her visit and took her alligator purse with relief. She stood at the door, ready to leave, "Why don't you sell the apartment, Dad? I worry about you here alone." Sometimes she said that he should come and live with her, but neither one of them believed that this was possible or that it was a serious suggestion. She put her hand to the slivered wood where the door had been jimmied. Twice they'd broken in — his own tenants most likely who knew when he was out with his cronies at the Knights of Columbus. They'd stolen her mother's silver plate and the portable TV from the bedroom.

"Don't worry about me," he said not looking up at her.

"But I'd be so much happier if you lived in a decent place."

"Decent!" he said. The word rumbled up through the phlegm in his throat. He was laughing at her. "The kids should have a decent summer and I should live in a decent place. How do you know what's decent anymore!"

Millie opened the door and turned once more to look at him with a heavy sigh, "Take care."

"Smile," the old man said, "I haven't seen you smile since you married that fella."

The car had been sitting in the sun so the seat was warm and comforting. After every visit Mill's heart swelled, joy leapt through her whole body. She was that glad to be out of there. It was over now for another week or ten days. She had only to call the old man in the mornings and she need not feel guilty about him for a while. Some days she shopped after she left her father, yearning for pretty things like a schoolgirl, appeasing herself with a new face cream or a blouse — some little thing for herself. As she drove down the block, her block, the scene of her girlhood, it looked familiar and soothing again in the soft spring light as it had long ago when the Murphys were in the yellow brick apartment across the way and the Fussellis who owned the grocery store were in the three-family house on the corner. Jack's family had lived in the next block, but that was ruined completely now — cheap cotton blankets were being aired out of the window from which he'd watched for her with a lover's eye.

On the corner the drugstore was gone where they'd lingered over coffee before they were engaged. Jack Cogan had waited for her there every day till she came home from work. It was summer and the drugstore was cool after the subway, the big fans whirring as a background to their foolish intimacies and the sweet jibes they took at one another. By Labor Day they were set for life. Herbs and perfume in the air, dignified, old-fashioned — the drugstore was gone for years now and a bodega took its place. Sheets of salted pigskin and green bananas hung in the window. Mill had not thought about the drugstore in years. Mr. Peck, the druggist, was a small Jewish man who'd been robbed constantly during the depression because he looked so helpless. His wife was tiny too, a romantic little woman with soft eyes, she sat crocheting at the counter all the while Millie and Jack were first in love and gave them a beautifully worked set of place mats that were too nice to use.

Today Mill could not escape the years she worked for Mr. Spears. Wonderful times, really. Let them laugh. Everyday was exciting, or so she thought now. Life had been opening before her — even the yearly inventory at the Minotaur Press, the CPA checking the books, had made the office bristle in a special way for a whole week. She had been so pretty then. Men turned to watch her as she walked from Grand Central to Murray Hill in the morning, her lovely red hair like a signal to them in the sunshine. What's gone is gone, Mill told herself, just as she might tell the children. No regrets. She decided that she would after all drive up to Connecticut and drop Dawson Spears's prayer book off at his house. Jack was wrong: though it did indeed mean something to her, it would mean so much more to his widow or to a child in the family. A grandson, she knew, had been named after the great man. Oh, great man to her alone, of course. Jack had made a joke of that when they were first married. To hell with his notions: she'd bring the book back.

One memory of Millicent Cogan's career was bitter to her always. She'd had a love affair with a young man in the office, a book salesman who represented the Minotaur Press in Chicago and was only in New York once or twice a month. Her shame in this matter was enormous for she was already engaged to Jack when it started and to this day he knew nothing about it.

The man, Morgan Barnes, was just out of Yale and very handsome in a beefy, athletic way. Treating her like the secretary she was, he'd started a flirtation with her which got her Irish up. They argued over the world series and bet against each other with uncalled for vehemence. Morgan Barnes was tall and broad, big compared to Jack Cogan. His ties were beautiful. The thrust of him when he came into the office was immense. He was a match for Mr. Spears: two important, powerful men, so alike. The other salesmen, though older, were subservient, worried about their progress at every turn.

When Millicent's Yankees lost, Barnes sent her a dozen roses and a sympathy card. She wired the twenty dollars he'd won to his Chicago address. A lot of money for a girl who was saving to get married. Next time he came to New York the excitement as they talked was demanding, insistent. He took her to a dark corner of the old Statler bar and she phoned to say that she would not be home — too many reports to type with the salesmen in town. There was never

154

anything like it for her again: her body was throbbing and swollen with desire by the second daiquiri. He put her hand on him to feel that he was already hard. Upstairs in his hotel room he told her that he'd stayed here for the first time instead of bunking with friends because he knew that she would come with him. At midnight he put her in a taxi for Brooklyn. She'd had nothing to eat.

In the next few months whenever Morgan Barnes came to town Millicent stayed with him. Their sex was uncluttered, pure: she knew little about him. His luggage was Mark Cross. His bottle of scotch on the night table was Black Label. At Yale he had belonged to a club and most of his friends were beginning jobs on Wall Street. They would eat a meal together at a dim French restaurant, a formality — and go directly to the hotel. She told her father and Jack that she was working late. In fact she *had* stayed in town two or three times on business and even gone out to the Spears's house for weekends when the work was heavy. While the affair with Barnes was on, Millicent was particularly loving to Jack Cogan, though she slipped the little diamond ring he'd given her into a compartment of her change purse every day. In all the years after, she'd been ashamed at the cool role that she had played. This bothered her more than the primary deception, the illicit nights at the Statler. She was not a simple, straightforward girl. She was duplicitous. Smooth. The lies rolled off her tongue because Mill wanted Morgan Barnes so much. She was free with him. The whole feel of the man came back to her at times — his shoulders were dense and muscular. She loved to sit on top of him as though in a saddle, and massage his back until he nearly fell asleep, her long red hair veiling them both. Then she would rouse him again: she wanted him so much. And kissed Jack in the hallway, let him open the top two buttons of her blouse. In the office she smoldered. Mr. Spears, who thought he had the sort of shy Irish girl who'd be with him for life, despaired and calculated the time he had left with his crackerjack secretary.

The end was painful and quick. Barnes took her along to a party with his friends. Rich, spoiled people. Young, but not funny or gay. Affected, set in their ways. The girls were all rather plain and found her flashy. She was more fashionably dressed. The men were amused for a while by the fact that her father had played for the Yankees, but on the whole they ignored her. She heard herself described as the girl Morgan's screwing.

"Where's Jane?" asked a sour female voice.

"Jane's in France. That's the point!"

Her humiliation was immediate and complete. When she looked into her lover's face to say that she was not feeling well he was impatient and took her down to a cab, tried to pay her fare to Brooklyn but she would not have it. It was all a mistake and she fled from those people to her own neighborhood and the safety of Jack Cogan.

A week before her wedding she went to confession in an obscure parish on Ninth Avenue. The priest behind the grillwork asked: "How many times? And was this with the same man, my child?" The absolution was technical: over the years her love affair haunted Mill Cogan: the fear of her own carnal nature. Barnes left the Minotaur Press soon after. She heard that he was off to Europe, that he had been accepted at the University of Virginia Law School, that he was, after all, from a big meat-packing fortune. Publishing bored him. He had toyed with his job as he had with her. In 1957, when Jimmy was a little boy, Mill read in the Sunday *Times* that Morgan Barnes was engaged to a girl with a hyphenated name, parents who had remarried and many places to live, a paternal grandfather who had been an ambassador to the Court of St. James's. Like the girls at that party she was pale, long-toothed, horsey. It gave Mill some satisfaction to note that she had not managed to graduate from college. Yes, it was many times with Morgan Seymour Barnes. The same man. For Christ's sake, she was not a whore. It had been a shock for Mill to discover that Jack Cogan came to their wedding bed a virgin.

The check she squeezed out of her father made things clear today. Ask and it shall be given. For too long she'd been passive letting life dribble away, sharing Jack's bad fortune, living off the past. Even the old love affair held some truth she'd never faced. How easy it was to say Barnes had used her when she was just as brutal in her use of him. It was purely sensual. She honestly didn't give a damn once it was over. He still appeared in her erotic fantasies — the strength of his shoulders under her hands, the solid athletic muscles in his buttocks — exciting her, yes, but with no more ardor than an expensive piece of meat. The memories of her working years in Manhattan had dragged her down, made her foolish to her children, a scourge to her husband. Why had she never learned? That she was once beautiful and bright, had made a charge upon the world, been scared off. So what? Her story was thin and self-defeating. She would take back Dawson Spears's boyish prayer book. What's gone is gone.

The Spears's house in Greenwich was the same: gray stone, large, not cheerful in its aspect. Inside it had been full of life — crowded with shells, rocks, plants (lima beans grew on strings to the ceiling), arrowheads, dogs, white mice and gerbils running mindlessly in their cages, a harpsichord — books everywhere. The children were all fair and growing tall like their father. Their mother was full-bosomed, matronly, expansive in the center of happy confusion.

Millicent was received by a shrunken Mrs. Spears in a

spare living room. The debris of her children tidied forever. The furniture was new: chrome, leather and glass. The old woman crossed a pair of shapely legs and looked at Mill. At first she did not remember. "Murray?" she asked.

"I was his secretary."

"The redhead!" exclaimed Mrs. Spears with delight.

"Yes," said Mill smiling and handed over the prayer book.

"My husband was never a religious man," said Mrs. Spears with quick good humor. Everything about her seemed brisk to Mill, as though she were pressed for time. Her whole person was diminished, yet more than naturally alive and she was smartly dressed in the costume of a gay old lady with appointments to keep. "No — if it wasn't for his name and a plausible date, I simply would not believe it. That old scoundrel with a prayer book!"

"You see," Mill explained, "it was from when he was a boy. He kept it in his desk always and gave it to me — because I still went to church."

"You did!" said Mrs. Spears. "I can't imagine. *Murray* was your name?"

"Yes," said Mill and stepped towards a chair but she had not been asked to sit down. "I came here on weekends sometimes when work was heavy at the Press."

"He often worked on weekends," Mrs. Spears informed Mill with a wicked laugh, "because he fooled around too much in town. He just never grew up. And this is his prayer book, you say."

"I shouldn't have troubled you." Mill had not imagined their meeting would be like this. The disappointment was too much to bear. She sank into a corner of the big modern couch while the sprightly little woman ran to the window, checked the time on a plexiglass clock without numbers. "It was sentimental of me to bring it, but it seemed too personal a thing to keep. I thought your children or your grandchildren should have it for their own."

"It was nice of you, but unnecessary," said Mrs. Spears, suddenly more sober. "Paul, my oldest, is dead —"

"Oh —" cried Mill.

"And I don't get on with the girls. I always thought that since I didn't get on with my husband, I would surely get on with my children. That hasn't been the case. We were just so polite and disapproving of one another — that I've called a halt to the whole thing." Mrs. Spears seemed delighted at her own good sense.

Millicent's eyes rested on the little worn black book that she had brought with her. The gilt cross stamped into the leather was irrelevant on the thick glass table next to a block of lucite with new pennies tumbling at all angles in its clear, mysterious mass. Life has glanced off this woman, Mill thought. That is why she looks so small and lively. She dismisses all the difficulties with a laugh. Her husband is dead. Her son. She doesn't see her own children. "Well," said Mill softly, "I do get on with my kids. It's a constant battle, but we do get on."

"Of course when they're *young*," replied Mrs. Spears. A navy blue Cadillac drove into the driveway and parked behind Mill Cogan's car. "You've just caught me on the run. I can hardly keep up with my social life now. That's the widow's plight."

"I admired your husband very much. I enjoyed working for him before I was married. Those years were a good time in my life." Without asking she picked up the old prayer book and put it back in her purse. Outside the Cadillac beeped. "I still go to church. Some of the prayers are the same that we say now —"

"Come," said Mrs. Spears and she led Mill by the arm gently, avoiding a scene.

"Some of the prayers are the same," Mill insisted. "Even then when I read it, when he first gave it to me, I noticed all the parts from the New Testament were the same — Saint John and the Sermon on the Mount."

"Blessed are the pure in heart," chirped Mrs. Spears.

"Yes," said Mill fiercely, "for they shall see God." She let the woman maneuver her out to the hall and she stood like a dummy while Mrs. Spears got her own purse and coat. They left the house together. Two grand old ladies waved at them from the front seat of the Cadillac.

"I do remember you, Miss Murray. You came on weekends."

"Yes."

"When the children were growing up. The place stank with life. You were beautiful."

Mill protested.

"Yes, you *were*. Beautiful." There was a glint of truth in the old lady's eyes, so slight, yet Mill was sure she saw — a flick of pain. "I always thought you were one of his women. There were so many. He was such a rotten man."

After they drove off, Mill stood alone by her car and of course, when she got her keys out, there it was — the damn prayer book. She was stuck with it now. It didn't mean that much to her after all. Another one of her stories, another unfelt moment: the great man reaching into his desk, handing it over to her. His height as he stood above her — his loss of faith. The desiccated scene preserved like a precious sliver of the true cross.

3

Co-op City

SIOBHAN'S SCHOOL would not get out until the last week in June, but she was restless at the end of May with four more weeks to go and yet another class trip to the Museum of Natural History for a gape at the dusty old brontosaurus with his small brain and broken hip bone. Then the appalling aspect of the whole long summer before her. At Easter the Cogan twins had turned thirteen and almost at once Siobhan had developed a histrionic streak which Cormac, who knew her completely, failed to understand. She would start to tell him something in their old conspiratorial whisper and her voice would rise, affecting a lack of control, until she was shrieking at him in an intemperate girlish speech spiced with "mod" words they had sworn never to use.

"Listen, baby," she screamed at him, "it's gross, it's absolutely gross what they have in mind for us this summer. We're going to have to split." She had blushed then to the roots of her brittle red hair. The words were hers. *She* had said that to Cormac and the sneer he gave her in return was justified.

It smarted like an open sore when she remembered it at night, lying alone on the fold-out couch in the living room. Recently Mill Cogan had placed a screen across the open doorway when Siobhan was ready for bed so that the child might undress in private, apart from her brothers. True to form, Millie kept to her own ways and wandered the house in her nylon nightie while the little girl stole behind her screen, sneaking out of her underpants and into the bottoms of her thin pajamas. Last week her mother had given her a training bra, come right round the screen after Siobhan was in bed and dangled it out of a flowered department store bag. She was made to try it on and was supposedly "seeing how it worked out" before they bought more. She had stuffed the thing back in its bag and not looked at it since. Two years ago her nipples had popped, first one and then the other — a great source of amusement to Cormac and herself. They had giggled till they were sick with the notion she might begin popping all over in bumps like their parents' chenille bedspread or the hobnail glasses the Esso station was giving out with a full tank of gas. But this spring the swelling had started again in earnest and no amount of pressing them down (she had tried the Holy Bible and *Webster's New Collegiate Dictionary* balanced spine to spine on her chest) had managed to slow the growth.

"Siobhan is like me and will sleep through the judgment," Mill said. It had always been so. Since they'd moved to this last flat in the Bronx, she'd had no bedroom of her own and slept through the late comings of Jim and her father, through all the traffic down on the highway, through her mother's eleven o'clock news and late movies on the portable out in the kitchen. Now the poor child counted the headlights that flashed across the ceiling and turned her angry face into the arm of the couch not to stare any longer at the hopeful bright and green and yellow that her mother had painted their old furniture. Every night now there seemed to be something weird to haunt her left over from the day. The freaky way she had started talking to her brother and sometimes she had the sensation of crying without shedding tears. A boy in school named Fred Monahan who played baseball with them had given her a pencil holder that he made in shop and she had accepted it and flushed red with the queer exciting sensation that she had to go pee. Across the ridiculous screen her parents' voices came to her in fragments as she lay waiting for her troubles to lull her to sleep. It was always Jimmy they were on about — Jimmy and the girl. Jimmy and the incense their mother had found in his closet which Millie knew kids used to cover the smell of pot. Jimmy and the girl again, the dirty girl. But one night she sat up and stole out of bed to listen: it was truly their names that had reached her. Cormac and Siobhan. Unnatural, unhealthy. Cormac and Siobhan with that Italian man like last summer.

"They must learn now to go their separate ways," her mother insisted.

"It's impossible dealing with them," Jack Cogan said. "They're like a force of nature."

"They're not babies anymore. It isn't right."

Her father, who was usually on their side, said, "I can see your point, Mill, but I don't want to be around when you tell them."

The weeks that followed were painful for the girl. She had tried to tell her brother, her twin, who had always been the other half of herself, that this summer they were condemned, but for the first time he had not responded. Cormac seemed mystified by her anguish. "They are sending us to camp," she

163

said. "You better believe it. I heard them and not to Regis, to some finky overnight place where I'll have to make tote-bags and teenie crap with the girls."

In a fury one afternoon she cut off her hair so that she would be like her brother again. Her mother had insisted that she let it grow during the winter and when it was scattered on the bathroom floor she flung the scissors down and cried behind the locked door because it had begun to look pretty down on her shoulders. Some of the kink had disappeared into heavy waves. Millie screamed at her that she was disfigured, but Siobhan took her brother aside and told him, "Now we are alike. Just alike." And in the afternoon when they came home from school they changed into jeans and matching shirts and, at her insistence, started to steal again at the five-and-ten and the drugstore. Cormac feared her new intensity and did what she asked. She controlled him now, could bend him to her will and at night when she counted the headlights from Bruckner Boulevard that flashed on her ceiling by the hundreds, she feared the worst — that he did not care as he once had, that their great bond had weakened, their composite nature had suffered a terrible change.

The more she understood this the more Siobhan clung to him, forced him to her way: It must be as it had always been. They must think again as one, step in the same direction without a sign, though the more she asserted herself, the more she hated herself and longed for the old balance, the indefinable spirit between them.

As the last weeks of school approached she grew bolder. Listening to her parents fears for Jimmy — his graduation had gone off with a good deal of strain. He had worn a black arm band on his gown and refused to pledge allegiance to the flag. This spunk had pleased his parents, but the whole schlocky scene at Bronx Science had offended Mill. People overdressed and vulgar. Jim of indifferent rank in the class among the bright kids who had won their National Merit Scholarships. In cleaning the closets Mill had turned up an embroidered Indian shirt and a dirty book called *The Garden of Love*. Another book by a fellow with burning eyes lay right on his bed. The man believed, as far as Mill could make out, that we'd be better off in an asylum, as madness was rampant in the streets. Jack had started to read this with some interest, saying they had better have it out in the open one night and not be ignorant at the time. He'd read all of Jim's books lately and said they weren't so bad. They'd give him something to think about when he got to college. Behind the screen Siobhan crouched listening until she could stay awake no longer.

It was thrilling to hear Jimmy accused by her mother. Jim who thought he was so great and never had been freaky in the eyes of the world. She would go to her couch full of hope for herself: if Jim were not all good, then she might not be all bad. Now memories of last summer began to be a comfort — when she and Cormac had Silvio, and the time together had been lovely and long as an endless Monopoly game. That too, was an idle dream: Silvio had his driver's license and a second-hand Pontiac Le Mans to free him from Angie. Angie had a baby boy who was up in their flat, the tiny possessor of an entire nursery suite delivered by Toddler's Inc., "Furniture for Mini-people." A couple of times in the last weeks Silvio had taken the twins for ice cream up at Carvel's and done a fast swing around the empty roads of Co-op City, the vast complex of high-rise apartments that rose out of the reclaimed swamps off Bruckner Boulevard. Their rides, Siobhan realized, were for old time's sake. She tried to make them last, saying, "Go down another road here — and another. It's like a whole city — a magic, horrible city. It's noplace. I want to live here," she insisted. "I want to put the address on my letters. Noplace, Noplace at all." She spoke in a marvelous way that was hushed and beguiling, though it was only to her brother and Silvio. "Come and we will live noplace together. In apartment three thousand fifteen we will make our nest." A feminine pleading. She sounded seriously seductive.

One Saturday Fred Monahan, whose pencil holder she placed beside her bed each night, called up and asked for her, asked if she would like to come play baseball over in his street. Siobhan who would normally have jumped at the chance said no she couldn't, that she and her brother had to go out. Monahan said, "See you in church." She was awkward, put the receiver down abruptly, yet she would like to have talked on to him. All week she'd noticed Fred Monahan's flesh. He had lots of moles on his arms which she liked, but none on his face. The skin on his face was pure and unblemished, darker than any boy she knew. His mother was Italian though his features were Irish and his eyes were blue. Blue was her favorite color. When she turned round from Fred Monahan's telephone call she said to her mother and Cormac, "It was nothing," and, head in a whirl, went straight to the pantry for a handful of Hydrox cookies though it was only nine in the morning.

Millie smiled at her daughter in a simpering way, then with an air of formality asked the twins to sit down. The breakfast things had been cleared away with marked efficiency and blank brown manila envelopes sat in the center of the table like an omen.

"I have a surprise," Mill said. "Your father's been doing so well with his marvelous machines —" (This they knew to be a lie) — "that we think this year we can send you to camp." And with that she produced brochures and applications from the brown envelopes. "Twin camps in the Poconos," she said, laughing, "I thought you'd go for that!"

Siobhan looked at Cormac with wild, accusing eyes. He was turning the pages of *his* brochure with interest: photos of boys swimming and sailing and singing round the campfire at Timber Trails. Her own brochure of Merimeechee which she opened dumbly showed the same activities with the substitution of lardy girls in leotards doing modern dance for the boys' baseball team. Their mother prattled on nervously, full of uplift as though she had memorized the slogans that lured her into Timber Trails and Merimeechee. "Self-motivation, development of individual resources and team spirit emphasized . . . set among the beautiful lakes and streams of the rolling Poconos."

Next, like a lady in a TV commercial, Millie produced sweat shirts in muddy green, Timber Trails, Merimeechee emblazoned on them and with special pride she turned out the neck of each shirt to show them their own printed name tapes already sewn in. Siobhan Cogan in dainty script. The name seemed much too odd to the girl. She didn't claim it as her own. She had always thought of her name along with Cormac's and in school they signed S. Cogan, C. Cogan to their papers. As little kids they knew instinctively that their full, given names were more of their mother's foolishness. Cormac Cogan — it was like a mouthful of nuts and bolts — you could not even say it. Now they were shown their absurd names on socks, on underwear. This was class, Mill's smile told them. To stitch on these name tapes she had stayed sober many an afternoon. Once again her dream was tangible. Good lisle socks, quality underwear. Her kids weren't going to be sweating it out on Bruckner Boulevard. The children at Timber Trails and Merimeechee came from good backgrounds, mostly in Riverdale and Westchester, thank God, not this weed and cement Siberia. For a moment their mother's familiar bitterness filled the kitchen: "I'd forgotten why we ever moved here. I guess it was in your Dad's territory for Merganthaller and we thought we'd look for a house in New Rochelle."

"Yes," Siobhan said smartly, "and it's not near the track, but you forgot the Yonkers Raceway."

"Ah, well," their mother said, folding her lovely green camp outfits. "I hope you're pleased. I know I am. There's one more thing," she said pushing a box at Cormac. "It was only on the list for Timber Trails."

"Cool," Cormac said, using a forbidden word. "Thanks a lot, Mom." His sister watched with a sneer as he fondled a canteen zipped into its own khaki jacket.

"Neat-o!" she said grabbing the canteen and guzzling air.

"Even stephen," Millie cried. "I'll get you something special, lady — don't forget it. God, what a trial you two are. Tit for Tat."

Cormac filled the canteen at the sink and Siobhan fled the room leaving them to gabble of summer fun. Later, when she was asked "Why? Why did you do it? When did you ever think of such an idea?" — she was able to say that she had not thought at all. Yet the idea was there, festering in the hours she lay behind her screen, dreamt perhaps, the malign dream of the princess of Bruckner Boulevard. She had gone to her bureau and taken sweaters, socks — she and Cormac were the same size still — a blanket from her unmade couch, then to the boys' room where she filched Jimmy's sleeping bag and all of the savings she and Cormac cherished, fifteen dollars and forty-five cents. She was sorry to steal from Jim. It occurred to her at the moment that he would never see his sleeping bag again. One further insight came to her as she waited for her brother to finish off with his enthusiasm for Timber Trails: could be that without the television they would be bored and she reached into

Jimmy's books and grabbed *Great Expectations,* a Christmas present he had never read, and *The Garden of Love,* a queer looking volume with a wonderful oriental tree on the cover, lushly bejeweled and fruited. Calmly she sat on the foot of Cormac's bed until her mother's slovenly flip-flop slippers were heard in the hall and the bathroom door locked. She listened to the water running, the buzz and wosh of the Water Pik on her mother's soft, puffy gums and ran out to the kitchen where she grabbed her brother with his silly boy scout canteen and had him out of the house before he understood what it was she had in mind with the sleeping bag and the malice in her eyes.

"Had you no mind of your own?" Jack Cogan asked his son in the end.

"Are you jelly? A spineless gray jellyfish?" asked Mill whose tongue was more practiced at accusation.

No, he was not spineless at all, yet the other was true: he had no mind of his own. Until this year his mind had been one with his sister's and when the fissure came it was like a hairline crack in an old cup that held even under the pressure of Siobhan's new theatrics, her bossy demands that they play at thieving and deceptions that were no longer of interest to him. On that famous Saturday morning he was dragged halfway down the block before it registered: she had Jim's sleeping gear and a shopping bag packed full.

"Where are you going?" Cormac asked.

"I'm getting out of here," she said. "I don't know about you anymore but I'm not having Merimeechee put over on me." They went first to the vacant lot they often played in. He felt entirely separate from her as he listened to her plan. They were running away. They were conspicuous, but she had figured it, she said. With a series of costume changes, with her Sunday shoes and a kerchief she could look a couple of inches taller. He knew that she was making it up as she went along, all the details of where they'd go, how they'd eat and sleep and dress. So impossible and childish. Stealing tuna fish, canned peaches, Franco-American spaghetti — all their favorites. She said they must buy a can opener at once.

"Why not steal it?" he mocked, but Siobhan was not in the mood. She pressed on, single-minded about the blanket she had brought, sweaters and socks, all of their cash. Cormac thought she had gone mad, but then that was like part of himself, his own mind distraught and burning as hers was now. He remembered the fresh green shirts and shorts that his mother had bought for Timber Trails, the pictures of little sailboats dotting the lake, the boys his own age lined up at the diving board. He would love to be off at camp by himself. Why was he squatting here in this dump behind a billboard, hiding and plotting like a little kid playing cops and robbers?

"Don't you see," Siobhan whispered with the old loving complicity, "all our stealing before and playing off two for one, it's as though we've been in training. I know. I know we can make it."

"They'll pick us up in a few hours. Two kids the same size, same description."

"All right, Cormac," she said. Her words rang hard on the stale city air. She had never, till this day, called him by his name. "I'll go it alone, Cormac." She got off her perch, an old truck tire, and swung the heavy shopping bag up. The weight pulled her shoulders back and there were two small firm breasts, the nipples knob-hard through her T-shirt. Her lips were fuller than his now and he had noticed that her lashes had darkened, had even suspected that she was fooling around with Millie's cosmetics, but she had grown different — that was all. A feeling of tenderness came over him.

"So long," she said. Her color was high, her eyes were the eyes of a zealot. With a fluttering, feminine gesture she twirled at the little curls above her left ear, hesitating.

"Give me the bag!" Cormac said. What could he do but go with her this one last time. It was only in his mind that he betrayed her: he knew from the moment he took the weight off her scrawny shoulders that they would not get far. Time had already caught them, sorted them out into the world of men and women. He was stronger and wiser for the moment. He thought to say, "Don't you know Mother will be worried out of her head?" Siobhan could no longer read his mind and he allowed himself to be swept along by her passionate will, feeling from the first block they hiked that he owed her this one last fling. A lover who is about to desert? A husband who knows that his wife is doomed? No such analogy came to the boy's mind. He dreamed during the nights that were to come of a movie he had seen on television where the monster watches dainty little people dancing in a nightclub, watches in fascination for a while before he crushes them in his enormous paw.

If Millie Cogan could put aside her anguish and Jack his self-recriminations they would laugh at the twins. The whole episode is funny with elements of the grotesque. On the first day the kids filched their cans of tuna, spaghetti with meat sauce and peaches in heavy syrup from the nearest Shopwell, paying only for a six-pack of chewing gum as they left the store. Their greed was a great mistake. The shopping bag began to tear, so while they were unloading some of the stuff into a mail box they were spotted by two lazy cops in a squad car who yelled and cruised after them for three blocks but didn't bother to follow when they ducked into a movie house. There they sat frozen with fear for five minutes and slumped for three hours after that getting their money's worth: two Disney productions featuring

171

hilarious automobiles. It was late afternoon when they came out into the light, stunned by the time they had wasted. Two skinny redheaded kids carrying a load between them like a body.

The same squad car came round the corner and they dashed into a beauty parlor. "We gotta wait for our mother," said Siobhan.

"We don't have more appointments for today," said a soft white woman who looked like a pillow in the middle. "Syl —" she called, "You don't have no one left on the books?"

"We don't have no one left on the books," the big woman told them. "Say, you kids twins?"

"Yeah," Cormac said. He wondered why they just didn't go out and ask the kind policemen for a ride home. One cop got out of the car and went into a coffee shop across the street. In the beauty parlor a last customer was under the dryer, another being combed out into fat silver curls. A girl about sixteen, a dim-wit, was sweeping the day's residue of hair along the floor, shorn locks of every false color. She stared straight at them as she came nearer and nearer with the dead sweepings. She gazed out from under a fringe of black hair plastered to her forehead with scotch tape. She saw the police car. "What you kids done?" she hissed.

The twins ran out. The other cop was asleep behind the wheel. Their whole afternoon a farce. They ended up in the bright June evening, conspicuously lugging their pack along the guard rails of Bruckner Boulevard heading towards the tendrils of Long Island Sound that separate the boroughs of Manhattan and the Bronx. The fumes were dense at rush hour, the thin strip of grass where they walked was edged with a thick black muck, the bodily discharge of traffic. Climbing an embankment to the steel rail, the force of each car passing pushed them further on their journey, their bodies bent down like the figures of two old wayfarers with their packs, marginal people walking in a land where no one walked, where the human body is too frail, too poor a thing. Across the highway the towers of Co-op City came in sight. A whole world rose before them, vast and complete.

Cormac lost his footing and the shopping bag wrenched off his arm and down the embankment. "Where the hell do you think you're going?" he cried out to his sister, tears of pain and exasperation in his eyes.

"What?"

He shouted above the din of traffic, "Where the hell are you going?" But it was no use.

Guessing at his question she shouted, "Noplace. Noplace. Noplace." They retrieved their bag and after a wild trip, dashing between cars across the highway, they slouched towards the new city of endless bright windows that seemed like noplace at all.

"If I thought about that," Siobhan said when they were safely across, "I would never have done it. We might have been killed. That was worse than the beauty parlor. And why —" she asked, her tongue suddenly come loose in her head, "Why did that fool girl hate us so. Because we looked like we were doing something of our own and she'd spent her whole Saturday sweeping up that filthy hair. Those bangs stuck to her head. She'll wow them tonight. God, she looked as though she's already in the hate business."

"Shut up!" Cormac cried. "Shut up. I've had enough of you. I want to go home. I'll call Daddy to come and pick us up. Where do you think you're going — some commune, some pad in the East Village where Jimmy goes? Where do you think you're headed anyway?"

"I'll be better off alone. Here," she said looking about her, "I'm staying here tonight."

"*Here*? In the exhaust fumes?"

"Don't be dumb," she said and pulled the bag from him. "Here. Right *here*." And she crossed an empty roadway and walked on into the complex of tall new apartments that still looked like cardboard models in the architect's project. Behind her the cranes and bulldozers were discarded for the weekend until they would pick up the job of filling the rest of the soft swampland for the foundations of more and more concrete shafts to hold the thousands of middle-class refugees. For these people the city itself had become so terrifying, glowing across the Triborough Bridge in its halo of filth that they had fled — the streets filled with screams, sirens, shots, horror all horror — in the elevators, behind chained doors, the creeping festering disease of fear. Fear of blacks, of pushers, of addicts, of kids, of madmen, of whores. Fear of death and disorder so great that they, the plain people, could not survive. Here in Co-op City the walls and doors, the linoleum and grass could be taken to heart again, cared for and owned, above all owned as things had been owned and guarded in the past. No Main Street *this*, yards and houses with family names. That was over — the shaded street with the big white houses — and this bleak, efficient pattern of towers was one idea at least of how it will be.

The Cogan kids had the time of their life. They followed the signs to a floor in building D, just off the highway to a set of magic apartments furnished and ready to live in, models set up by the real-estate corporation with every semblance of model life in the rooms but no bodies to sleep in the bed or heads to soil the bright little decorator pillows.

"The television has no antenna," Cormac said as though that were enough to lure his sister away at once. Indeed, when he looked, it had no plug, just the wire snipped off, castrated, an abomination in a big carved cabinet. They settled this first night in a modest one bedroom model with solid oak table and comfortable club chairs upholstered in moss green plush. The bedroom was all high-polish mahogany and though they switched to other models for safety on the following nights, Siobhan loved this apartment best of all. The neat bourgeois placement of ashtrays and lamps was the very opposite of her mother's quixotic housekeeping and zany creative touches — paper flowers in an old tin can, coffee tables the color of egg yolks — anything to be different.

"I could live here forever," she said to Cormac after supper.

"Yes," he said. Though he was still annoyed about the television she saw that he had accepted the night ahead. She went to the sink like a housewife while Cormac, the good husband, got down under the kitchen cabinet and turned the valves so that they would have water. Happily she washed the plates they had used for their tasty supper of tuna and cold Franco-American. She'd set the freestone peaches on salad plates, for the table in the dining L had been all set up for two in an ordinary white china with gold rims and ordinary water goblets with the kind of squat sterling silver candlesticks her mother said you give as wedding presents when you don't care about the people. They looked fine to Siobhan with pristine white candles which, if they were to remain undiscovered, she could not light. After she washed the dishes and dried them with a clean undershirt out of the shopping bag, she set the table up again exactly as she found it, waiting for two ordinary people. "I could live here forever," she said.

Her brother was sitting in one of the plush chairs reading *The Garden of Love.* She looked over his shoulder: "The erotic zones of the female's body are intricate and beautiful, given to her for her delight and for her lover as a sweet bouquet, her special gift." She flinched. She had thought when she swiped it off Jim's shelf that it was about all the

Indian stuff — more of the Creative Love talk that she and Cormac laughed at. Her eye skipped down the page: "Under the breast the abdominal region of the woman lies like an unsullied white field, the plain of special pleasure to some who desire a stroking or soft kneading of the flesh to open the more intimate zones of love."

"Disgusting!" she said. Cormac read on, turning the page to "The Inner Garden of Ecstasy." "I'm, surprised Mommy didn't throw that out."

Cormac read on.

"Tomorrow we'll buy a pack of cards," she said to distract him, "and grab a couple of Hershey bars."

"Yeah," he said and went back to the vaginal bower.

"Gross!" She spit the word on his cheek like a spoiled kiss.

They turned from each other in confusion. She settled in the other chair and they sat like a couple who have quarreled, letting the damage sink in. He would like to have gone on with *The Garden of Love*. It was their parents' new policy to encourage Jim in having all the books he wanted around the house and in the last few weeks the bookshelf in the bedroom that he shared with his brother had sprouted forth a lot of great stuff — parapsychology, astrology, sex. *The Garden of Love* was terrific. He had read it four times. He sat avoiding his sister's eyes across the chasm of spiffy orange carpet. He wanted so much to be free to go to Timber Trails.

"Tomorrow," she said with a pout, "we should get paper napkins and two cans of soda."

"Tomorrow?"

"Yes. We must do everything now before the light fades to leave this place exactly as we found it. At nine o'clock these models are open to the public but you can never tell, they might check them earlier."

176

"Tomorrow," Cormac said, "I'm going home."

"Don't be dumb. Even if we do go back, one night's not nearly enough to convince them we won't go to their concentration camp. We've got to scare them sick . . ."

Cormac closed his eyes and let her rattle on. He decided that he would never marry, that it would be like this, listening to Siobhan say what she thought and what he should do while he rested from the battle in bitter isolation.

"What I'd like to know is where she got the money?" she asked and answered herself quickly. "From Grandpa. Poor old Grandpa with his rents and taxes on that tenement. He doesn't want to give us a dime, but she can get 'round him still. Daddy'd kill her if he thought she took money from him, but she cheats and goes over to Brooklyn and comes back smiling like an old tabby cat with her purse full. That's how she'll get the college money we've been hearing about till our ears fall off. And Daddy has to make believe he doesn't notice like a chump."

"He is a chump," Cormac cried, leaning towards her suddenly. "He should slam her. I don't blame him for gambling. She's so superior. Oh, she married beneath her that's for sure. He should throw her downstairs."

His sister sat primly on the edge of her chair, a bit frightened of him.

"Oh, I don't mean really," Cormac said.

"Of course you didn't," she replied in a ladylike way.

The light faded mercifully and they were left to the excitement of feeling their way in the dark among unfamiliar objects. In the blacked out bathroom they read with the flashlight behind the shower curtain their one other book. The text was hard for them, not Dickens retold as it was in their school readers, but the original with long involved sentences and the odd talk of English people. They found the effort worthwhile. They loved Pip, and being thieves themselves, appreciated his difficulties in stealing the pork pie for Magwitch. He was a brave, beautiful little boy and wonderful adventures lay ahead for him. Before going to bed they looked out over the black infested waters of New York. The faceless inhabitants of Co-op City took the foul night air on the blank walkways far below. Drained and tired, the Cogan twins lay down carefully beside each other on the double bed. There were no sheets or blankets, only a spread of gold satin stuff which they put aside. It was meant for the model couple, not for them.

"I'm going home tomorrow," Cormac said.

"Oh," said his sister quietly, "I'll miss you." They held hands firmly as they had done when they were little kids crossing the Brooklyn streets and soon Cormac was asleep. For two years now he'd slept in with Jimmy and his short, asthmatic breath, mouth agape, was unfamiliar to Siobhan as a man's night-breathing might be to his bride. It was certain pain — she would go alone to Merimeechee and he to Timber Trails. Lost to each other, she would feel the kiss of Fred Monahan on her untouched lips and discover the moles on his arms with her fingers. Her stomach was a white field for him (or a boy not yet imagined), her breasts shallow buds to be gathered and her dark love, all her desire, lay in forbidden brambles. She held back her tears, not to stain the pure mattress of this perfect place, the ordinary life they could not lead together.

They were found three days later huddled under the sleeping bag for warmth in a big two-bedroom model gaily done with Italian pottery and plastic ferns. Two uniformed patrolmen stood at the bottom of the bed with Silvio who had brought them here. Silvio, their lost friend, the informer who had turned them in. It was so early that he was in his baker's suit, white from head to toe with a powdery chin. "I'm glad I find," he said, all very chummy with the cops.

They were his pals now. "Not bad kids. They make up stories. Most things they tell me I don't believe."

Their discovery was reported on a walkie-talkie. The room filled with piercing static and a list of coded numbers blasted back — three-forty-six. Three-forty-six, seven-nine, over.

"Come, you big enough gangsters now?" Silvio said to the Cogan twins with a laugh.

The police car drove them out Co-op Boulevard onto the highway and they passed the huge dump of industrial garbage, a nifty arrangement of mashed cars and rusted oil drums, where they had spent the last safe days, playing cards and reading Dickens till the night.

4

Cogan Wins

WHAT A PAIR: Yes, one might say strange bedfellows —
Hoshie Feinmark and Jack Cogan. Sitting together in the
back office; one pale teakwood desk, two swivel chairs upholstered in Swedish wool the color of tomato juice, wall to
wall industrial carpet, top grade, in a stunning charcoal
gray. Here the architect and his sidekick designer had been
given *carte blanche*. We want the best looking office in the
building, Feinmark's sons said with pride. So now that the
old man wore glasses thick as the bottom of the crystal
tumblers in the built-in bar, his office, the best looking office
in the building, was a blur.

"Don't tell me the cost," Feinmark said to his sons. "The
Lord is merciful. It's better I'm blind." Still Feinmark saw
enough to keep complaining, "Marble floors in the toilet!
Such excess! Never be extravagant in business. The one
thing I tried to teach you boys was restraint and I see that I
failed. A couch! I'll be having cocktail parties here — young

girls, the secretaries perhaps. I can't see which ones are pretty anymore."

"You can take a nap, Poppa," said Jay, the older son.

"I've never been a lazy man."

"The walls are pebbled concrete, Poppa, like Saarinen used up at Yale," said Pauli. He was the youngest Feinmark child, a grown man always suing for favor. Pauli had majored in art history at Amherst and given it all up for Harvard Business. "An arched skylight up there, Pop, with fiberglass shades. Great for your eyes. You control the light from this panel. You deflect the rays of the sun in the middle of the day."

The old man looked up. There a dome rose to God, like a temple. The ceiling of his new office began to dim, fuzzed down to gray. In a moment it blazed open again and the sunlight overwhelmed the old man's clouded eyes like an angel of pain. He winced and made a joke of it, for he knew he was to be more than grateful. He was supposed to be thrilled: the light control, his own thermostat — for his circulation was poor and he suffered from the cold. His sons had made the heavens arrange themselves: paradise had come to him before his time. He might as well be dead. This lifeless luxury at the back of the new building was his resting place and out front Jay and Pauli would continue to buy and sell land, to build towns, to rent skyscrapers for millions, to scatter both coasts with shopping plazas, to enlarge the empire he had started fifty years ago.

When a contract was large enough the old man was still present at the signing. Last year the Feinmark boys had bought a Fifth Avenue landmark which they intended, with the enlightened largesse of the very rich, to restore to its Beaux Arts splendor. Their father on such a prestigious occasion was led forth as chairman of the board, his hand guided to the document. While Jay held a tasteful silver magnifying glass over the closing papers, he signed, Harold J. Feinmark, the bold, steady signature of a self-made man. The capitals were flamboyant. It had been a name to reckon with. One day soon, a day that Feinmark did not look forward to, he would be chauffeured into the city with the boys to receive a plaque from the New York Historical Society. The three of them would be pictured in the *Times*.

None of this business was after Hoshie's own heart. He had ruined whole blocks of Federal houses in his day to build capacious office buildings that were considered wonderful at the time. He was not sorry: the city was growing and his fortunes grew with it. He was smart then and smart now. So much dignity — the awards, the dinners, the donations, the responsibility of his station — was false fruit of labor to the old man. The family was in business. Why be fancy? When he left Columbia College in 1920 he didn't want to be Rockefeller. Culture — he worshipped it. All day long his recordings of Horowitz, the Rubinstein Chopin Mazurkas, Richter's Prokofiev concert blared through the door of his new office. The scratched Lotte Lehmann Schubert lieder on an old thirty-three made Hoshie cry. But his sons and daughter bought the stuff up — paintings, sculpture, an empty box at the opera, the Philharmonic. Feinmark on the program. Patron of the Arts. Fashion and art were confused by his children. They moved from one social event to the next in a stupor. His daughter, dressed like a gypsy, twice divorced, trying to pass for a girl, was pictured on the arm of an Italian dress designer at the Guggenheim Museum. She was happy. She telephoned: "Poppa, it's Sondra. I wore the right thing!" She was so happy. His sons built modern palaces to accommodate the large simple-minded canvasses of the sixties.

One day in the middle of May, Jack Cogan knocked lightly on Mr. Feinmark's door and let himself in. They were friends. The old man was caught with his magnifying glass in the act of studying the Piranesi etching of the Spanish Steps which hung on his pebbled wall.

"Until this day," said Feinmark, "I have refused to *see*, ha! — to *see* the pictures they hung here. Come, Cogan," he said, "hold the glass. My arm is tired. For six months I've sat here and every day I say that I'm going to look at the pictures these fellows put in and every day I know it will upset my stomach. How many thousands have they spent on a blind man?"

"Nonsense," Jack Cogan said.

"Please don't flatter me. I get quite enough adulation from my children. They should put me out in the lobby with the Lipchitz. I'm part of the museum. A work of art. This old man in the cashmere jacket and silk shirt is Poppa, a success. They never called me Poppa when they were little but it's quaint now, Jewish. Sometimes I want to laugh. My daughter from Vassar with the Yiddish phrases. They wish I'd been raised in some stetl, half-drowned in chicken soup. My mother never went near a temple. Karl Marx, Bakunin hung over her stove. A cold woman, so high-minded I never got a meal. She wrote editorials for the anarchist papers and got out pamphlets for the unions. Hundreds of them. I drew in the margins while my father held meetings in the back of tailor shops and bakeries."

Jack Cogan had heard it before. Hoshie was old and repeated himself, the same stories rewound. His own children didn't want to listen, but to Cogan he was an exotic, a colorful, eloquent bird, brilliant horn-rimmed blind balker. Cogan, as a gambler, was easy with fantasy and often thought how different things would be if Hoshie were his father. He loved the old man. What bastards the Feinmark boys were to deny the riches of their past. Their grandfather had died of tuberculosis distributing greasy syndicalist

183

pamphlets to the coal miners out in Scranton. A sickly intellectual Jew in a fine black broadcloth coat, head blazing with theories, he collapsed and bled into the snow as the workers teamed by. A refined wealthy girl, Hoshie's mother had taken Emma Goldman as her role-model when he was still toddling about in baby smocks. As a delicate strawberry blond, a Venetian Jewess of great beauty and intensity, she had encountered her husband and his cause at the Kurpark in Wiesbaden midst parasols and tea tables, but all her son knew of her was her coarse role in America, badly played. The filthy house, starvation by choice, flagrant love affairs, the walls stuck with pictures of Marx and Engels, Trotsky and Juàrez like so many music hall stars. Nothing was thought through. She was seldom in the flat on the lower East Side where she and her young German husband imitated the abject poverty of the truly poor.

"There was never such a happy orphan," said old Mr. Feinmark to Cogan.

"Your mother died?"

"No — she went to prison. That's what she wanted all along. Real misery, martyrdom. She walked like a princess out into the street with the police detective who came to get her. Like they were going to a ball. Charges of sedition. Her greatest moment. Mamma forgot to say goodbye and since my father was dead the neighbors took me right up to my grandmother on Fifth Avenue. I was twelve."

"So you weren't an orphan," Jack Cogan said.

"She disappeared off the face of the earth. It was just as good for me. My children don't want to believe in her cruelty. I want to tell them about it now that I'm an old man — look how you can survive your history I want to say, but they won't listen."

Cogan saw the story as an omen. He was all set up, programmed like one of his wonderful machines to believe in magic, the gambler's psychology of romantic lore: "Once a man just walked into this bar," he said, "and a bottle of Teacher's crashed from the top shelf and he didn't have a nickle and he put his money on Near Disaster, twenty-five to one at Belmont, and made a pile, and once the numbers on a license plate suggested a serial — plus three minus two pattern — like the serials in Jimmy's math book at the time and I bet on a cereal that day, Cheerios, and cleaned up. Once a fellow I knew got a pain in his knee before a Rose Bowl game and took his money off the favorite from UCLA and bet a narrow victory. The hulk was carried off with a broken knee cap in the first quarter."

"Magic," said Feinmark. "Ridiculous for a man of your age. This is the technological era. Get out and sell your machines. Why sit here all day and tell me your voodoo stories. Think of your wife and children."

"At least I'm not at the track," Jack Cogan said. "I'm wasting my time with you."

"Because you're playing a hunch. More supernatural garbage. You betting on *me*," said Hoshie Feinmark. "That you're going to get a lot of orders from the corporation."

Cogan hung around until it was time to go out for lunch, to guide the old man slowly up the steps of the Red Coach Grill for a steak on the Feinmark account. In the afternoons they argued, played records and read until it was time for Jack to go home to his family in the Bronx. Here was the intelligent loving man who could never be Cogan's father. Here was the sweet failure, the charming ineffectual boy of forty who could never be Harold Feinmark's son.

"You're putting your money on me this time," the old man said. His smile was guileless now that his eyes were weak and watery. But I don't have power anymore. I would never go to my sons and say that they should buy so much as an adding machine from you. The business is theirs and you know it, Cogan."

"You've got a swell place here."

"Beautiful isn't it? A toy for an old man who can't sit home and take the doctor's orders."

Jack said, "It still reads Feinmark and Sons on the front door."

"Work the ceiling again. The light makes me cry out in pain. Oh, you drive me crazy, Cogan. You are trying to lose again. Hiding out here. You're gambling on me. Read Freud!"

"I've read it," Cogan said. "The masturbation theory. I've read every piece on gambling from the *Reader's Digest* to Dostoevski and I'm not a reader."

"If you really want to lose your job with Merganthaller why don't you quit?"

"I can't do it that way," Jack Cogan said, "and besides I'm going to win."

"Go to work!" Hoshie yelled. "Oh, I see it's not magic. This way you can have your family and friends dangling from day to day." The old man accused Cogan of being a power monger. Cogan said for his part he believed the gambling meant that he was not directly responsible for anything.

Together they went to Grant's to buy the old man a cheap bulletin board to stick up in his office. He saved all the revolutionary tracts that his grandchildren sent to him from college with special care. "To me it's wonderful. Two generations and it turns up again. Trotskyites, Maoists. My mother would have been proud. Two of Jay's boys in prison in 'sixty-eight. Jennifer, the little darling, investigated by the F.B.I. up at Bennington. The amount of history in one family and my own children are dead to it."

When they brought the bulletin board to the beautiful back office of Feinmark and Sons, there was no way to fix it to the wall. Cogan chipped at the concrete while the old man gazed helplessly through misty eyes. The nails bent

186

back at them like toothpicks. They settled on Elmer's glue. With the help of his magnifying glass and thumbtacks like little ladybugs, Mr. Feinmark posted an editorial from the *Berkeley Barb*, the newest resolves of the S.D.S., Jennifer's letter from the Congress of the Fourth Internationale in France where she spent her summer vacation, advice from the Yippies' bible (Bubble gum in toll machines blocks highways) and a brown-edged crumbling pamphlet with the famous words of Proudhon, *Property is theft.*

Hoshie had found the pamphlet stuck in with his father's clothes when the body was shipped back from Scranton, Pa. He went, then, at the age of twelve to live with his German grandmother in a fine big apartment up on Fifth Avenue. He vowed to avenge the movement that had killed his father, had made him a virtual orphan from the day he was born. He went to Columbia, quit to become a dough-boy with a surefire patriotism that would have scandalized his parents, serving at Château-Thierry and Verdun. When he finally got through college he took his graduation present, a check for five hundred dollars, and put it down on a tenement which became part of a parcel for the City Trust skyscraper in nineteen twenty-four, a quarter of a million. And he never stopped buying — Florida, then Arizona and Southern California, the great sunshine places. Who couldn't see it? But New York was home: he bought during the twenties in Manhattan, the streets for him were gold. Prices were down in the Depression and he bought as though he were gorging himself on the city, reaching out greedily after the Second World War for the suburbs — Long Island, Connecticut.

His marriage, too, was a revenge on his mother. Her sticks and crates in the old flat. The worn pans and broken plates. Harold Feinmark married the girl of his grandmother's choice, a jolly round-faced German Jewish girl, puffed

187

with prosperity. She loved him, he supposed, but was truly passionate about possessions — heavy silver, thick rugs, paintings, draperies, collections of jade, of blood red Bavarian crystal and Staffordshire figurines. She filled their New York apartment and then went to work on a house in Scarsdale and another in Palm Springs. The children and servants were moved from place to place in a routine of Edwardian splendor.

Hoshie told Cogan it was a happy marriage, remote but full of good will. All of his energy went into business. He liked to come home from a day's appointments and smell the money in the rooms of his own house. His babies were always in pale sweet costumes with ducks or flowers sewn on, clean and orderly at their supper. In each house his wife had a monster grand piano, the Harvard Classics, linen napkins with substantial initials in the corners. Together they bought and bought. Not a day went by in his adult life that he didn't think of his mother, the willful dreamer who made him eat out of cracked bowls and left him hungry to be taken in by the neighbors. His mouth was full of sores as a little boy and the poor woman across the hall washed it out and gave him a clean shirt to wear — she often fed him in the evening with her family, a poor illiterate woman who could only speak Yiddish and (his mother's words) "babbled to God before each meal which is appropriate for an idiot who tacks pictures of the American presidents on her parlor walls when she doesn't have enough to eat."

When Jack Cogan came to the Feinmark Corporation for the first time the new building was not complete. It was an impressive square structure of brown stone and amber glass panels that sat upon a hill in Westchester like a small chateau. Workmen were everywhere with the Feinmark crest stenciled on their helmets, laying in a forest of birches and installing the pipes for the fountains that were to play along the loggia. The receptionist was cute but not the sort of girl he ran into every day on his rounds. She seemed to Cogan gracious beyond the call of duty, yet too informal, as though she might pick up her book where she left off reading with no offense intended. She was well into a collection of essays on the silent film with a shot of D.W. Griffith in a slouch hat on the cover.

Cogan said: "I always thought he looked like Woodrow Wilson."

"Yes! You're absolutely right." Her hair was dark and very shiny. Through the top of the smoke glass reception desk Cogan saw that she was barefooted, in jeans worn to a soft baby blue at the knees. "But I think that was a face of the time," the girl said. "You know — like there was a pre-Raphaelite face and a decadent face and that hard-jaw young hero face of the Second World War."

"You've got some theory going there!" Cogan said in a hearty salesman's voice. He wondered if he was in the right place.

"My great-grandfather looked *exactly* like Griffith," the receptionist said, "and he only invented a couple of engines in Detroit. They were skinny-faced artists then. Total squares, but I mean brilliant artists masquerading as businessmen." She smiled and swung around in her chair. If she shut up, he thought she'd be like a gorgeous college girl on a magazine cover. "It was the last time America could afford such independent genius," she said portentously.

When they finally got down to Cogan's business she said that the purchasing department had not moved out from the city yet, but he could make an appointment. Embarrassed, Jack Cogan said he should have called. The girl made him feel as though the situation was purely social. He had faked it — had driven over knowing that the Feinmark move was incomplete, but he had to throw the day away. A suspension of time and purpose came over him like a desperate daydream. The scene receded. He had no right to be here, talking to this lovely girl. Her ease reminded Cogan of his wife years ago when she was a self-assured working girl. There was nothing then that Mill couldn't handle. He had fooled her into marrying him in a courtship that seemed afterwards like a shell game — trickery, sleight of hand. The receptionist asked Jack Cogan if he was into film.

He mustered the charm, "No," he said, "I'm not *into* anything like that. Griffith was before my time and I'm too old to catch him at the Museum. You guys will just have to take me with my hockey games and a glass of beer in front of the set."

"That's OK."

She showed him around the building, padding down the corridors in her bare feet. The offices were tranquil open spaces. Nothing had the look of commerce about it, the large expensive plants in Indian baskets, the malachite ashtrays, the almost oppressive good taste.

"Awful, isn't it?" the girl asked.

It was a peculiar afternoon altogether. Jack Cogan learned that she was living with one of the Feinmark kids and they were into urban renewal. The new headquarters of the largest real estate firm in the country was a piece of shit. Totally dishonest. But they'd had it with the radicals. She and Louis were really into working within the system.

As an afterthought she took Cogan to the back of the building. "Wait till you get this ceiling!" she said.

A very frail old man sat at his desk industriously reading the large print edition of the *New York Times*, his head like a small brown bird's, pecking at words.

"Do you mind if I show off your Las Vegas skylight, Mr. Feinmark?"

As the sun zoomed in like a trick stage effect, Jack Cogan realized that the old man covering his eyes now like a frightened creature was the legendary Harold Feinmark.

"I'm retired," Feinmark said as an opening gambit. "I can't sit home so I come to the office. This place," the old man said unnecessarily, "is new." He seemed startled, even wounded by his surroundings and fumbled among the beautiful objects on his desk till he found a plastic calendar with the date in bulbous white numbers. "My sons won't be out here till the end of the week."

Cogan's wildest dreams had not projected a scene in which he'd meet one of the Feinmarks, never mind the old man. At best he'd leave the extravagant five-colored brochure with a minor flunky in purchasing, go to the track, and call it a day.

"They're moving the whole operation out here. I'm retired." Mr. Feinmark said, "Believe me, I can't do you any good."

"I didn't intend to bother you," Cogan said almost irritably. He wanted to run in shame from the unseeing eyes of Mr. Feinmark. The girl had deserted them. He felt a fool without the usual response to his quick smile, his jaunty looks.

"Sit down! Sit down!" Feinmark urged. "I have no authority here," he said and began negotiations with Jack Cogan that lasted for three weeks. They talked in the millions — two professional four-flushers who had time on their hands. The old man matched Cogan's glibness at every turn. A meeting of champions: the real estate king who in the old days had sold mosquito infested swamps for state hospitals, the penny-ante gambler who had talked fast all his life for a buck. On paper Cogan contracted for photographic processing machines, tape deck files, microfilm libraries for the entire Feinmark enterprise, here at the palatial Westchester site as well as the whole West Coast and Atlanta operations. When Jay and Pauli Feinmark came out to look over the new building they found their father in better spirits than they had seen him in years: he made jokes about his pacemaker and introduced them to his friend. The Feinmark boys were big, impressive men, taller than Hoshie had ever hoped them to be. They looked to Jack Cogan like figures in national politics, governors or members of some powerful committee in the Senate.

In the months that Cogan observed the Feinmark sons, they seemed always to be on the way to Kennedy airport. At least a dozen times they came into Hoshie's office to say goodbye, patronizing the old man with their solicitous concern. Jay, the aggressive older son, thought that his father's mind had begun to fail and smiled at Cogan knowingly — anything that keeps "them" amused he indicated with his extra warm handshake. Pauli, whose confidence was as external as the tailoring of his suits, was sure that Poppa had met this fellow after Mamma died when he took those courses in alienation at the New School.

"Go bet on the Knickerbockers, my friend!" Hoshie cried as a greeting one day when Cogan stopped for their bargaining session, "I'm not buying anything and you know it."

"Who's selling?" Cogan shrugged. "Your organization happens to be in my territory."

"What's the name of that young man they've got for an office manager?"

Cogan wasn't sure.

"And where's the purchasing department?" Leaning into his prey Harold Feinmark laughed, for he could see that Cogan had not even bothered to find out you took a left turn past the Braque. He felt his way to his chair and swiveled back and forth like a nervous child. "Please go

192

sell your smart machines. While we've been discussing they've already bought from your competitor."

"Ah —," Cogan's sigh was triumphant. The bet was lost. Wasn't that what he had wanted all along?

"It's my fault," Hoshie rocked in his bright red chair which engulfed his shrunken body like a womb. "I'm a foolish old man. But it was good, lovely to be talking deals again and I knew you were ready to waste the time. It was like flexing muscles where the strength's been gone. It was like seeing again." And he took off his glasses, staring blindly ahead. His eyes, drained of life, expressed none of the remorse he felt. Facing the wrong direction, he cried out to Cogan, "It was a cruel thing to do and I didn't give a damn for your product. All that ever gave me a thrill in the old days was the purchase of property, real property."

"Thanks," Cogan said. The old man could hear that he was at the door.

"Listen! I'll make it up to you. I have never interfered with the business since my sons took over, but I'll break precedent. I'll tell them that I want my old files put on tape I can listen to — You name it. What's a fair commission for the time you've put in?"

"I wouldn't take a dime," Jack Cogan said. Disgrace was not new to him.

"Come back! Come back, my friend. What's done can be undone."

"I'm a loser," Cogan's voice was tight. "And you just said you were foolish and cruel. That all sounds right to me."

"But *I* don't believe it! There's the difference between us." Hoshie found his glasses and put them on again. "There! I see you now —" he called to Cogan gaily as if playing with a baby, but behind the thick lenses, a last hope of light, the old eyes were misted. "I don't believe we are so set in our ways, my friend."

Cogan had no place to go. They faced each other again in the tomato red chairs, princes of idleness.

"I don't believe we are so set in our ways. When my wife died," Harold Feinmark told Cogan, "I looked in her closet for the first time. It was the size of a small room and there with the coats and dresses and furs, I counted one hundred and twenty-eight pairs of shoes. All kinds. All colors. Many of them unworn. That was what was left after a life. Oh, and a hospital wing for children in Israel, but that was inevitable — with the solid Jewish background and so much money to spend. Out of guilt now I keep the membership to Emmanuel. She only got me in a temple once to marry me. I could remember her when she was in good health, ready to play golf or go off to lunch with her women friends. I could remember good times — ordering a silver punch bowl with her in Florence, or our sons' graduations, our daughter's first marriage to a boy in medical school. All these memories seemed shallow and the shoes began to bother me. She had bought those shoes, every pair, and after the funeral I went immediately out to the house in Westchester and found one hundred and twelve more pairs of shoes — shoes for every activity and time of day. There were no comfortable old shoes. All of them new . . . many with tiny heels and pointed toes . . . that was the style, you see. My mind was so clear. I recalled a magazine rack in her bathroom that was stacked with the latest fashion magazines which I studied at once and all the shoes for that year, for that season were like her shoes. My wife was six-and-a-half B, a common size I found. I was on the next plane to L.A. and my children said Daddy was stricken with grief, running from his sorrows. I knew what I would find: there were ninety-seven pairs of shoes and three boxes from

Magnin's as yet unopened making it another even hundred. I sobbed for a while, collapsed completely in the house out here, those stale rooms. The furniture all shrouded. She'd had a passion, my wife. Her name was Ruth. A full-fledged passion and I never knew. I hadn't looked at her feet, just presumed she had feet at the end of her legs like everyone else."

Hoshie's eyes were tearing again and Jack Cogan went into the marble bathroom to bring him a hand towel with the Feinmark monogram. "Why don't we go to lunch," he said to the old man. "Come on. We'll get a nice steak."

"Don't patronize me!" Hoshie cried, When his glasses were in place he looked hard at the red Fs woven in the towel. "It's terrible. My name's a household word. My office looks like a cultural center. Six months after my wife died every aspect of the corporation was signed over to my sons. I, personally, didn't own one piece of property. I *rented* in an apartment built by U.S. Steel."

"Calm down . . . it's bad for your heart," Cogan said. "So you perpetrated a hoax on me . . ."

"I don't own a thing. Don't bet on me." But the denial was terrific, like a perfect bluff at the poker table and Cogan feeling lucky placed his bets. A long chance. The thrill was enormous and all that winter Jack came to visit Hoshie, bringing with him the books he found hidden in Jimmy's room for the old man to study with his feeble eyes.

For Harold Feinmark, having divested himself of his property, lusted next after wisdom. For years after his wife died he had been chauffeured to the Twelfth Street entrance of the New School to face the complexities of the twentieth century . . . alienation, loss of identity, urban blight, anxiety, entropy and self-renewal were met full on. He sat in the cafeteria forgetting to take off his hat, like an old Jew in the garment district bent over a corn muffin and Kafka. He reckoned in a lighthearted moment that *Metamorphosis* had been assigned four times, *Waiting for Godot* six. For the first time he read the hated Marx and found him reasonable, lucid — nothing to inspire his mother's mad dedication there. His copy of the *Interpretation of Dreams* was frayed, spineless, a corpse of a book — exhausted from being shared out in many directions. To Hoshie, Sartre was cold, but ultimately correct with his "fundamental choice." He grew old thinking. He saw no one. There wasn't time. He left financial statements unopened and sent the rest of his mail on to his sons to do with as they saw fit. Late into the nights he read in his sparsely furnished apartment. His eyes went back on him and he hired a college girl to read to him — her sweet accentless voice droning on over the great questions, the impossible answers.

In the end he fell over a footstool and his children took him to live in Pauli's house out in New Rochelle where rooms were perfectly set so he could find his way. Blinded, he saw for the first time that the text of his life was simply this: he had loved property to spite a woman who had abandoned him. He had not known his wife. He did not know his children. Often he dreamt of the shoes, three hundred and thirty pairs. Didn't you know, he chided himself, that Ruth loved shoes? If he had been a poor man they might have argued over the bills. Perhaps other secrets were locked in her heart . . . a lover even, but that did not disturb him. It was the waste. The waste of her life and his. The doctors opened him up and put a pacemaker in to regulate his numb, faltering heart. He refused to pay the bill and never knew who made out the check. Where would he have learned love anyway? The little bit he knew from his father, the poor man flushed and coughing in a coal cellar, his father cradling him under his overcoat while he read to dark ragged figures, passages from some revolutionary text in his educated British accent, a touch of the German poking through.

"You begin sorting your life out now," the old man exhorted Cogan. "My grandchildren laugh at me. Like some old fellow in a parable I wanted to be rich and then I wanted to be wise."

"Well, you are wise," Cogan said.

"Too late. My children are strangers. My grandchildren amuse me. They live off the fruits of my empire with all their leftist jargon, my mother's talk again. Free love by the heated swimming pool. But you, Cogan, you could know your wife still. Your children!"

"I know them," Jack Cogan replied with a smirk and a quick soft-shoe step across the carpet, the old clownish routine. But it was only a matter of days before he came by to see Hoshie with a manifesto by P. J. Clauson he had found in Jimmy's room and he was genuinely moved by his wife's boozy fears that the boy would be destroyed, her helpless cries echoing in his ears.

"All variegated manifestations of multifarious categories of energy, both animate and inanimate, spring from the all-inclusive cognizant fountainhead of Creative Love." Cogan caught his breath and read on: "There are innumerable progressive phases of cognizance of the Supreme Cognizant, and these phases are reflected in the material world linked in various species and pervaded by desires springing from various quantities of knowledge. With Krishna Nuru the living being comes to his natural full complement of cognition and bliss."

"The words of a lunatic," Hoshie pressed his temples in disbelief. "Read Carlyle," he sighed. "There is nothing to fear. 'Cagliostros do prosper by their quackery for a day.'"

Soon after that it was *The Witches' Almanac.* Feinmark read the title. "Terrible print. I can't make out a word."

197

"Potions. Incantations. Look," Cogan cried, "he's underlined the declining moon for the next weeks and written 'glycerine and household roaches'!" Another day it was the *I Ching* or the flowery dreams of a Mexican Indian or a mystic preacher with a holy entourage in a VW bus.

"Magic," the old man said. "You should understand with your gambling that your son has lost faith in the rational. What's so different in your hunches. Flaunting yourself in the face of reason."

"My wife is afraid he's sleeping with a dirty girl who calls him up."

"Don't bother me with that. It's all magic — his roaches and mumbo jumbo may bring him peace. It's too hard. The world is too hard for us — it's too hard without magic."

"But he hasn't sent in his acceptance for college," Cogan was worked up that day, full of accusations about his son, evasive details. "He has hidden Indian garments in the back of his closet. Peace! Why does he need peace at his age. I need peace with three children and a wife with her bottle stashed behind the breadbox. Merganthaller all but fired me this week."

"Ah —" said Harold Feinmark.

"But they can't get rid of me because of your sons . . . your sons requested that I stay on. Your sons who thought I sold file cabinets and carbon paper till a few weeks ago, and Feinmark signs with my competitor."

"What do they want you for?" the old man asked.

"For *you*," said Cogan. "I'm trapped listening to your wisdom. They have purchased our friendship. I've been bought. They'll throw a little business to Merganthaller and the company will put me on a retainer."

"Why don't you quit?" Hoshie asked.

"That's too easy, my friend," said Cogan in his most winning manner. He nudged Feinmark out of his chair.

Lately he touched the old man a great deal, prodding him on when the way was safe, caressing the shrunken blue hand when they waited for the doors of the palace to swing open. "You want to get out in the air?" Jack Cogan asked.

"Don't bet on me," Feinmark spoke softly from his shadowed world and let himself be buttoned into his topcoat to be taken for a ride in the spring sunshine.

"Too late," Cogan whispered, "the bets are made."

On the day that Harold Feinmark died, Jack Cogan was met at the front door of the new building by the sons. They stood together in black ties behind the row of fountains. The willows' first faint green, the azaleas in full bloom, the beds of tulips looked as though they'd been there forever — a public park of long standing.

The tears burned down Jack Cogan's face before they spoke. His briefcase was stuffed with pamphlets and mimeographed sheets found under Jimmy's bed. The Eclipse of God. The need to destroy knowledge and enter the state of grace. The great energy flow. The urgent call to violent passivity. Peace to the spirit. Consciousness to the soul. A babble of hysterical beliefs. He had wanted to talk to the old man, to take the wasted hand in his today, to read aloud the madness. I am your eyes. You perceive what I cannot see. Though his family didn't know, he had not put his money on a horse or touched a card in weeks. He knew that he was off it now forever. The old man would be proud of him.

". . . no pain at all. The mechanism wasn't foolproof." Jay, the older son, broad-shouldered, gray-templed, duly solemn, summed up his father's final scene. "When he knew that he wouldn't make it through the night, he told us that he had an appointment with you. He sent apologies."

"A thing so small —" said Pauli, dry-eyed, bemused. They

went into the marble lobby and stood together as though none of them belonged, stiff figures of grief.

"He was a great man," said the younger son.

"Yes," Cogan said.

"We knew for months that he could go at any moment."

"I didn't know. I didn't know." Jack Cogan cried again. He could not stop. Without shame, without fear he wept as Hoshie's sons should have wept. They took him to the old man's office. Was there anything here he'd like. Cogan went to the bulletin board and pulled off the old anarchist pamphlet exhorting the coal miners to action in nineteen-fourteen. This he carefully put into his briefcase with the crazed messages from Jimmy's room.

The funeral was the following morning at Temple Emmanuel. Cogan attended sitting apart, the only gentile aside from the motley official delegations from the city and the state, trustees of Lincoln Center and the Preservation Society. A pair of Rabbis made Harold Feinmark into a religious man . . . a man of vision, engaged in the building of America, the great dream realized, wise in the ways of the world he had given all his worldly possessions away and become wise in the spiritual realm. Devout husband, loving father. The foundations were invoked — as a child of Israel he gave to the children of Israel. Thus does a name live on . . . the patriarchal Jew that was good box office emerged. How Hoshie would have laughed, the weak eyes and failing heart would have fluttered with mirth at this preposterous scene. Now wouldn't Cogan love to rise up and tell them of the old man's greed, his cruelty and vengeance on his mother's name, the leaky cellars and wasteland the Feinmark glories were built on, but he said only the short Catholic refrain — *May he rest in peace.*

The mourners waited to be sorted into the line of black limousines at the curb. When the hearse doors had closed on Hoshie's casket flanked with bright red roses, Cogan silently took his leave, but he got no further than a few steps when a woman grabbed him by the elbow. This was the Feinmark daughter. He knew her though they had never met.

"My father left you something," she said crisply. "He left you his books."

"What?" Cogan asked.

Her manner was pure bitch. "He left you his books, a bunch of paperbacks mostly, nothing of value."

"No first editions!" Cogan quipped.

She smiled. It was the hard smile of a woman who likes to be put down. Dieted, tanned, brittle as dried bones, fashion and money blazed from her face. She was curious to distraction. "Why did my father love you?" was her question. Her plain dress and black silk veil aped the costume of the notorious weeping women of the sixties. Then, almost flirtatious, she said to Cogan, "I hear you have a deal."

"What's that?"

"My brothers said you're getting a big contract out of them." Her voice rose quickly to a society pitch. She talked angrily at Cogan. The cars were ready to leave for the cemetery. A young man with his hair in a braid and sandals, but otherwise conventionally dressed, waited for her at the door of the last limousine.

"It's only fair," said Feinmark's daughter. "You were good to him. We're decent people."

"What's fair?" Cogan asked.

"That all that business should be thrown to you, to Merganthaller."

"It's a pity . . ." A stab of intense pleasure charged through Cogan's breast, and he said, ". . . then it's a pity I don't work there anymore." Miraculous! Beyond reason — he seemed to levitate, to soar up over the row of black cars on Fifth Avenue, over the impatient grandchildren, the angry daughter and bored Feinmark executives who must ride out to Valhalla, to hover in great peace over the big black hearse with the body of his friend.

III

SCENARIO: *Before My Time*

FROM THIS POINT on — to the end let us say — I would like to picture for you quick-moving scenes. It is not so much that they pass before me swiftly but that these images sometimes fill my mind at once or follow one upon another with an insistence like motion, like pages flipping over or the suggestion of motion in a coil of black film. Running time: undetermined . . . for there are places where I like to stop and look at one face, replay the moment when the head turns, slightly off-axis, thrown by a quick response, to see again the eyes that fill with tears. A woman in tears. *I*, I too, have licked the salt from the corners of my grieving mouth. To satisfy myself with that vision and then refreshed, move on. My projection of the waking dream: he will sit . . . she will stand above him . . . and the kiss when it comes will be a kiss she wants to tear from her cheek. Again: the bemused smile as she turns, eyes fill with tears. Like an ending, a completion for me . . . not quite. And in the dark his voice. — Stay here. Speak of familiar things awhile.

Start with the big city — a view of the center at the end of a summer day, framed by the tinted glass windows of a new building. The elegant safety, the psychic warmth of being inside while the city is out there in amber — too nice. The people here will be smudged with glamour. It will be hard to care, to trust the depth of their feeling. The city of Boston. A gentle mechanical hum. Harry Quinn stands at the window of his office, amber glass cased in anodized aluminum (the window I have looked through) and he sees the meager scattering of cars like scarabs in the parking lot below. He looks at his watch and clicks off the tape on his desk, takes the jacket off the back of his chair and buttons himself into it formally. A lean man with a rigid body, rather slick good features like an actor, fair skin and sandy hair, but a face not distinct enough to be memorable, eyes that are red-rimmed with trouble. A mature face, guarded and professional but kind. The office is dim and silent. Harry moves in the dark paneled room with unnecessary force closing up for the day, exerting a brutal control on the window blinds and desk drawers. His locked desk. His high leather chair. Law books. Prints of old Boston and the Harvard Yard — I see the little colonial people walking under half-grown trees. Merchants and scholars and men of God.

Harry starts for the door of his office and with relief turns back to the desk, clicks on the machine. The gentle hum of the tape again as it absorbed his words which are spoken with great purpose in an unbroken stream.

— I want the letters by noon and the file on the Mayer separation goes to Lewis now. I haven't time for it: a note to the effect that it's not my kind of law, that I'm a personal friend of both parties and I'll advise . . . can't foresee any complications and so forth. Get McMahon and tell him I want a solid commitment from his delegation. It's a bad year and we have to look good. The reapportionment gets killed in the first round or the Democrats in this state will be caucusing in a phone booth. He stands stiff shouldered, at attention. There is nothing more to attend to, nothing Harry can think of to hold him and he leaves.

The outer office is dark. One sharp streak of lamp light on the last papers of the day to be signed and mailed. In the shadows a demure looking girl in a neat white blouse with a cardigan over her shoulders against the air-conditioned atmosphere. A pale girl with recessive blond coloring, slight chin — she waits in a typing chair, straight as a post, purse in her lap, shopping bag of extras at her side. She is Elizabeth, diligent and good. When Harry knocks the shade of the desk lamp scribbling his signature, the light flares up on her and the secretary is surprisingly old — a woman in her middle years whose features are too sweet to be true, an arrested life, harrowed by emptiness.

— The tapes are for noon, Harry says.

— Tomorrow's Saturday, she complains in a high childish voice, and I want to get the ten o'clock ferry for Provincetown with some girls.

— There's not so much there. You'll get them done. They go out through the still corridors and down in the elevator which is a searing blue enamel box. Music plays when the doors shut — a soupy will-destroying music that carries them to the ground floor. Elizabeth feeling wronged studies Harry Quinn with an angry glare that quickly turns to gentle sorrow, yearning.

— Last year, she says with a sigh, we never went in on Saturdays after Memorial Day. I went up to Gloucester to see my sister and the kids. I was relaxed then. I had a tan. She holds a pale arm out to him.

— Last year wasn't an election year.

— I've been through a few elections, she says. She has pushed her cause as far as she will. They go out through the hollow lobby, approaching their images in the glass doors. Their cars lie at opposite ends of the vast parking lot. Mysterious white papers flutter over the asphalt pavement. Harry Quinn turns to his secretary to say good-night. Now he is direct — the stiffness, the self-absorption fade. As he looks at her with concern, his face comes alive with a practiced charm. This change in him, however contrived, is like a blessing and Elizabeth smiles.

I feel the reality of all exterior scenes: a harsh light in day, a terrifying darkness streaked with artificial light at night. There is no hiding place in the natural light. Out-of-doors faces are coarse-grained, the women made-up, the men ordinary against buildings and automobiles. The interiors are warm and protective, wrapping the Quinns and their story in a soft light, that surface glow I have come to expect from color film. The order and harmony that ease hard facts. There are no costumes. No relief from the contemporary save in two scenes which I savor for their theatrical pitch.

Now in the parking lot the heat that Harry and Elizabeth have been spared all day presses down on them, and he asks — How is your mother?

— She's the same. Waiting for it to be over.

— Yes. We all are, Harry sighs.

— Nonsense. Elizabeth laughs at him, pouts like a coquette but it won't do. Her lips are thin, unsatisfied. The sunlight is painful in her eyes. She squints then hides behind giant dark glasses. — You're only waiting for the election. She laughs at him. — That's what you're waiting for. You've worked too late everyday this week. You didn't play golf on Wednesday and there's some damn thing on the calendar every night. You'd think you were running for office. You have one hour — one hour to get home and come all the way back to town for the fund raising stint.

— What's the matter, Liz? Aren't you a good Democrat anymore?

— It's not that, she says miserably. They move a few steps away from each other in their separate directions.

— How's the new nurse, Harry asks.

— Oh, she weighs about two hundred pounds. Mother loves her. They sit together and watch people dying on television all day. It's awkward, this personal talk between them, and yet he must. This directness is part of his calculated and real charm, and she must assume the pity and hatred that she has for her narrow life. — Momma's just propped up there on her pillows, Elizabeth says, watching them all divorce and die.

— Don't come in tomorrow. You have enough to think about.

— Thanks, Harry. She has what she wants from him — sympathy, attention. She says — Maybe I'll get them done on Sunday. I hate to be home all day Sunday. Harry Quinn tells her emphatically that next week things will ease off and it will be over and though she doesn't understand his insistence they say good-night pleasantly as they have done for years. In the windshield wipers of their cars they each find a piece of white paper like those scattered over the parking lot: Madam Aurelia predicts and she also fully guarantees to tell you how you are standing and banish your luck if you are held back from the things that are rightfully yours. Don't sit in the darkness crying and worrying when you can be helped, for it is not God's will nor way that sorrow should follow you around. Satisfaction guaranteed. You must be pleased.

Now HARRY QUINN IN HIS CAR, a suave brown Mercedes, his way of showing the world. He is an aggressive driver, cutting in and out of traffic, impatient at stoplights — the only area of his life that is reckless. Enclosed with the leather seats and chrome fixtures of his dashboard Harry is complete as he is at his desk. Indeed, I see him there, too, back in the office, an overlay — the car and the desk interchangeable mise-en-scènes, his world — surrounded with manly equipment in the filtered false light, shored up by his belongings. The excitement of downtown life, the exhaustion at the end of a hot day's work are all outside of his vision. I see him alternately at his desk, in the car, justifying himself in a bold revealing monologue. One face. Stay with one face. My forced, then willing attention. One story. I'm sick of the constant movement that becomes mere entertainment, the nervous idea that I might be bored unless the scene moves on. His face, his words hold me.

— I've been driving myself hard, Harry says, with good reason. We are in a weak position at the State House this year and I have never found romance in supporting the underdog. I like to win. There's a sick tradition in this country among a lot of smart people of wanting to lose as though they don't quite believe what they stand for, as though it would be a shame to be right. As long as I can remember, I have always wanted to win, but it now seems that to say so is simpleminded, crass. At the age of forty-five I'm locked into myself. I can't think any other way and that's it.

— It would be impossible for me now to retreat to a position where every strategic move is a fine moral decision or to wince for example at the old notion of balancing the ticket, dragging in the Italians, the Irish vote. You can't be easily offended and win. Roosevelt knew that and Kennedy. Every pol in Dorchester knows it, there's no point pulling out the big guns. If you want to get a housing project through for the poor then you'd better be pretty sharp in dealing with the middle class. It's dirty and deceptive, full of intrigue if you want to think of it that way, but I don't. I think that you will get the goddamn housing project *built,* or the school, or the highway. It's nonsense to play at politics like cops and robbers and if things get too real you quit the game. We are the good guys — I believe that — and I know that if I told the men and women on the Democratic Committee in my district what I really wanted for this state, or for the country, I would get a vote of no-confidence. But believe me, I don't want to lose: I don't want to be superior and powerless. There's nothing in it. Nothing at all.

The unrelieved study of Harry's face. The strength drains as I look at it from different angles, the light blue eyes and thin sandy hair seem weak, a flickering sort of beauty, a man's vulnerable beauty is impressed on me until I finally accept, even grow to love this face. Then at a stoplight, one outward glance — a small band of sweet hip kids with a young priest are sitting on the steps of a public building with signs flopped down so that their cause is not known. They begin to sing and Harry rolls up the windows to keep out the noise. On Memorial Drive his car seems to swallow up the miles, the city as backdrop, the car (the office) his safe place where he can *tell me* — for that's the sense of it I have, a feeling of our intimacy. His pale eyes on me, so direct and yet the professional tone never quite disappears.

— It's strange, Harry says, that I can't run for office . . . not personally. I have to content myself with being the man behind the scenes. Once I entered the congressional race from the Sixteenth District and got badly beaten. When I faced people to speak for myself I went dry. A disgusting, humiliating fear came over me and my limbs were heavy and wooden. I spoke without feeling or conviction on issues of ultimate concern — civil rights, the education of our children and the war . . . even the war, that great oozing sore became a dispassionate subject. No one believed in me — how could they? And at the same time . . . while I was out there meeting them in shopping centers, at village fairs and riding in parades I believed more than ever in my cause. After the election I collapsed. I simply didn't function for some weeks. I couldn't remember the process by which I buttoned my shirts, or didn't have the will — and saw that there were hidden meanings in the stars and in the movement of the planets. I have never put myself before the people again.

— So that's why Elizabeth is sore at me. She's been with me for fifteen years and knows the whole story better than my wife. I've been driving myself lately with good reason. I don't believe for a minute that she's going to Provincetown. She's protecting me. If I died tomorrow Elizabeth could carry on — write the letters I write, phone the people I phone, everything but appear in court — if I dropped out again, but I don't intend to. I intend to be appointed Judge of the Federal Court by the first of January. My wife's father was a judge in this district, which is amusing since she did not love and respect the old man at all.

iii

THIS IS THE HEIGHTENED SCENE: Evening in the Quinns' house — here Laura, in a sinuous white gown, looks and behaves like a high-strung heroine of the old days, the old untrue movies. Bette Davis say — pettish, shrill, oddly beautiful and affected as hell. And that dress, the dress of a haughty society bitch or a neurotic actress.

Laura is in their bedroom unhappy about the evening ahead. She sits on a low chair reading peevishly in the dim light of a boudoir lamp. The rest of the room is in darkness. The long white dress falls in graceful folds on the carpet. Her hair is unkempt. Her face polished and raw. With an eyebrow pencil she marks a passage in the book and reads on. Suddenly she takes the book and throws it across the room. Something smashes in the dark and she rests her head on her hand in a gesture that is anguished but not quite genuine for a woman alone in her bedroom. She sits up and turns in a dummy-like way to stare at herself in the mirror of her dressing table. A voice calls from below, but Laura does not answer. The voice comes nearer and calls again — Can they skip their baths? Laura sits at the dressing table with her eyes half-closed and reaches out to touch her face in the mirror with a clawing that accomplishes nothing, then digs her nails into her palms and stares down at the painful red crescents she has cut into her flesh.

Frieda, a plump energetic woman of sixty, comes to the door of the bedroom with Laura's children. She wears a flowered housedress which might as well be a servant's uniform. The boy is seven, the girl nine, golden, healthy kids half-hidden by Frieda's bulk. The three of them stand on the threshold looking in as though at someone who is at a remove from their world. It is the darkness of the room that holds them there, the illumination of the white dress, Laura's startled look as she turns to them.

— I said, can they skip their baths tonight?
— Yes, Laura replied.
— Yes, they can, or yes, you heard me.
— They look all right.
— Right then, says Frieda. She watches as the boy puts something down his sister's neck and the girl begins to squeal. He then starts to run for his mother but Frieda grabs him, slaps his arm — We don't go near your mother

in that dress, she says, and then as a grievance — You'll come and say good-night to them, I'm sure.

Laura doesn't bother to reply but says to the little girl — Come, Mary. Come here. Mary walks through the darkness and into the arc of light where her mother sits, standing away from the white dress. She wriggles and a terrible realistic rubber toad falls from her dress onto the carpet. She is a solemn child with clear round eyes and a plain face, straight thick hair in a dutch bob, an obedient old-fashioned child with secret ways.

Laura rummages through a tray of jewelry and holds out a necklace — Here's something pretty, she says. And here's another for you. She puts a bracelet on Mary's arm. The girl is pleased but restrained and turns to show Frieda and her brother but they've gone.

— You're going to be a beautiful girl when you grow up, Laura says. Your bones are like the Murrays' and they were all beautiful.

Mary looks at herself in the mirror and sees her plain face. Something smells, she says. She goes to the corner where Laura threw the book. — It smells here and it's messy, Mary says. I think we have rats.

— We don't have rats.

— Yes, the child says, big ones out in back and when it gets cold they'll come into the house.

— Those are field mice. Benjamin catches them . . . you've seen. They are little gray mice he carries in his mouth.

— No, Mary shakes her head no. Jim Cogan says we have rats.

— Oh, well then, Laura laughs. Was Sam bad tonight? Mary comes back into the light and doesn't speak. — I don't mean you should tattle, Laura says, but he's little and doesn't understand sometimes.

214

— He put ketchup in my milk at supper. She takes the bracelet off her arm and holds it up like a monocle. With one wise eye she looks at her mother and says, Daddy's home.

— No!

— Yes, Mary says, because I heard his car and he came up the back walk and looked at us through the window. She turns away and leaves her mother abruptly, triumphant at knowing more than an adult, and runs out through the darkness to her bedtime rituals.

Laura begins to brush her hair, lets the brush drop. She stares at herself in the mirror again . . . herself in the mirror, but this time she is alive, turning her face slowly to see the flesh under both eyes. With expert fingers she explores the down at the sides of her mouth, a small round scar on her cheek from a childhood accident, an oddly adolescent pimple below her right ear. It is a sad narcissistic moment — a caress that yields nothing.

iv

HARRY QUINN swings into the driveway of his house, a long drive that leads to the garage, an elflike cottage in a thicket of ivy. He walks slowly to an elongated terrace at the back of the house that is covered with bicycles and toys. Within, his children are sitting at the table with Frieda. The boy kicks his sister fiercely under the table and when the motherly woman is busy closing up the milk carton, he gets a chance to fling a spoon of Jell-O across the table. Mary puts in a complaint and Frieda slaps the little boy's hand while smoothing his hair and then kisses him on the hand she has punished. Harry draws a wicker chair up to the window and remains in the shadow watching his children

215

eat and quarrel. The little girl's face is unemotional as she watches Frieda finishing the last of her Jell-O, her fat cheeks wobbling as she chews. Then, Mary gets down from the table and goes secretly to a cupboard where a doll is hidden in a pot and drops bread and scraps of her meal into the doll. She smiles squatting over the hidden pot until she is called and both children are taken off. Before Mary leaves she turns to the window and stares straight into the darkness at her father, but gives no other sign.

v

THE LIGHT GOES ON suddenly in the bedroom. — Why are we in darkness, Harry says. In the corner a little table has been knocked over by Laura's book and a bottle of white almond-scented lotion lies in a pool on the carpet. They both dash to the spot and Laura retrieves her book before Harry can see. She stands with it hidden in the folds of her skirt.

— I'm going to get so fucking mad, Harry says with neat control, that one night I'll strike you.

— I'm ready to go, Laura says.

— You don't look it.

— I could have driven into town to meet you.

— I wanted a shower. He has torn off his shirt and tie. Laura with quick guilty movements hides the book she had been reading and flies about the room assembling his dinner jacket, black tie.

— I wanted to come home, Harry says, and watch the decay of my family.

She brushes her hair, puts on her rings with a superb abstraction. I'm going to say good-night to the children, she says.

Harry stands before her naked with a dressing gown over his shoulders like a prize fighter — I had lunch with Lewis and the girl today. She's not even pretty, a feckless, frog-eyed girl. She's got big boobs. Lewis hangs on her words . . . the ordinary stuff . . . the world is fake and she's real. The world is vulgar, mechanized . . . all made-up, lifeless talk. God it was boring. Lewis is trivial when he's with her. He looks about ten years older. Harry comes close to Laura and breathes his words on her like a threat. She's not a bad girl, he says. Kids like that have no hooks into the world, no direction. There's no reason for her except sex.

— I'm going to say good-night to the children. I'll be in the car.

vi

THE CHILDREN'S ROOM is too sweetly and lightly imagined, like rooms of unreal children in technicolor movies. Frieda has established a fantastic order here. Things are as she wants them — toys lined up in a joyless parade. She turns back the beds while Laura with her book in hand watches from the doorsill. The closet door moves and the children begin to giggle. A hand comes out in a red sock. The door shuts on the hand. The hand is in agony. Frieda turns, her fat face trembling with rage and yanks Jim Cogan out of the closet.

Here I see that I've come to the hero, or at least the star. A big grinning kid of eighteen, square Irish face, shy American male, plenty of personality, but muted, easy manners that make me believe in him, and a shallowness, that makes me beg for more. Frieda's complaints about the boy run on, though they are not serious, while Jim Cogan tries to kiss her fat old cheek and the kids laugh.

— Let them be, Laura says. It was only a game.

— We've had enough games for one day, Frieda says smartly, but she allows Jimmy to put his arm around her.

— I want something to eat, he says.

— Well, supper's been served, my dear, while you were deep in your meditation. Frieda folds the red sock against her bosom and says with a thin layer of exasperation over the tenderness she feels for the boy — You can't imagine the order we had here before you came.

They laugh when she leaves and then Mary comes to pick up the folds of her mother's dress. It is stained from the book cover and smells faintly of almond.

— No one will see, Laura says. No one will even know. I'll carry a scarf over it there and we'll sit up at a big table and the cloth will cover everything. She is acting for them now — Only the politicians get up and speak. The Senator is wonderful and handsome . . . big jokes about the Republicans, little jokes about his wife, stories about his naughty children. No one will see me. I'll hardly be there.

Jimmy takes the book out of her hand and smooths the ruined cover. — It's a great book, he says. He had it in mind that Laura would accept this book, Laura whom he respects and loves, so different from his own dull parents, so sympathetic, yet honest with him, confessional. He's a terrific guy, Jimmy says.

— I threw it across the room. It's a muddle-headed, illiberal manifesto against our lives. It's a dangerous book. The man's no more mystic than I am. He's just an aging queer who wants to stay young, who wants the license to do as he pleases.

— You can't say that without finishing the book, Jim says. He's not just some hip guy.

— I tried, but you see he didn't convince me on a line-to-line basis that his transpersonal, transrational should be my heart's desire. His arguments aren't arguments at all . . . it's polemic . . . it's a sermon . . . religion again.

Laura and Jim's voices argue on while Mary puts herself to bed. The shades have been drawn to cut out the light of the long June evening. She turns out the lamp above her bed, then gets up and goes to her brother, tucks him in, turns off his lamp and kisses him on the forehead. Laura smiles at her motherly ways but the child cannot see in the sudden darkness.

— You have to *give* yourself to it, Jimmy says moodily. He sits down on a little chair at a miniature table laid out with crayons and coloring books. He accuses Laura, You live in your head.

— You don't understand a thing I say, Laura replies, near tears. There is a wild honking of the car horn. — My God, we're so late already! She rushes to Jim and bends to kiss him, but he turns away. With some violence she wrenches his chin around so that he faces her and kisses him on the forehead. Her tears run freely, the emotions of the day unleashed and the day not over. Jimmy Cogan wipes her face with his hands and the horn sounds again — a call to duty. With a self-involved touch of the theatrical Laura suffers a wan smile.

Now I watch carefully, *precisely,* for it's fast, but not to be missed at any cost as she turns back to the room and looks at the children pretending sleep, the big boy sulking at the little table over his much loved book . . . the dolls, the trains, a puppet theater. Pictures on the walls of orderly Victorian children rolling hoops, riding docilely in dogcarts, and listening like perfect dears to a great circus calliope which I hear in the distance too, far away but exciting.

This is how it will be (as Laura knows): When it is dark and Frieda is asleep then the children will steal out of bed and Jim Cogan will push their bedclothes and pillows out

219

through the window onto a flat roof that runs over the back porch. There the three of them will sleep under the stars in the soft June night, close to each other for safety, the white curtains fluttering out to them like the membranes of dreams. Laura's face.

vii

A LINEUP OF STAINLESS STEEL serving carts. Hundreds of covered dinner plates. Stamped-out sameness. Waiters leaning against the walls. Gray institutional scene. The two waiters at the top of the line peek through the glass window of the door, sigh, and signal that it is not yet time. The food is already cool to the touch. The lead man, an older waiter, is a sickly fellow whose red jacket hangs loose on him. He watches a young waiter lift the serving dome and pop an olive into his mouth. "Pig," he says with a faint European accent, which only goads the young man into opening the dish again and eating a fried potato.

— I intend to report you, the old man says with dignity.

— I'm doing them a favor, eating this food, the young man says. He is ugly, pimply, already balding at twenty, full of spite. The only gesture of contempt possible in his waiter's uniform is to wear an outrageously dirty and frayed macrame bracelet which dangles over the roast beef dinners as he steals more olives and potatoes. — At a hundred dollars a plate I want them to get their money's worth . . . anyways the Senator's wife doesn't eat this shit.

— *I* serve the Senator's wife, the old man draws himself up with professional pride. I have always, always served the dignitaries at the head table. In this instance I get the Cardinal, the Senator, the Chairman of the Democratic Committee *and* the Senator's wife.

— See what's down her front and give me the news, the

young waiter snorts and gets a feeble laugh out of his comrades . . . the old fellow sighs and leans against the wall. Silence. Applause. The doors swing open. The trays are carried high. The parade of roast beef specials enters the dazzling grand ballroom. Hundreds of diners who have put down a hundred dollars a head for the party. Bursts of laughter, coughs, catarrh. Laura Quinn sits at the far end of the head table drawing lines into the linen with her knife and listening to a fat, florid man who purses his mouth in a wet kiss, a rosy anus. She has known a dozen men who looked like this during her life — politician friends of her father's when she was a little girl, more recently unwilling advocates of her husband's policies — venal men, gorged on public funds, puffed with their own importance, dangerous men who would do you in with a smile. Drawing little lines into the tablecloth she thinks deliberately in order not to attend to him and her words are the words that I hear while the man talks to her . . . that she will bring home the folder of mementos, stickers, campaign buttons, banners and a nice little gold pen for the children to play with and keep the folder, made of some suede-like cardboard, that cost a hundred dollars, for herself.

— Yes, she says indifferently to the fat man when he persists, pressing her for an answer, sucking up air with his mouth, furious that he has been placed next to her, a woman of doubtful importance. He is through and he knows it. All the time he talks on about her father . . . those were the days. Jokes about Mayor Curley and the Judge, the time Jim Farley came out to the house and the Judge . . .

— My father was a fool, Laura says to the man, means it to be a slap in the face. He doesn't understand or pretends he doesn't, hearing gone bad and the waiter comes between them, the insolent acne-faced boy with dirty cords hanging from his wrist into the food. The Cardinal and Negro Minister have blessed the tepid roast beef, these Thy

221

gifts. The fat man eats greedily, everything — parsley, olives, frill of carrot. Pictures are taken of the important people, those at the center of the table: Harry Quinn and Black Baptist, Senator's wife laughing it up with Catholic Cardinal and Episcopalian mucky-muck. Stunned with envy the old politician turns to Laura with hurt, squashed eyes. Next year he will be floundering down in the sea of tables among the regulars.

— They don't have a Rabbi, she says sarcastically.

— What's that?

— I said, they forgot to have a Jew.

— Yes, we have, he says, paying her back at last — we have that psychiatrist from Harvard who spends all that money on the niggers out in Roxbury. He turns from her then, scraping his chair around so that the broad of his back is to her and she sits in dreamy isolation at the end of the table, drawing a design of stars into the linen with her knife. The psychiatrist from Harvard is Harry's pet project, his best friend. She smooths the place in front of her, smooths the white cloth over and over again in a comforting motion while the Senator speaks in the background . . . a rousing patriotic speech about the future . . . how great the goals, how ready the people, how able and enlightened the leaders . . . our way is still intact, still special and best, but the moral stagnation of our opponents is to be feared, the self-seeking, the callous disregard for human life. Let us not comply with the abuse of our rights . . . as good Democrats . . . the tradition is strong in theory and in fact.

viii

LAURA SMOOTHS THE TABLECLOTH, looks out over the noisy, overdressed women and hearty men. A memory of the recent past. Here the effect is staged, ceremonial: Laura's hand smoothing an identical white cloth, that same gesture in the sunlight. The scene moves up and I see the most magical of countrysides, wild daisies in a field, high grass, orchard in full leaf, filtered light over all, silent as a painting. Frieda and the children in large straw hats sitting in perfect harmony against an apple tree. The picnic table set with wine and fruit and big red cold lobsters, their claws boiled harmless. All of this unreal. Laura dressed like a farm woman of the last century, checks, apron, baskets of bread. Jim Cogan like a youth in from the fields. I love the whole scene. I love it and can't help thinking it's foolish, the masquerade for this party, the chic bucolic atmosphere, and they are, after all, as I see now, only out in the backyard, the back of the house, one car in the driveway and Harry's car coming up the drive to park behind it. He's in his suit from the city and walks wearily across the lawn as though he doesn't want to be drawn into this fantasy.

Games. Party hats. Litter of lobster shells. More games for the children. The cake! Both Laura and Jim blow the candles, head to head, the breath of intimacy between them. Their shared birthday. It begins as a joke, for the children's delight, arm wrestling between Jim Cogan and Harry Quinn — and then turns brutal. Faces and bodies, no sense of the country charm now. Close shots of the older man straining until his thin sandy hair fringed with white begins to curl with the sweat, his temples pounding with the effort, his arm pale against the boy's, pressing with an awful determination, a will that never lets up, a force from within, against the odds, his tongue like a half-sheathed weapon between his teeth. Their breathing and the silence of their audience a nearly peaceful audience, passive, unable to imagine the hatred that has come to the surface before them. The boy, Jim Cogan, powerful, brown from the sun,

the unbeatable aura of youth, but doubt in his face, fear
that this transgression, this passion is beyond him. Laura's
face like stone. Frieda stunned — the little boy rests his
head down into her skirt, but Mary looks steadily on and
on, watching the sweat pour into her father's eyes. The
contest goes on, a sharp yell of triumph from Harry Quinn
as he presses Jim Cogan's arm to the table, and I see on a
re-play the moment when the young man can no longer hold
to his purpose, a flicker of indecision and the game is lost.
Laura's face betrays her anger at the loss. In the full sun
the first delicate lacework of wrinkles that surround her
eyes. Once more the lilting calliope music and the country
scene, the cake passed again, a toast to another year.

ix

Now she moves through the crowds after the fund-
raising dinner and stands with the Senator's wife. The two
women protect each other, one with the wooden composure
of a pretty doll, perfectly dressed, pointedly dressed for the
dais, the camera, smiling into the air, the other woman
plain in her plain white dress, hair combed but no more
fuss, the folds of the dress, clutched awkwardly with one
hand — this is Laura Quinn, old Boston, the handsome
woman, well-educated, vibrant, reassuring in public — the
old manners really pull these ladies through. As she walks
along with the Senator's wife the red stain on her skirt falls
loose, displayed like an open wound. They greet the people
who come to them like royalty and move out into the lobby
waiting for their husbands, waiting for it to be over.

Still waiting. Laura is now in the car sitting in the hotel
parking lot. The summer night harshly illuminated by over-
head lights, the sudden flash of headlights on her as cars

drive away. Voices calling good-bye, good-night, coarse laughter. Harry stands on a little island of grass completing the last deal of the evening with an obese couple, the woman in a glittering satin gown. She is young with brown curls bouncing on her forehead and fans herself with the dinner program while her husband writes down Harry's instructions. Then Harry comes to the car. It's hot in here, he says. Why don't you put the windows down?

— I don't want to hear any more blather. That's all it was, Laura says.

They drive out to the street in silence. Harry slides the roof of the Mercedes open and the breeze blows Laura's hair, the folds of her dress.

— I'm sorry you got Quigley at your end of the table. I know he annoys you.

— I insulted him, Laura says. I said my father was a fool and by extension they were all fools. (Pause.) In that time. Her face is a mask of suppressed anger, her eyes drawn shut in some inner pain. In the mirror Harry sees his wife as though she were behind him . . . a double image of her blank profile and her contorted face.

— There's worse than Quigley, Harry says. He's a harmless fool.

— I don't believe that anymore.

Bright yellow sodium lights flare on them as they drive up the ramp to the highway. Harry waits at the yield sign and they look at each other in shocked silence. Their argument seems stark and ugly.

— When I was young, Laura says, I always wanted to insult one of the corrupt fat faces and when I finally get the chance, twenty years later, it backfires, sandbox quibbling. Much later, to break the silence, she asks, with a light sarcasm — Did you "get all the people tonight?"

— What?

— Did you get them to do what you want, to do the right thing, to make them feel they had decided that the overpass, or the referendum or the aid to parochial schools was of benefit to mankind, not juggling for power, political hokum . . . but good in a large sense, the goodness that is forgotten.

— You should have made a speech, Harry says.

The Mercedes seen driving up the dark road to their house and into the drive. One dim light downstairs in the kitchen. Harry stops short of the garage. The headlights off — a sudden darkness. He puts his hand up to close the top of the car.

— It's a beautiful night, Laura says, as though to stop him.

— It's a beautiful night, Harry says, but that doesn't help, does it?

— Oh, nothing helps. They sit in the confined darkness of the car.

— I want that kid out of the house, Harry says.

— He goes on Sunday. You know that.

— That's why all the brooding. The soulful lady with the rich interior life . . . the stained dress.

She reaches out to hit him, but hesitates and her hand, like some cumbersome tool, drops in her lap.

— I want to stop loving Irishmen . . . who want the world to be different. Never my world or my . . . mine. Hunched over, she cries. The zipper of her dress has come undone if it was ever done this evening and her back is exposed before Harry, the shoulder blades pinched and heaving, like the back of a trapped animal. He spreads his hands on her flesh gently and the heaving subsides.

— Stay here, he says. Stay awhile. He bends to kiss her white skin reverently, like a priest kissing the starched white cloth of the altar. It will be over when he goes, Harry says.

226

That boy will go back to his family, back to New York and face the charges. Nothing will happen to him . . . it's all been arranged. The guilty will be judged deranged. It's absurd to think a baby like that ever meant any harm. He will go to college and it will become his memorable experience. His scrape with the law. We'll go to the Vineyard in a few weeks. You'll sit down in the quiet of the day after Frieda takes them to the beach and turn off the telephone on your desk and open the pages. . . .

Laura straightens, listens to Harry's story in the dark, closes her eyes and sees the projection of herself, of herself willed —

x

DRESSED IN BLACK PANTS and shirt she closes herself into her study, a plain white room and goes to a cabinet where she stoops and takes a tape recorder out of its case. Squatting like a child at play she plugs the machine in and listens.

A woman's voice, distant, uninspired: . . . very thrilling, very exciting, unlike any other experience in that it must be fought for, not simply earned . . . ah, I would say an exhilarating experience.

Laura's voice: You won by a wide margin, so that clearly (pause) clearly you felt that the voters had given. . . .

She reverses the tape, listens to the babble, then stops it, hearing her own voice again: . . . a modest view of our society, a modest European position that we are improvable, but not perfectable?

A woman's deep hard voice: Everything is wrong with that. We can do anything. With the resources we have there is no reason why, given the time, given the will. . . .

Laura jumps the tape and hears her voice again: . . . not

able to solve. Acceptance, resignation then . . . diminishing
. . . diminish . . .

Now she presses the erase button. In a frenzy she pulls
other tapes out of the cabinet and stacks them beside her.
I find all of this is terrifying to watch, awful destruction,
something private I should not see and yet the fascination
— it is pornographic, this scene. The black and white of it,
the lack of protection this room gives her. Later she is sitting with the tapes all around her . . . all erased now . . .
many of them pulled off their reels, trailing out of a waste
basket. She goes to the shelf above her desk and takes down
a photograph of a three-year-old boy, not her son, but an
old photo of her brother long dead and looks at it. At the
window she stands with the photo in full light. The little
boy has an odd private smile, a broad high forehead, a
clever superior looking child. Laura draws her hand down
over the boy's face slowly, lovingly as though shutting the
eyes of the dead. Squatting again she puts the tape recorder
and the photograph in the low cabinet and closes the door.

xi

IN THE STILL DARKNESS of the car Harry Quinn holds his
wife to him, like a patient, caressing her face which is
withdrawn now, distant and smooth in the dim light.

— I have always imagined that in the old days, Harry
says, when people suffered a loss of faith it was like this.
They knew what to call it and we don't. Remember, I've
had my breakdown. Remember you drove me in the car to
the hospital and you were afraid for your life.

— Yes.

— And came to see me though I didn't know you were
there.

—Yes.

— And *I* am here like that now. I am here.

Laura sits up and pulls the dress off her shoulders. Her bare breasts are even whiter than the white of her dress. She is offering herself in remorse to her husband. She smiles. She takes his hand and places it on her breast. His mouth seeks her cold comfort.

Then I see the children asleep on the roof of the porch, Jim Cogan watching from above as the Quinns make love like high school kids in the car. He turns quickly away and stares straight at the heavens, hardly breathing, in torture until it is over and he hears the car door shut, their footsteps to the house. It is obscene.

xii

No SOUND. The face of the secretary, Elizabeth, in bright sun laughing. She puts on dark glasses, looks worldly, even a bit racy. She ties a kerchief over her wild hair. The sound begins. Holidaymakers on the boat to Provincetown. Her companions are two sisters with identical pug Irish faces, one fat, one thin as though they are a carnival joke, women near fifty, gay and loud . . . and a pretty, delicate cripple who is much younger, a girl like Elizabeth once was, who has canceled out most possibilities. They are laughing together. The four women look up and I see that their focus is a group of lesbians on the deck above, wearing backpacks, smoking black cigarillos and trailing an enormous male dog as a mascot. The fat sister takes a bag of Cracker Jacks out of her purse and they begin to laugh again, uncontrollable, infantile. Elizabeth turns from her friends abruptly and walks down the deck to the bar. It is a dark quiet place, the only place of shabby dignity on the worn excursion boat.

She sits up at the bar and a man moves towards her, a hard thin man with a thin mouth, graying hair, the dishonest eyes of a make-out artist. They drink and talk and smile at each other. Elizabeth seems very open, very free. The pretty, crippled girl has come to find her and stands in the doorway watching them. With a large gesture to illustrate some point in his story the thin man at the bar opens his arms and brings one hand down on the light material of Elizabeth's blouse, the other on her knee and moves it up under her skirt. A sharp word spits from her mouth and she raises her hand against him, but the man moves quickly out of range. In the doorway the crippled girl turns quickly, but she is seen and Elizabeth calls to her. They go out together into the vast glimmering sunlight.

— Men like that are filth, scum, Elizabeth says. She takes the crippled girl's arm and leads her to the rail, saving her from a boisterous group of children. Her manner with the girl is conspiratorial and instructive. You want a moment's peace, Elizabeth says, maybe a drink or two. It seems so little to ask and they ruin it. All they want is the thrill, to be able to say something with a dirty mouth.

— What did he say?

— Never mind, Elizabeth says. There's the rim of the Cape . . . it won't be long now before it's over. They walk down the deck past parties of vacationers and find the two look-alike sisters stretching on deck chairs in the sun. They have put gaudy kerchiefs over their heads and peer out at the world, laughing.

Elizabeth holds the pretty girl aside. — I should have stayed at home, but I couldn't, she says.

— You need to get out, the girl says sweetly.

— Tomorrow the nurse is off and I'll be with her all day.

— You've got to get away now and then.

— My sister hasn't been down from Gloucester for six

weeks, Elizabeth complains. Six weeks of excuses. It's so unfair.

— It *is* unfair. Happy with their grievance they take the last steps to join the pug-faced sisters who have produced an enormous feast out of their gear. Turning to the bright unfettered sun, Elizabeth bites into a thick white sandwich and closes her eyes in peace.

xiii

THE MORNING SUN EARTHBOUND, held in branches, eerie, low slanted streaks of light. A deceptive moment: old trees, expanse of grass but the grass is chained off, and above the trees the city, gray smogged light. Heat, heaviness, bums sleeping on the benches. Pigeons strutting the walks. No sound. No ordinary people yet. Jim Cogan stands on the steps of Bryant Park confused by the quiet city pastoral before him, waiting until at last at the far end of the Library near Forty-first Street a band of white figures comes round the corner, fifteen or twenty people, most of them young, but a half-dozen middle-aged zealots clothed in white flowing garments. Their leader a plump man, bald, smooth-faced, gleaming with purpose marches them to the little platform of benches and bushes directly at the center back of the New York Public Library. There he speaks to his people. No sound, only the pantomime of their fervor, bowed heads, hands touching. Jim Cogan watches, his lips moving silently as though he too is praying and then he runs towards them. The action is fast. No sound now other than his steps against the pavement, the flutter of pigeons. No music, no . . . to induce a false sense of excitement, the oppressive silence and passivity of the white-robed people. The noises of the city beyond the park.

231

Jim Cogan runs up to a blond tangle-haired girl in a soiled white garment. She is sluttishly appealing with an angry, neurotic face. He pulls her forcibly away from the others and they stand apart. The setting is justly theatrical — the raised area of the park where they perform, like a little arena theater, with the classical colonnade of the library itself, huge green-encrusted statue. The girl hisses, bites at him but there are no words, as though neither of them will break the mood of peace and meditation in the group by their private struggle. Without warning, the girl's eyes change to a sweet compliance. She throws her arms up around the boy's neck in a passionate embrace. Her face is thick with lies he cannot discern, sly, conniving as an old courtesan twice his age. She presses close and kisses him boldly on the lips and by the time the purr of police cars is heard she has transferred two cigarette packs into the pockets of his loose summer shirt.

Clauson and his sect have seen the police cars too. They drive up on the pavement where cars are not allowed, closing off the park. Slowly a phalanx of policemen on the right, on the left, down the broad pavements of Bryant Park. The bums make a getaway. Clauson's people join hands and say their prayers as the police come at them. Like the completion of a ritual, their explosives are surrendered. Their faces, young and old alike, shine with crazed sweetness . . . tears of joy from one woman's pale, ill-nourished face. Their hands are held high in tribute to their gods. The silence penetrates even the uniformed men and a young cop clears his throat in embarrassment and calls to the squad car on his radio that they will need a paddy wagon. Music now — the formality of a Mozart sonata establishing itself and restating the neat theme. The harmless melody of old music. The consolation of refrain. An audience has gathered out of the city's morning crowds, has found the excitement. I see faces in the crowd, anxious, vicarious eyes, the break of a smile lusting for the punishment of wicked people. The faces of the crowd look up at the beatific faces on the stage. Jim Cogan is herded in with the religious white robes who have lowered their heads once more.

— I am not, he cries. I did not. The music goes on, set on its course to a balanced perfection and young Cogan cries out over and over again, words I cannot hear, words that cannot be heard, like supplications in a dream. I am not . . . I did not . . . and then the soft whisper of his voice comes directly to me, behind the music.

— I am not one of them. I did not betray them.

xiv

THE SHARP REALISTIC SETTING of the Quinns' kitchen. A friendly scene. Time of departure. Harry and Laura wait at the door while Frieda puts sandwiches into the top of Jim Cogan's duffle bag. He sits with the children on the floor, three limp figures propped against the cabinets.

— He'll be home in a couple of hours, Laura says.

— Well, he's eaten everything in the house. He might as well clean us out completely.

Jim comes to Frieda and hugs her. — I'm not hungry, he says. Her fat face trembles with emotion, all too predictable.

— You're going to be all right, she says. They won't hurt you. You'll be all right. I put in a couple of salami and cheese.

— There won't be time, Laura repeats.

Jim slings the duffle bag over his shoulder and turns to the children, but Mary with her wise old lady's face avoids him, stands up and stiff as a weather vane swings to the back door and points to Elizabeth.

An apparition. The secretary is like a sleepwalker come into their midst, in a drooping old housecoat, hair pinned crazily out of her face. She carries a sheaf of papers and envelopes in front of her like an offering. — The letters are done, Elizabeth says. I wanted to do them. Oh, they all came down from Gloucester this time and they said no, I mustn't . . . but I got right out of the house away from them. I wanted to get the letters done. They are all stamped. They can go in the evening mail. I'm so glad I got the letters done today, she insists.

Harry starts toward her. She puts her hands out to him and the letters and envelopes flutter over the kitchen floor. — My mother died, Elizabeth says. I went away and when I came back she was dead. She stands back from them all and looks at Jim Cogan, a timid smile of recognition.

Laura takes the keys from her husband. — I'm sorry, Liz. I'm terribly sorry.

— You're going to the airport now, Elizabeth says. *I* called for the summer schedule. This to show perhaps how far she is into their lives. I typed the last letter to Glickman this morning. The lawyer in New York. The case will be dismissed against Cogan. There's never been any real danger. Misdemeanor. First offense. The basketball coach and the priest come and speak for him. All along I've known what they do with cases like this . . . a boy with good connections . . . dismiss him with a lecture. This morning when they took her body out of the bed I went along to the office and did my letters.

Harry controls her, holds her now. That's what she wants. All the years she has denied herself his embrace . . . death is the occasion for it, sanctions the fatherly touch. Wipe my tears, comfort me. Already she looks better, sitting at the table like a little girl with a cut on her knee. Her grief and guilt pour out, a poor offering to the man she

234

loves. They are alone. Laura has prodded Jim Cogan out of
the back door. Frieda has taken the kids away.

xv

Now THEY GO TO THE AIRPORT. Jim Cogan and Laura
Quinn. She has romanticized the weeks of his visit. How
ephemeral her despair was then and how real, how wearing
it seems now on this hot brassy Sunday evening. His face is
heavier, older with a dull cast to the eyes. What visions has
he seen through her to ruin him so? Why did she envy his
youth? Feed off the foolishness of his tender years, a genteel Brahmin vampire. It is perfectly just that her melo-
dramatic thoughts, as they drive back the way they came,
are broken by his simplicity, his fresh smile not gone yet.
— This will be my second time in a plane, he says.
Yes, that's all it comes to, his boyish enthusiasm and her
studied sobriety. They start a litany of apologies . . . that
she was not open, that he was irreverent. Her love for him
is dribbling away. In her face a slackness, a loss of interest.
She cannot hold to what they have meant to each other.
She, too, looks much older, that part of her that was virgin
still at forty, taken at last. Tough luck. Now she knows how
it is to be spread eagle to the world.
— The Murrays really must have been something, the
boy says.
— Why?
— They weren't ordinary, he says. Look at your mother.
She was so beautiful and when she left Brooklyn she really
struck out on her own, came up here where she didn't know
people, where she didn't belong. And my grandfather played
for the Yankees when it was really a game, when they really
had a team. He radiates an empty cheeriness, a sense that

235

his visit to Boston, his experiences here have already ended. The time with Laura in the car is an obligation. Brother and sister, he says, there were only the two of them, your mother and Skip Murray, and one of them was born in Ireland.

— I didn't know that, Laura says dryly.

— Yes, but I'm not sure. Didn't you ever hear that story about the Murrays, that the oldest one of them was born the day before they took the boat?

— I don't know about all that. After a pause she says in sorrow and self-defense — The past is theoretical. I don't know all that family history. That was before my time.

They come to their starting point, where they met on their first day. The modest back-end of Logan airport with a few taxis circling for fares. The light is blinding here in the open space and squinting up at the boy, Laura takes an envelope out of her purse, the plane ticket and a note that she rips up. The envelope is stuffed with money, a wad of bills.

— I don't want you to take the plane, she says.

— Oh, I'm coming up to see you, up to the Vineyard before school starts.

— I want you to take the next shuttle. The one that goes to Newark.

— My parents will be at La Guardia!

— I thought Harry would be with us, Laura continues, and it would be our last little intrigue. I wrote you this letter to explain . . . you should run off like you planned, take the money and go to Newark. Get a plane out West. There are thousands of kids traveling the country.

— No way, Jim says. My hearing is tomorrow. Even if all their plans go wrong and I get sent to jail, I want to go back. My mother and father are pitiful, but I miss them. My old man has a new job with IBM and they think they're moving out to New Rochelle. I want to see my brother and sister,

236

can you believe it? They were fools, but it wasn't their fault what happened to me. I want to see them all. It's an idea you gave me, that it's my life, my real life.

They wait in silence and finally Laura asks — Did you love her? That Shelley Waltz?

— I couldn't let her alone. I don't know — her whole form, her body was into me.

— Yes, Laura says, the whole feel of the person is on you and you want to keep them with you — to save them. She takes the money out again and presses it on him.

— It isn't *reasonable*, the boy cries and pulls away from her.

— Listen to me now, Laura pleads. Please take the money. Take the money and run.

xvi

AGAIN THE SCENE GOES BACK to the familiar and yet I find it hard to place this room, white, spare . . . a studio or workroom. An entrance, like a staged entrance only close to me — her movements slow, larger than an actress at a distance, her whole large shape in the doorway, moving in the dead stark room. Laura Quinn in her study. She is in black, the same shirt and pants that she wore when she erased the tapes, the material for her book on women elected to public office or whatever. As though at an interview, I watch her move to the desk and take her place. I watch her throughout, watch her face with full attention, the features that I have seen over and over again in various lights. A plainness emerges, a symmetry in the bones, large mouth, not beautiful, a mouth that is too mobile, self-mocking, a face that responds to every mood of her story, sensual, bitter, sometimes cracked wide with the smile of a glib comedienne.

237

Her eyes are steady, a light English blue, intelligent Yankee eyes that see and see and see with a clarity and fade against the emotion of her words. The room dims, closes in about her — the feeling that I am in there with her and her voice to me is hushed and private.

— I wanted then, she says, to thrust the envelope at him, slip the money into his pocket. But it was too obvious and I couldn't. That she, the slut whose shape was on him, had put her cheap wares into his pocket, was in my mind. And he did not love her. Here Laura pauses, smiles — anyway he did not answer that question when I asked. Still I could not force myself and my desire on him. It was a considerable amount of money from the legacy my father left me — money I never wanted, never touched, money my brother should have shared and there would have been that extra satisfaction, a fillip — she smiles out at me childishly superior — in the notion, she says, that all the money would flutter away in the pursuit of pure madness, mumbling bunkum, growing beans in the desert, a vision of man like pure thin air, exhilarating, free and almost . . . almost unattainable. A life my father would never recognize as life at all. I could not and he pushed my hand away and I stuck the envelope back into my purse and said — OK, You win. The sun washed over him, washing his feelings for me away. Someday this moment would be useful to him, but not now.

Laura looks down and after awhile I realize that there are notes, something . . . words . . . she is using to prompt herself. Her eyes come back, cynical, begging my pardon. A change of tone now, large voice, funny story to pass off on me, a story which is not so funny after all.

— Then we kissed, Laura laughs at the mention of it, cheeks together, kisses off balance in the air, and because he thought I wanted it he said, — I wish I'd been twenty years older. — Fallen Adam. The rot of it . . . the stupidity. *That* false note. The inevitable artificial coloring. I wanted to start one of the old arguments again but departures are too long, never long enough and I couldn't. He went running off across the asphalt field to his plane, on his way home. The sun had faded at last; it was near the summer solstice, a long day. I have never been that lonely, though I could still feel his embrace, not the false kiss, but the embrace that came before, before the spoiling of the day. A hug, ungraceful hug, close as kind animals we were, domestic animals surely, wanting nothing from each other. The imprint of him on me like a lover, but not . . . the imprint of his youth. How sour I was when I first lost the sense of my world and Harry's cause and couldn't justify the tidy vision I was to pass on to my children, the message . . . oh, that something can be done, that it can all be rebuilt stone by stone.

She pauses. The rustle of pages, hesitation on the words as though they are not set, not permanent and the projection of her story continues, scenes of sober reality, no fantasy, no poetic touches in the sequence with soft focus or fade-outs. The city again, not as I saw it to begin with in condensed amber, but raw, fringed with dirt and tired people at the end of the weekend.

— I drove around Boston, Laura says, like a common gull, circling the port that is my home, that scene of all my long history, distant, indifferent to the place . . . and when it was finally dark, as though I had been waiting for the light to fade mercifully away, I drove out to the house, drove past the house because I could not make myself go in, and parked down the road and walked alone, like a stranger down the road past houses and trees and stones I had never seen, going by as I always do in a car. The good girl I despised in me was dead, the good girl who must be as good if not better, as good if not better . . . the secret was out. I rattled around the neighborhood like a stray, and thought with fleeting happiness that I might stay out there in the dark forever or go back to the good life, that it didn't matter because I had the doubt and the doubt itself was sweet.

Up over the side lawn where I have not walked in years, on the far side of the house where nothing grows in the shade, where the dog that died rutted the earth. They are at the kitchen table, Harry and the children. Frieda has gone for the Sunday night visit with her son. He is playing a game with them, a board with dice, little soldiers who advance over the printed landscape, moats and streams, get lost in the woods and take the castle in the end, an ugly gray plastic castle that sets up in pieces and enchants no one at all. It is a troubling scene — that of a father who spends little time alone with the kids, being instructed: this is how we play. I felt sorry for the man, his awkwardness there under the light with his children and the smile he gave them, his little constituents, the automatic grin that would bend them to his way. Later I cried, filled with such pity, such forgiveness as I watched him, for I saw that he made the supreme sacrifice, that he moved his soldiers foolishly so that his children could win.

xvii

Now THE MUSIC, the calliope tune that set the picnic off, but the orchard is blank, stripped clean, cobwebs, trees, wet grass, moonlight, a haunting empty place now and Laura Quinn sits like a spectator watching the lights go out in her house. The time dwindles from her and with a terrific resolution she gets up, out of the cold grass and runs home. Darkness, the fluttering curtains of the children's room, the discovery of mysteriously empty beds. Silence as she stands framed in the window. A little of the Mozart now, the completion of the theme. Like so many American heroes she fixes on the one flickering light on the horizon, her doubt like new knowledge in her heart. But there are Harry and the kids camping out on the roof.

He turns to her in his sleep. — Come out, he says. It's fun out here. That's all he says, and she steps through the window and stands above him looking out over the cultivated gardens, as though she were on a ship looking out to the wild sea.